D1395953

A Miscellany of Sense and Nonsense

"'E was a-standin' there, at the other end of the punt, a-smokin' a cigar."

[See page 92.

A Miscellany of Sense and Nonsense

Jerome K. Jerome

Alan Sutton
1983

Alan Sutton Publishing Limited
17a Brunswick Road
Gloucester GL1 1HG

First published 1923

Copyright © in this edition 1983 Alan Sutton
Publishing Limited

ISBN 0-86299-080-7

Printed in Great Britain

Dedication

TO THE GENTLE

GUIDE

WHO LETS ME EVER GO MY OWN WAY, YET BRINGS ME RIGHT—

TO THE LAUGHTER-LOVING

PHILOSOPHER

WHO, IF HE HAS NOT RECONCILED ME TO BEARING THE TOOTHACHE
PATIENTLY, AT LEAST HAS TAUGHT ME THE COMFORT THAT
THIS EVEN WILL ALSO PASS—

TO THE GOOD

FRIEND

WHO SMILES WHEN I TELL HIM OF MY TROUBLES, AND WHO
WHEN I ASK FOR HELP, ANSWERS ONLY " WAIT ! "—

TO THE GRAVE-FACED

JESTER

TO WHOM ALL LIFE IS BUT A VOLUME OF OLD HUMOUR—

TO GOOD MASTER

Time

THIS LITTLE WORK OF A POOR
PUPIL
IS DEDICATED

(*Three Men on the Bummel.*)

Index

From " THREE MEN IN A BOAT "—   PAGE

The Man Who was a Hospital   15
Under Canvas   33
Uncle Podger Hangs a Picture   47
The Rule of the World   53
Harris and the Maze   120
Henry VIII. goes A-Wooing   138
The Thing that Spoilt the Picture   159
The Good Fisherman   168
George gets up too Early   195
Sailing ! Sailing !   211
Talk about the Weather   222
Learning the Bagpipes   232
In Rain Time   242
Saint Montmorency   330

From " THREE MEN ON THE BUMMEL "—

The Caution of Captain Goyles   106
The Polite Art of Buying Boots   162
Verboten   262
Morning at " Beggarbush "   265
The Wisdom of Uncle Podger   270
Harris to the Rescue   285
A Lost Leader   304
Uncle Podger goes to Town   357

From " NOVEL NOTES "—

A Disturber of the Peace   20
The Perfect Dancer   37
Wet to Stormy   82
James : A Simple Soul   91

From " IDLE THOUGHTS OF AN IDLE FELLOW "—   PAGE

    On Babies 56
    Vanity 86
    Cats and Dogs 99
    Advice to Edwin and Angelina 103
    Idle Thoughts on Memory 142

From " SKETCHES IN LAVENDER "—

    A Charming Woman 189

From " OBSERVATIONS OF HENRY AND OTHERS "—

    Choosing a Profession 235

From " DIARY OF A PILGRIMAGE "—

    How to Go to Bed in Germany 200
    At Ober-Ammergau 249
    See England First 347

From " PAUL KELVER "—

    How Paul Kelver came to Write a Story . . . 23
    Paul Talks with a Writer of Books . . . 125
    Paul's First Chum 147
    Noel Hasluck 156
    An Evening at the Play 171
    His First Engagement 184
    Paul is Invited to a Marriage Feast . . . 215
    Humour and " The Penny-a-Liner " . . . 258
    The Princess sends Paul a Ring 272
    How to Write a Play 316

From " MALVINA OF BRITTANY "—

    Malvina of Brittany 298
    The Return 337
    The Fawn Gloves 365

From " SECOND THOUGHTS OF AN IDLE FELLOW "—

    The Dwellers in the Elms 62
    On the Art of Making up One's Mind . . . 69
    On the Inadvisability of Following Advice . . 341

INDEX

From " THE ANGEL AND THE AUTHOR "—   PAGE
    The Angel and the Author   292
    How to be Healthy and Unhappy   368

From " IDLE IDEAS "—
    Swallow Street   133
    Should we Say What we Think ?   152
    Why Didn't He Marry the Girl ?   361

From " TEA TABLE TALK "—
    Too much Lover   115
    Man and his Relations   180
    Does Art Elevate ?   206
    To What End ?   245

From " THEY AND I "—
    The Billiard Lesson   275
    Robina on Marriage   326
    Dream Children   351

From " ALL ROADS LEAD TO CALVARY "—
    The Window Ajar   283
    The Makers of War   312
    The Unknown   332
    All Roads Lead to Calvary   373

From " JOHN INGERFIELD "—
    The Music Hall of the Old Regime   74
    Silhouettes   226

A Miscellany of Sense and Nonsense

The Man who was a Hospital.

IT was my liver that was out of order. I knew it was my liver that was out of order, because I had just been reading a patent liver-pill circular, in which were detailed the various symptoms by which a man could tell when his liver was out of order. I had them all.

It is a most extraordinary thing, but I never read a patent medicine advertisement without being impelled to the conclusion that I am suffering from the particular disease therein dealt with in its most virulent form. The diagnosis seems in every case to correspond exactly with all the sensations that I have ever felt.

I remember going to the British Museum one day to read up the treatment for some slight ailment of which I had a touch—hay fever, I fancy it was. I got down the book, and read all I came to read ; and then, in an unthinking moment, I idly turned the leaves, and began to indolently study diseases, generally. I forget which was the first distemper I plunged into—some fearful, devastating scourge, I know—and, before I had glanced half down the list of " premonitory symptoms," it was borne in upon me that I had fairly got it.

I sat for awhile, frozen with horror ; and then, in the listlessness of despair, I again turned over the pages. I came to typhoid fever—read the symptoms

—discovered that I had typhoid fever, must have had it for months without knowing it—wondered what else I had got ; turned up St. Vitus's Dance—found, as I expected, that I had that too,—began to get interested in my case, and determined to sift it to the bottom, and so started alphabetically—read up ague, and learnt that I was sickening for it, and that the acute stage would commence in about another fortnight. Bright's disease, I was relieved to find, I had only in a modified form, and, so far as that was concerned, I might live for years. Cholera I had, with severe complications ; and diphtheria I seemed to have been born with. I plodded conscientiously through the twenty-six letters, and the only malady I could conclude I had not got was housemaid's knee.

I felt rather hurt about this at first ; it seemed somehow to be a sort of slight. Why hadn't I got housemaid's knee ? Why this invidious reservation ? After a while, however, less grasping feelings prevailed. I reflected that I had every other known malady in the pharmacology, and I grew less selfish, and determined to do without housemaid's knee. Gout, in its most malignant stage, it would appear, had seized me without my being aware of it ; and zymosis I had evidently been suffering with from boyhood. There were no more diseases after zymosis, so I concluded there was nothing else the matter with me.

I sat and pondered. I thought what an interesting case I must be from a medical point of view, what an acquisition I should be to a class ! Students would have no need to " walk the hospitals," if they had me. I was a hospital in myself. All they need do would be to walk round me, and, after that, take their diploma.

Then I wondered how long I had to live. I tried to examine myself. I felt my pulse. I could not at first find any pulse at all. Then, all of a sudden, it seemed to start off. I pulled out my watch and timed it. I made it a hundred and forty-seven to the minute. I tried to feel my heart. I could not feel my heart. It had stopped beating. I have since been induced to come to the opinion that it must have been there all the time, and must have been beating, but I cannot account for it. I patted myself all over my front, from what I call my waist up to my head, and I went a bit round each side, and a little way up the back. But I could not feel or hear anything. I tried to look at my tongue. I stuck it out as far as ever it would go, and I shut one eye, and tried to examine it with the other. I could only see the tip, and the only thing that I could gain from that was to feel more certain than before that I had scarlet fever.

I had walked into that reading-

It was my liver that was out of order.

B

room a happy, healthy man. I crawled out a decrepit wreck.

I went to my medical man. He is an old chum of mine, and feels my pulse, and looks at my tongue, and talks about the weather, all for nothing, when I fancy I 'm ill; so I thought I would do him a good turn by going to him now. "What a doctor wants," I said, "is practice. He shall have me. He will get more practice out of me than out of seventeen hundred of your ordinary, commonplace patients, with only one or two diseases each." So I went straight up and saw him, and he said:

"Well, what 's the matter with you ? "

I said:

" I will not take up your time, dear boy, with telling you what is the matter with me. Life is brief, and you might pass away before I had finished. But I will tell you what is *not* the matter with me. I have not got housemaid's knee. Why I have not got housemaid's knee, I cannot tell you; but the fact remains that I have not got it. Everything else, however, I *have* got."

And I told him how I came to discover it all.

Then he opened me and looked down me, and clutched hold of my wrist, and then he hit me over the chest when I wasn't expecting it—a cowardly thing to do, I call it—and immediately afterwards butted me with the side of his head. After that, he sat down and wrote out a prescription, and folded it up and gave it to me, and I put it in my pocket and went out.

I did not open it. I took it to the nearest chemist's

and handed it in. The man read it, and then handed it back.

He said he didn't keep it.

I said :

" You are a chemist ? "

He said :

" I am a chemist. If I was a co-operative stores and family hotel combined, I might be able to oblige you. Being only a chemist hampers me."

I read the prescription. It ran :

> " 1 lb. beefsteak, with
> 1 pt. bitter beer
> every 6 hours.
> 1 ten-mile walk every morning.
> 1 bed at 11 sharp every night.

And don't stuff your head with things you don't understand."

I followed the directions, with the happy result—speaking for myself—that my life was preserved, and is still going on.

(Three Men in a Boat.)

A Disturber of the Peace.

An old corncrake lived near to us, and the way he used to disturb all the other birds, and keep them from going to sleep, was shameful. Amenda, who was town-bred, mistook him at first for one of those cheap alarm clocks, and wondered who was winding him up, and why they went on doing it all night ; and, above all, why they didn't oil him.

He would begin his unhallowed performance about dusk, just as every respectable bird was preparing to settle down for the night. A family of thrushes had their nest a few yards from his stand, and they used to get perfectly furious with him.

" There 's that fool at it again," the female thrush would say ; " why can't he do it in the day-time if he must do it at all ? "

The way he used to disturb all the other birds and keep them from going to sleep was shameful.

(She spoke, of course, in twitters, but I am confident the above is a correct translation.)

After a while, the young thrushes would wake up and begin chirping, and then the mother would get madder than ever.

"Can't you say something to him?" she would cry indignantly to her husband. "How do you think the children can get to sleep, poor things, with that hideous row going on all night? Might just as well be living in a saw-mill."

Thus adjured, the male thrush would put his head over the nest, and call out in a nervous, apologetic manner :—

"I say, you know, you there, I wish you wouldn't mind being quiet a bit. My wife says she can't get the children to sleep. It's too bad, you know, 'pon my word it is."

"Gor on," the corncrake would answer surlily. "You keep your wife herself quiet ; that's enough for you to do." And on he would go again worse than before.

Then a mother blackbird, from a little further off, would join in the fray.

"Ah, it's a good hiding he wants, not a talking to. And if I was a cock, I'd give it him." (This remark would be made in a tone of withering contempt, and would appear to bear reference to some previous discussion.)

"You're quite right, ma'am," Mrs. Thrush would reply. "That's what I tell my husband, but" (with rising inflection, so that every lady in the plantation might hear) "*he* wouldn't move himself, bless you— no, not if I and the children were to die before his eyes for want of sleep."

" Ah, he ain't the only one, my dear," the blackbird would pipe back, " they 're all alike " ; then, in a voice more of sorrow than of anger : " but there, it ain't their fault, I suppose, poor things. If you ain't got the spirit of a bird you can't help yourself."

I would strain my ears at this point to hear if the male blackbird was moved at all by these taunts, but the only sound I could ever detect coming from his neighbourhood was that of palpably exaggerated snoring.

By this time the whole glade would be awake, expressing views concerning that corncrake that would have wounded a less callous nature.

" Blow me tight, Bill," some vulgar little hedge-sparrow would chirp out, in the midst of the hubbub, " if I don't believe the gent thinks 'e 's a-singing."

" 'Tain't 'is fault," Bill would reply, with mock sympathy. " Somebody 's put a penny in the slot, and 'e can't stop 'isself."

Irritated by the laugh that this would call forth from the younger birds, the corncrake would exert himself to be more objectionable than ever, and, as a means to this end, would commence giving his marvellous imitation of the sharpening of a rusty saw by a steel file.

But at this an old crow, not to be trifled with, would cry out angrily :—

" Stop that, now. If I come down to you I 'll peck your cranky head off, I will."

And then would follow silence for a quarter of an hour, after which the whole thing would begin again.

(*Novel Notes.*)

How Paul Kelver came to Write a Story.

At the corner of a long, straight, brick-built street in the far East End of London—one of those lifeless streets, made of two drab walls upon which the level lines, formed by the precisely even window-sills and doorsteps, stretch in weary perspective from end to end, suggesting petrified diagrams proving dead problems—stands a house that ever draws me to it ; so that often, when least conscious of my footsteps, I awake to find myself hurrying through noisy, crowded thoroughfares, where flaring naphtha lamps illumine fierce, patient, leaden-coloured faces ; through dim-lit, empty streets, where monstrous shadows come and go upon the close-drawn blinds ; through narrow, noisome streets, where the gutters swarm with children, and each ever-open doorway vomits riot ; past reeking corners, and across waste places, till at last I reach the dreary goal of my memory-driven desire ; and, coming to a halt beside the broken railings, find rest.

The house, larger than its fellows, built when the street was still a country lane, edging the marshes, strikes a strange note of individuality amid the surrounding harmony of hideousness. It is encompassed on two sides by what was once a garden, though now but a barren patch of stones and dust, where clothes it is odd anyone should have thought of washing hang in perpetuity ; while about the door continue the remnants of a porch, which the stucco falling has left exposed in all its naked insincerity.

Occasionally I drift hitherward in the daytime, when slatternly women gossip round the area gates, and the silence is broken by the hoarse, wailing cry of " Coals—any coals—three-and-sixpence a sack co-o-o-als ! " chanted in a tone that absence of response has stamped with chronic melancholy ; but then the street knows me not, and my old friend of the corner, ashamed of its shabbiness in the unpitying sunlight, turns its face away, and will not see me as I pass.

Not until the Night, merciful alone of all things to the ugly, draws her veil across its sordid features will it, as some fond old nurse, sought out in after years, open wide its arms to welcome me. Then, the teeming life it now shelters hushed for a time within its walls, the flickering flare from the " King of Prussia " opposite extinguished, will it talk to me of the past, asking me many questions, reminding me of many things I had forgotten. Then into the silent street come the well-remembered footsteps ; in and out the creaking gate pass, not seeing me, the well-remembered faces ; and we talk concerning them ; as two cronies, turning the torn leaves of some old album where lie faded portraits in forgotten fashions, speak together in low tones of those now dead or scattered, with now a smile and now a sigh, and many an " Ah, me ! " or " Dear, dear ! "

This bent, worn man, coming towards us with quick, impatient steps, which yet cease every fifty yards or so, while he pauses, leaning heavily upon his high Malacca cane : " It is a handsome face, is it not ? " I ask, as I gaze upon it, shadow framed.

In and out the creaking gate pass, not seeing me, the well-remembered faces.

C

" Aye, handsome enough," answers the old House ; " and handsomer still it must have been before you and I knew it, before mean care had furrowed it with fretful lines."

" I could never make out," continues the old House musingly, " whom you took after ; for they were a handsome pair, your father and your mother, though, Lord ! what a couple of children ! "

" Children ! " I say in surprise, for my father must have been past five-and-thirty before the House could have known him, and my mother's face is very close to mine in the darkness, so that I see the grey hairs mingling with the bonny brown.

" Children," repeats the old House irritably, so it seems to me, not liking, perhaps, its opinions questioned, a failing common to old folk ; " the most helpless pair of children I ever set eyes upon. Who but a child, I should like to know, would have conceived the notion of repairing his fortune by becoming a solicitor at thirty-eight, or, having conceived such a notion, would have selected the outskirts of Poplar as a likely centre in which to put up his door-plate ? "

" It was considered to be a rising neighbourhood," I reply, a little resentfully. No son cares to hear the family wisdom criticised, even though at the bottom of his heart he may be in agreement with the critic. " All sorts and conditions of men, whose affairs were in connection with the sea, would, it was thought, come to reside hereabout so as to be near to the new docks ; and had they, it is not unreasonable to suppose they would have quarrelled and disputed with one another, much to the advantage of a cute solicitor convenient to their hand."

"Stuff and nonsense!" retorts the old House shortly, "why, the mere smell of the place would have been sufficient to keep a sensible man away. And"—the grim brick face before me twists itself into a goblin smile—"he, of all men in the world, as 'the cute solicitor,' giving advice to shady clients, eager to get out of trouble by the shortest way, can you fancy it?—he who for two years starved himself, living on five shillings a week—that was before you came to London, when he was here alone: even your mother knew nothing of it till years afterwards—so that no man should be a penny the poorer for having trusted his good name. Do you think the crew of chandlers and brokers, dock-hustlers and freight-wreckers would have found him a useful man of business, even had they come to settle here?"

I have no answer; nor does the old House wait for any, but talks on.

"And your mother! Would any but a child have taken that soft-tongued wanton to her bosom, and not have seen through acting so transparent? Would any but the veriest child that never ought to have been let out into the world by itself have thought to dree her weird in such folly? Children! poor babies they were, both of them."

"Tell me," I say—for at such times all my stock of common sense is not sufficient to convince me that the old House is but clay. From its walls so full of voices, from its floors so thick with footsteps, surely it has learned to live; as a violin, long played on, comes to learn at last a music of its own. "Tell me, I was but a child to whom life speaks in a strange tongue, was there any truth in the story?"

"Truth!" snaps out the old House; "just truth enough to plant a lie upon; and, Lord knows, not much ground is needed for that weed. I saw what I saw, and I know what I know. Your mother had a good man, and your father a true wife, but it was the old story: a man's way is not a woman's way and woman's way is not a man's way, so there lives ever doubt between them."

"But they came together in the end?" I say, remembering.

"Aye, in the end," answers the old House. "That is when you begin to understand, you men and women, when you come to the end."

The grave face of a not too recently washed angel peeps shyly at me through the railings; then, as I turn my head, darts back and disappears.

"What has become of her?" I ask.

"She? Oh, she is well enough," replies the House. "She lives close here. You must have passed the shop. You might have seen her, had you looked in. She weighs fourteen stone, about; and has nine children living. She would be pleased to see you."

"Thank you," I say, with a laugh that is not wholly a laugh; "I do not think I will call." But I still hear the pit-pat of her tiny feet, dying down the long street.

The faces thicken round me. A large-looming, rubicund visage smiles kindly on me, bringing back into my heart the old odd mingling of instinctive liking held in check by conscientious disapproval. I turn from it, and see a massive, clean-shaven face with the ugliest mouth and the loveliest eyes I ever have known in a man.

"Was he so bad, do you think as they said?"
I ask of my ancient friend.

"Shouldn't wonder," the old House answers. "I
never knew a worse—nor a better."

The wind whisks it aside, leaving to view a little
old woman, hobbling nimbly by aid of a stick. Three
corkscrew curls each side of her head bob with each
step she takes, and as she draws near to me, making
the most alarming grimaces, I hear her whisper, as
though confiding to herself some fascinating secret,
"I'd like to skin 'em. I'd like to skin 'em all. I'd
like to skin 'em all alive!"

It sounds a fiendish sentiment, yet I only laugh,
and the little old lady, with a final facial contortion
surpassing all dreams, limps beyond my ken.

Then, as though choosing contrasts, follows a
fair, laughing face. I saw it in the life only a few hours
ago—at least not it, but the poor daub that Evil has
painted over it, hating the sweetness underlying.
And as I stand gazing at it, wishing it were of the dead
who change not, there drifts back from the shadows
that other face, the one of the wicked mouth and the
tender eyes, so that I stand again helpless between the
two I loved so well—he from whom I learned my
first steps in manhood, she from whom I caught my
first glimpse of the beauty and the mystery of woman.
And again the cry rises from my heart, "Whose fault
was it—yours or hers?" And again I hear his mocking
laugh as he answers, "Whose fault? God made us."
And thinking of her and of the love I bore her, which
was as the love of a young pilgrim to a saint, it comes
into my blood to hate him. But when I look into his
eyes and see the pain that lives there, my pity grows

stronger than my misery, and I can only echo his words, " God made us."

Merry faces and sad, fair faces and foul, they ride upon the wind ; but the centre round which they circle remains always the one : a little lad with golden curls more suitable to a girl than to a boy, with shy, awkward ways and a silent tongue, and a grave, old-fashioned face.

And, turning from him to my old brick friend, I ask : " Would he know me, could he see me, do you think ? "

" How should he ? " answers the old House ; " you are so different to what he would expect. Would you recognise your own ghost, think you ? "

" It is sad to think he would not recognise me," I say.

" It might be sadder if he did," grumbles the old House.

We both remain silent for a while, but I know of what the old House is thinking. Soon it speaks as I expected.

" You—a writer of stories, why don't you write a book about him ? There is something that you know."

It is the favourite theme of the old House. I never visit it but it suggests to me this idea.

" But he has done nothing ? " I say.

" He has lived," answers the old House. " Is not that enough ? "

" Aye, but only in London in these prosaic modern times," I persist. " How of such can one make a story that shall interest the people ? "

The old House waxes impatient of me.

" ' The people ! ' " it retorts, " what are you all but children in a dim-lit room, waiting until one by one you are called out to sleep ? And one mounts upon a stool and tells a tale to the others who have gathered round. Who shall say what will please them, what will not ? "

Returning home with musing footsteps through the softly breathing streets, I ponder the words of the old House. Is it but as some foolish mother thinking all the world interested in her child, or may there lie wisdom in its counsel ? Then to my guidance or misguidance comes the thought of a certain small section of the public who often of an evening commands of me a story ; and who, when I have told her of the dreadful giants, and of the gallant youths who slay them, of the woodcutter's sons who rescue maidens from ogre-guarded castles, of the princesses the most beautiful in all the world, of the princes with magic swords, still unsatisfied, creeps closer yet, saying : " Now tell me a real story," adding for my comprehending : " You know—about a little girl who lived in a big house with her father and mother, and who was sometimes naughty, you know."

So perhaps among the many there may be some who for a moment will turn aside from tales of haughty heroes, ruffling it in court and camp, to listen to the story of a very ordinary lad who lived with very ordinary folk in a modern London street, and who grew up to be a very ordinary sort of man, loving a little and grieving a little, helping a few and harming a few, struggling and failing and hoping ; and if any such there be, let them come round me.

But let not those who come to me grow indignant

as they listen, saying, " This rascal tells us but a hum-drum story, where nothing is as it should be " ; for I warn all beforehand that I tell but of things that I have seen. My villains, I fear, are but poor sinners, not altogether bad ; and my good men but sorry saints. My princes do not always slay their dragons ; alas ! sometimes the dragon eats the prince. The wicked fairies often drove more powerful than the good. The magic thread leads sometimes wrong, and even the hero is not always brave and true.

So let those come round me only who will be content to hear but their own story, told by another, saying as they listen, " So dreamed I. Ah, yes, that is true, I remember."

(*Paul Kelver*.)

Under Canvas.

CAMPING out in rainy weather is not pleasant.

It is evening. You are wet through, and there is a good two inches of water in the boat, and all the things are damp. You find a place on the banks that is not quite so puddly as other places you have seen, and you land and lug out the tent, and two of you proceed to fix it.

It is soaked and heavy, and it flops about, and tumbles down on you, and clings round your head and makes you mad. The rain is pouring steadily down all the time. It is difficult enough to fix a tent in dry weather : in wet, the task becomes herculean. Instead of helping you, it seems to you that the other man is simply playing the fool. Just as you get your side beautifully fixed, he gives it a hoist from his end, and spoils it all.

" Here ! what are you up to ? " you call out.

" What are *you* up to ? " he retorts ; " leggo, can't you ? "

" Don't puil it ; you 've got it all wrong, you stupid ass ! " you shout.

" No, I haven't," he yells back ; " let go your side ! "

" I tell you you 've got it all wrong ! " you roar, wishing that you could get at him ; and you give your ropes a lug that pulls all his pegs out.

" Ah, the bally idiot ! " you hear him mutter to

c*

himself ; and then comes a savage haul, and away goes your side. You lay down the mallet and start to go round and tell him what you think about the whole business, and, at the same time, he starts round in the same direction to come and explain his views to you. And you follow each other round and round, swearing at one another, until the tent tumbles down in a heap, and leaves you looking at each other across its ruins, when you both indignantly exclaim, in the same breath :

" There you are ! what did I tell you ? "

Meanwhile, the third man, who has been bailing out the boat, and who has spilled the water down his sleeve, and has been cursing away to himself steadily for the last ten minutes, wants to know what the thundering blazes you 're playing at, and why the blarmed tent isn't up yet.

At last, somehow or other, it does get up, and you land the things. It is hopeless attempting to make a wood fire, so you light the methylated spirit stove and crowd round that.

Rainwater is the chief article of diet at supper. The bread is two-thirds rainwater, the beefsteak-pie is exceedingly rich in it, and the jam, and the butter, and the salt, and the coffee have all combined with it to make soup.

After supper, you find your tobacco is damp, and you cannot smoke. Luckily you have a bottle of the stuff that cheers and inebriates, if taken in proper quantity, and this restores to you sufficient interest in life to induce you to go to bed.

There you dream that an elephant has suddenly sat down on your chest, and that the volcano has exploded and thrown you down to the bottom of the sea—the elephant still sleeping peacefully on your bosom. You wake up and grasp the idea that something terrible really has happened. Your first impression is that the end of the world has come; and

Your first impression is that the end of the world has come.

then you think that this cannot be, and that it is thieves and murderers, or else fire, and this opinion you express in the usual method. No help comes, however, and all you know is that thousands of people are kicking you, and you are being smothered.

Somebody else seems in trouble, too. You can hear his faint cries coming from underneath your bed. Determining, at all events, to sell your life dearly, you struggle frantically, hitting out right and left with arms and legs, and yelling lustily the while, and at last something gives way, and you find your head in the fresh air. Two feet off, you dimly observe a half-dressed ruffian, waiting to kill you, and you are preparing for a life-and-death struggle with him, when it begins to dawn upon you that it 's Jim.

"Oh, it 's you, is it ? " he says, recognising you at the same moment.

"Yes," you answer, rubbing your eyes ; "what 's happened ? "

"Bally tent 's blown down, I think," he says. "Where 's Bill ? "

Then you both raise up your voices and shout for "Bill ! " and the ground beneath you heaves and rocks, and the muffled voice that you heard before replies from out the ruin :

"Get off my head, can't you ? "

And Bill struggles out, a muddy, trampled wreck, and in an unnecessarily aggressive mood—he being under the evident belief that the whole thing has been done on purpose.

(*Three Men in a Boat.*)

The Perfect Dancer.

THIS story comes from Furtwangen, a small town in the Black Forest. There lived there a wonderful old fellow named Nicholaus Geibel. His business was the making of mechanical toys, at which work he had acquired an almost European reputation. He made rabbits that would emerge from the heart of a cabbage, flap their ears, smooth their whiskers, and disappear again ; cats that would wash their faces, and mew so naturally that dogs would mistake them for real cats, and fly at them ; dolls, with phonographs concealed within them, that would raise their hats and say, " Good morning ; how do you do ? " and some that would even sing a song.

But he was something more than a mere mechanic ; he was an artist. His work was with him a hobby, almost a passion. His shop was filled with all manner of strange things that never would, or could, be sold —things that he made for the pure love of making them. He had contrived a mechanical donkey that would trot for two hours by means of stored electricity, and trot, too, much faster than the live article, and with less need for exertion on the part of the driver ; a bird that would shoot up into the air, fly round and round in a circle, and drop to earth at the exact spot from where it started ; a skeleton that, supported by an upright iron bar, would dance a hornpipe ; a life-size lady doll that could play the fiddle ; and a gentleman with a hollow inside who could smoke a pipe and drink more lager beer than any three average German students put together, which is saying much.

Indeed, it was the belief of the town that old Geibel could make a man capable of doing everything that a respectable man need want to do. One day he made a man who did too much, and it came about in this way.

Young Doctor Follen had a baby, and the baby had a birthday. Its first birthday put Doctor Follen's household into somewhat of a flurry, but on the occasion of its second birthday, Mrs. Doctor Follen gave a ball in honour of the event. Old Geibel and his daughter Olga were among the guests.

During the afternoon of the next day, some three or four of Olga's bosom friends, who had also been present at the ball, dropped in to have a chat about it. They naturally fell to discussing the men, and to criticising their dancing. Old Geibel was in the room, but he appeared to be absorbed in his newspaper, and the girls took no notice of him.

" There seem to be fewer men who can dance, at every ball you go to," said one of the girls.

" Yes, and don't the ones who can give themselves airs," said another ; " they quite make a favour of asking you."

" And how stupidly they talk," added a third. " They always say exactly the same things : ' How charming you are looking to-night.' ' Do you often go to Vienna ? ' ' Oh, you should, it 's delightful.' ' What a charming dress you have on.' ' What a warm day it has been.' ' Do you like Wagner ? ' I do wish they 'd think of something new."

"Oh, I never mind how they talk," said a fourth. "If a man dances well he may be a fool for all I care."

"He generally is," slipped in a thin girl, rather spitefully.

"I go to a ball to dance," continued the previous speaker, not noticing the interruption. "All I ask of a partner is that he shall hold me firmly, take me round steadily, and not get tired before I do."

"A clockwork figure would be the thing for you," said the girl who had interrupted.

"Bravo!" cried one of the others, clapping her hands, "what a capital idea!"

"What's a capital idea?" they asked.

"Why, a clockwork dancer, or, better still, one that would go by electricity and never run down."

The girls took up the idea with enthusiasm.

"Oh, what a lovely partner he would make," said one; "he would never kick you, or tread on your toes."

"Or tear your dress," said another.

"Or get out of step."

"Or get giddy and lean on you."

"And he would never want to mop his face with his handkerchief. I do hate to see a man do that after every dance."

"And wouldn't want to spend the whole evening in the supper-room."

"Why, with a phonograph inside him to grind out all the stock remarks, you would not be able to tell him from a real man," said the girl who had first suggested the idea.

"Oh yes, you would," said the thin girl, "he would be so much nicer."

Old Geibel had laid down his paper, and was

listening with both his ears. On one of the girls glancing in his direction, however, he hurriedly hid himself again behind it.

After the girls were gone, he went into his workshop, where Olga heard him walking up and down, and every now and then chuckling to himself; and that night he talked to her a good deal about dancing and dancing men—asked what they usually said and did— what dances were the most popular—what steps were gone through, with many other questions bearing on the subject.

Then for a couple of weeks he kept much to his factory, and was very thoughtful and busy, though prone at unexpected moments to break into a quiet low laugh, as if enjoying a joke that nobody else knew of.

A month later another ball took place in Furtwangen. On this occasion it was given by old Wenzel, the wealthy timber merchant, to celebrate his niece's betrothal, and Geibel and his daughter were again among the invited.

When the hour arrived to set out, Olga sought her father. Not finding him in the house, she tapped at the door of his workshop. He appeared in his shirt-sleeves, looking hot, but radiant.

"Don't wait for me," he said, "you go on, I'll follow you. I've got something to finish."

As she turned to obey he called after her, "Tell them I'm going to bring a young man with me—such a nice young man, and an excellent dancer. All the girls will like him." Then he laughed and closed the door.

Her father generally kept his doings secret from everybody, but she had a pretty shrewd suspicion of what he had been planning, and so, to a certain extent, was able to prepare the guests for what was coming. Anticipation ran high, and the arrival of the famous mechanist was eagerly awaited.

At length the sound of wheels was heard outside, followed by a great commotion in the passage, and old Wenzel himself, his jolly face red with excitement and suppressed laughter, burst into the room and announced in stentorian tones:

" Herr Geibel—and a friend."

Herr Geibel and his " friend " entered, greeted with shouts of laughter and applause, and advanced to the centre of the room.

" Allow me, ladies and gentlemen," said Herr Geibel, " to introduce to you my friend, Lieutenant Fritz. Fritz, my dear fellow, bow to the ladies and gentlemen."

Geibel placed his hand encouragingly on Fritz's shoulder, and the lieutenant bowed low, accompanying the action with a harsh clicking noise in his throat, unpleasantly suggestive of a death rattle. But that was only a detail.

" He walks a little stiffly " (old Geibel took his arm and walked him forward a few steps. He certainly did walk stiffly), " but then, walking is not his forte. He is essentially a dancing man. I have only been able to teach him the waltz as yet, but at that he is faultless. Come, which of you ladies may I introduce him to, as a partner ? He keeps perfect time ; he never gets tired ; he won't kick you or tread on your dress ; he will hold you as firmly as you like, and go as quickly or as slowly as you please ; he never gets giddy ; and he is full of conversation. Come, speak up for yourself, my boy."

The old gentleman twisted one of the buttons of

his coat, and immediately Fritz opened his mouth, and in thin tones that appeared to proceed from the back of his head, remarked suddenly, " May I have the pleasure ? " and then shut his mouth again with a snap.

That Lieutenant Fritz had made a strong impression on the company was undoubted, yet none of the girls seemed inclined to dance with him. They looked askance at his waxen face, with its staring eyes and fixed smile, and shuddered. At last old Geibel came to the girl who had conceived the idea.

" It is your own suggestion, carried out to the letter," said Geibel, " an electric dancer. You owe it to the gentleman to give him a trial."

She was a bright saucy little girl, fond of a frolic. Her host added his entreaties, and she consented.

Herr Geibel fixed the figure to her. Its right arm was screwed round her waist, and held her firmly ; its delicately jointed left hand was made to fasten itself upon her right. The old toymaker showed her how to regulate its speed, and how to stop it, and release herself.

" It will take you round in a complete circle," he explained ; " be careful that no one knocks against you, and alters its course."

The music struck up. Old Geibel put the current in motion, and Annette and her strange partner began to dance.

For a while everyone stood watching them. The figure performed its purpose admirably. Keeping perfect time and step, and holding its little partner tightly clasped in an unyielding embrace, it revolved steadily, pouring forth at the same time a constant flow of squeaky conversation, broken by brief intervals of grinding silence.

" How charming you are looking to-night," it remarked in its thin, far-away voice. " What a lovely day it has been. Do you like dancing ? How well our steps agree. You will give me another, won't you ? Oh, don't be so cruel. What a charming gown you have on. Isn't waltzing delightful ? I could go on dancing for ever—with you. Have you had supper ? "

As she grew more familiar with the uncanny creature the girl's nervousness wore off, and she entered into the fun of the thing.

" Oh, he 's just lovely," she cried, laughing, " I could go on dancing with him all my life."

Couple after couple now joined them, and soon all the dancers in the room were whirling round behind them. Nicholaus Geible stood looking on, beaming with childish delight at his success.

Old Wenzel approached him, and whispered something in his ear. Geibel laughed and nodded, and the two worked their way quietly towards the door.

" This is the young people's house to-night," said Wenzel, as soon as they were outside ; " you and I will have a quiet pipe and a glass of hock, over in the counting-house."

Meanwhile the dancing grew more fast and furious. Little Annette loosened the screw regulating her partner's rate of progress, and the figure flew round with her swifter and swifter. Couple after couple dropped out exhausted, but they only went the faster, till at length they were the only pair left dancing.

Madder and madder became the waltz. The music lagged behind : the musicians, unable to keep pace, ceased, and sat staring. The younger guests applauded, but the older faces began to grow anxious.

"Hadn't you better stop, dear," said one of the women, "you'll make yourself so tired."

But Annette did not answer.

"I believe she's fainted," cried out a girl, who had caught sight of her face as it was swept by.

One of the men sprang forward and clutched at the figure, but its impetus threw him down on to the floor, where its steel-cased feet laid bare his cheek. The thing evidently did not intend to part with its prize easily.

Had anyone retained a cool head, the figure, one cannot help thinking, might easily have been stopped. Two or three men, acting in concert, might have lifted it bodily off the floor, or have jammed it into a corner. But few human heads are capable of remaining cool under excitement. Those who are not present think how stupid must have been those who were ; those who are, reflect afterwards how simple it would have been to do this, that, or the other, if only they had thought of it at the time.

The women grew hysterical. The men shouted contradictory directions to one another. Two of them made a bungling rush at the figure, which had the result of forcing it out of its orbit in the centre of the room, and sending it crashing against the walls and furniture. A stream of blood showed itself down the girl's white frock, and followed her along the floor. The affair was becoming horrible. The women rushed screaming from the room. The men followed them.

One sensible suggestion was made : "Find Geibel —fetch Geibel."

No one had noticed him leave the room, no one knew where he was. A party went in search of him. The others, too unnerved to go back into the ballroom, crowded outside the door and listened. They could hear the steady whir of the wheels upon the polished floor, as the thing spun round and round ; the dull thud as every now and again it dashed itself and its burden against some opposing object and ricocheted off in a new direction.

And everlastingly it talked in that thin ghostly voice, repeating over and over the same formula : " How charming you are looking to-night. What a lovely day it has been. Oh, don't be so cruel. I could go on dancing for ever—with you. Have you had supper ? "

Of course they sought for Geibel everywhere but where he was. They looked in every room in the house, then they rushed off in a body to his own place, and spent precious minutes in waking up his deaf old housekeeper. At last it occurred to one of the party that Wenzel was missing also, and then the idea of the counting-house across the yard presented itself to them, and there they found him.

He rose up, very pale, and followed them ; and he and old Wenzel forced their way through the crowd of guests gathered outside, and entered the room, and locked the door behind them.

From within there came the muffled sound of low voices and quick steps, followed by a confused scuffling noise, then silence, then the low voices again.

After a time the door opened, and those near it pressed forward to enter, but old Wenzel's broad shoulders barred the way.

" I want you—and you, Bekler," he said, addressing a couple of the elder men. His voice was calm, but his face was deadly white. " The rest of you, please go—get the women away as quickly as you can."

From that day old Nicholaus Geibel confined himself to the making of mechanical rabbits and cats that mewed and washed their faces.

(Novel Notes.)

Uncle Podger Hangs a Picture.

You never saw such a commotion up and down a house, in all your life, as when my Uncle Podger undertook to do a job. A picture would have come home from the frame-maker's, and be standing in the dining-room, waiting to be put up ; and Aunt Podger would ask what was to be done with it, and Uncle Podger would say :

"Oh, you leave that to *me*. Don't you, any of you, worry yourselves about that. *I 'll* do all that."

And then he would take off his coat, and begin. He would send the girl out for sixpen'orth of nails, and then one of the boys after her to tell her what size to get ; and, from that, he would gradually work down, and start the whole house.

"Now you go and get me my hammer, Will," he would shout ; "and you bring me the rule, Tom ; and I shall want the step-ladder, and I had better have a kitchen-chair, too ; and, Jim ! you run round to Mr. Goggles, and tell him, ' Pa's kind regards, and hopes his leg 's better ; and will he lend him his spirit-level ? ' And don't you go, Maria, because I shall want somebody to hold me the light ; and when the girl comes back, she must go out again for a bit of picture-cord ; and Tom !—where 's Tom ?—Tom, you come here ; I shall want you to hand me up the picture."

And then he would lift up the picture, and drop it, and it would come out of the frame, and he would try to save the glass, and cut himself ; and then he would spring round the room, looking for his handkerchief. He could not find his handkerchief, because it was in the pocket of the coat he had taken off, and he did not know where he had put the coat, and all the house had to leave off looking for his tools, and start looking for his coat ; while he would dance round and hinder them.

" Doesn't anybody in the whole house know where my coat is ? I never came across such a set in all my life—upon my word I didn't. Six of you !— and you can't find a coat that I put down not five minutes ago ! Well, of all the——"

Then he 'd get up, and find that he had been sitting on it, and would call out :

" Oh, you can give it up ! I 've found it myself now. Might just as well ask the cat to find anything as expect you people to find it."

And, when half an hour had been spent in tying up his finger, and a new glass had been got, and the tools, and the ladder, and the chair, and the candle had been brought, he would have another go, the whole family, including the girl and the charwoman, standing round in a semi-circle, ready to help. Two people would have to hold the chair, and a third would help him up on it, and hold him there, and a fourth would hand him a nail, and a fifth would pass him up the hammer, and he would take hold of the nail, and drop it.

" There ! " he would say, in an injured tone, " now the nail 's gone."

And we would all have to go down on our knees and grovel for it, while he would stand on the chair, and grunt, and want to know if he was to be kept there all the evening.

The nail would be found at last, but by that time he would have lost the hammer.

" Where 's the hammer ? What did I do with the hammer ? Great heavens ! Seven of you, gaping round there, and you don't know what I did with the hammer ! "

We would find the hammer for him, and then he would have lost sight of the mark he had made on the wall, where the nail was to go in, and each of us had to get up on the chair, beside him, and see if we could find it ; and we would each discover it in a different place, and he would call us all fools, one after another, and tell us to get down. And he would take the rule, and re-measure and find that he wanted half thirty-one and three-eighths inches from the corner, and would try to do it in his head, and go mad.

And we would all try to do it in our heads, and all·arrive at different results, and sneer at one another. And in the general row, the original number would be forgotten, and Uncle Podger would have to measure it again.

He would use a bit of string this time, and at the critical moment, when the old fool was leaning over the chair at an angle of forty-five, and trying to reach a point three inches beyond what was possible for him to reach, the string would slip, and down he would slide on to the piano, a really fine musical

" There you are," he would say, stepping heavily off the chair on to the charwoman's corns.

effect being produced by the suddenness with which his head and body struck all the notes at the same time.

And Aunt Maria would say that she would not allow the children to stand round and hear such language.

At last, Uncle Podger would get the spot fixed again, and put the point of the nail on it with his left hand, and take the hammer in his right hand. And, with the first blow, he would smash his thumb, and drop the hammer, with a yell, on somebody's toes.

Aunt Maria would mildly observe that, next time Uncle Podger was going to hammer a nail into the wall, she hoped he 'd let her know in time, so that she could make arrangements to go and spend a week with her mother while it was being done.

" Oh ! you women, you make such a fuss over everything," Uncle Podger would reply, picking himself up. " Why, I *like* doing a little job of this sort."

And then he would have another try, and, at the second blow, the nail would go clean through the plaster, and half the hammer after it, and Uncle Podger be precipitated against the wall with force nearly sufficient to flatten his nose.

Then we had to find the rule and the string again, and a new hole was made ; and, about midnight, the picture would be up—very crooked and insecure, the wall for yards round looking as if it had been smoothed down with a rake, and everybody dead beat and wretched—except Uncle Podger.

" There you are," he would say, stepping heavily

off the chair on to the charwoman's corns, and surveying the mess he had made with evident pride. " Why, some people would have had a man in to do a little thing like that ! "

(Three Men in a Boat.)

The Rule of the World.

IT seems to be the rule of this world. Each person has what he doesn't want, and other people have what he does want.

Married men have wives, and don't seem to want them ; and young single fellows cry out that they can't get them. Poor people who can hardly keep themselves have eight hearty children. Rich old couples, with no one to leave their money to, die childless.

Then there are girls with lovers. The girls that have lovers never want them. They say they would rather be without them, that they bother them, and why don't they go and make love to Miss Smith and Miss Brown, who are plain and elderly, and haven't got any lovers ? They themselves don't want lovers. They never mean to marry.

It does not do to dwell on these things ; it makes one so sad.

There was a boy at our school, we used to call him Sandford and Merton. His real name was Stivvings. He was the most extraordinary lad I ever came across. I believe he really liked study. He used to get into awful rows for sitting up in bed and reading Greek ; and as for French irregular verbs, there was simply no keeping him away from them. He was full of weird and unnatural notions about being a credit to his parents and an honour to the school; and he yearned to win prizes, and grow up and be a clever man, and had all those sorts of weak-minded ideas. I never knew such a strange creature, yet harmless, mind you, as the babe unborn.

Well, that boy used to get ill about twice a week, so that he couldn't go to school. There never was such a boy to get ill as that Sandford and Merton. If there was any known disease going within ten miles of him, he had it, and had it badly. He would take bronchitis in the dog-days, and have hay-fever at Christmas. After a six weeks' period of drought, he would be stricken down with rheumatic fever; and he would go out in a November fog and come home with a sunstroke.

They put him under laughing-gas one year, poor lad, and drew all his teeth, and gave him a false set, because he suffered so terribly with toothache; and then it turned to neuralgia and ear-ache. He was never without a cold, except once for nine weeks while he had scarlet fever; and he always had chilblains. During the great cholera scare of 1871, our neighbourhood was singularly free from it. There was only one reputed case in the whole parish: that case was young Stivvings.

He had to stop in bed when he was ill, and eat chicken and custards and hot-house grapes; and he would lie there and sob, because they wouldn't let him do Latin exercises, and took his German grammar away from him.

And we other boys, who would have sacrificed ten terms of our school-life for the sake of being ill for a day, and had no desire whatever to give our parents any excuse for· being stuck-up about us.

couldn't catch so much as a stiff neck. We fooled about in draughts, and it did us good, and freshened us up ; and we took things to make us sick, and they made us fat, and gave us an appetite. Nothing we could think of seemed to make us ill until the holidays began. Then, on the breaking-up day, we caught colds, and whooping cough, and all kinds of disorders, which lasted until the term recommenced ; when, in spite of everything we could manœuvre to the contrary, we would get suddenly well again, and be better than ever.

Such is life !

(*Three Men in a Boat.*)

On Babies.

OH yes, I do—I know a lot about 'em. I was one myself once—though not long, not so long as my clothes. *They* were very long, I recollect, and always in my way when I wanted to kick. Why do babies have such yards of unnecessary clothing? It is not a riddle. I really want to know. I never could understand it. Is it that the parents are ashamed of the size of the child, and wish to make believe that it is longer than it actually is? I asked a nurse once why it was. She said—

"Lor', sir, they always have long clothes, bless their little hearts."

And when I explained that her answer, although doing credit to her feelings, hardly disposed of my difficulty, she replied—

"Lor', sir, you wouldn't have 'em in *short* clothes, poor little dears?" And she said it in a tone that seemed to imply I had suggested some unmanly outrage.

Since then I have felt shy of making inquiries on the subject, and the reason—if reason there be—is still a mystery to me. But, indeed, putting them in any clothes at all seems absurd to my mind. Goodness knows, there is enough of dressing and undressing to be gone through in life, without beginning it before we need; and one would think that people who live in bed might, at all events, be spared the torture. Why wake the poor little wretches up in the morning to take one lot of clothes off, fix another lot on, and put them to bed again ; and then, at night, haul them out once more, merely to change everything back ? And when all is done, what difference is there, I should like to know, between a baby's nightshirt and the thing it wears in the day-time ?

Very likely, however, I am only making myself ridiculous —I often do ; so I am informed—and I will, therefore, say no more upon this matter of clothes, except only that it would be of great convenience if some fashion were adopted, enabling you to tell a boy from a girl.

Why do babies have such yards of unnecessary clothing ?

At present it is most awkward. Neither hair, dress, nor conversation affords the slightest clue, and you are left to guess. By some mysterious law of Nature you invariably guess wrong, and are thereupon regarded by all the relatives and friends as a mixture of fool and knave, the enormity of alluding to a male babe as " she " being only equalled by the atrocity of referring to a female infant as " he." Whichever

D

sex the particular child in question happens *not* to belong to is considered as beneath contempt, and any mention of it is taken as a personal insult to the family.

And, as you value your fair name, do not attempt to get out of the difficulty by talking of "it." There are various methods by which you may achieve ignominy and shame. By murdering a large and respected family in cold blood, and afterwards depositing their bodies in the water companies' reservoir, you will gain much unpopularity in the neighbourhood of your crime, and even robbing a church will get you cordially disliked, especially by the vicar. But if you desire to drain to the dregs the fullest cup of scorn and hatred that a fellow human creature can pour out for you, let a young mother hear you call dear baby "it."

Your best plan is to address the article as "little angel." The noun "angel" being of common gender, suits the case admirably, and the epithet is sure of being favourably received. "Pet" or "beauty" are useful for variety's sake, but "angel" is the term that brings you the greatest credit for sense and good feeling. The word should be preceded by a short giggle, and accompanied by as much smile as possible. And, whatever you do, don't forget to say that the child has got its father's nose. This "fetches" the parents (if I may be allowed a vulgarism) more than anything. They will pretend to laugh at the idea at first, and will say, "Oh, nonsense!" You must then get excited, and insist that it is a fact. You need have no conscientious scruples on the subject, because the thing's nose really does resemble its father's—at all events quite as much as it does anything else in nature— being, as it is, a mere smudge.

Do not despise these hints, my friends. There may come a time when, with mamma on one side and grandmamma on the other, a group of admiring young ladies (not admiring you, though) behind, and a bald-headed dab of humanity in front, you will be extremely thankful for some idea of what to say. A man—an unmarried man, that is—is never seen to such disadvantage as when undergoing the ordeal of "seeing baby." A cold shudder runs down his back at the bare proposal, and the sickly smile with which he says how delighted he shall be, ought surely to move even a mother's heart, unless, as I am inclined to believe, the whole proceeding is a mere device, adopted by wives to discourage the visits of bachelor friends.

It is a cruel trick, though, whatever its excuse may be. The bell is rung, and somebody sent to tell nurse to bring baby down. This is the signal for all the females present to commence talking "baby," during which time you are left to your own sad thoughts and to speculations upon the practicability of suddenly recollecting an important engagement, and the likelihood of your being believed if you do. Just when you have concocted an absurdly implausible tale about a man outside, the door opens, and a tall, severe-looking woman enters, carrying what at first sight appears to be a particularly skinny bolster, with the feathers all at one end. Instinct, however, tells you that this is the baby, and you rise with a miserable attempt at appearing eager. When the first gush of feminine enthusiasm with which the object in question is received has died out, and the number of ladies talking at once has been reduced to the ordinary four or five, the circle of fluttering petticoats divides,

and room is made for you to step forward. This you
do with much the same air that you would walk into
the dock at Bow Street, and then, feeling unutterably
miserable, you stand solemnly staring at the child.
There is dead silence, and you know that everyone
is waiting for you to speak. You try to think of something to say, but find, to your horror, that your
reasoning faculties have left you. It is a moment of
despair, and your evil genius, seizing the opportunity,
suggests to you some of the most idiotic remarks
that it is possible for a human being to perpetrate.
Glancing round with an imbecile smile, you sniggeringly
observe that " It hasn't got much hair, has it ? "
Nobody answers you for a minute, but at last the
stately nurse says with much gravity—" It is not
customary for children five weeks old to have long hair."
Another silence follows this, and you feel you are being
given a second chance, which you avail yourself of
by inquiring if it can walk yet, or what they feed it on.

By this time, you have got to be regarded as not
quite right in your head, and pity is the only thing
felt for you. The nurse, however, is determined that,
insane or not, there shall be no shirking, and that you
shall go through your task to the end. In the tones of
a high priestess, directing some religious mystery,
she says, holding the bundle towards you, " Take her
in your arms, sir." You are too crushed to offer any
resistance, and so meekly accept the burden. " Put
your arm more down her middle, sir," says the high
priestess, and then all step back and watch you intently
as though you were going to do a trick with it.

What to do you know no more than you did what
to say. It is certain something must be done, however,

and the only thing that occurs to you is to heave the unhappy infant up and down to the accompaniment of " oopsee-daisy," or some remark of equal intelligence. " I wouldn't jig her, sir, if I were you," says the nurse ; " a very little upsets her." You promptly decide *not* to jig her, and sincerely hope that you have not gone too far already.

At this point, the child itself, who has hitherto been regarding you with an expression of mingled horror and disgust, puts an end to the nonsense by beginning to yell at the top of its voice, at which the priestess rushes forward and snatches it from you with, " There, there, there ! What did ums do to ums ? " " How very extraordinary ! " you say pleasantly. " Whatever made it go off like that ? " " Oh, why you must have done something to her ! " says the mother indignantly ; " the child wouldn't scream like that for nothing." It is evident they think you have been running pins into it.

The brat is calmed at last, and would no doubt remain quiet enough, only some mischievous busybody points you out again with, " Who 's this, baby ? " and the intelligent child, recognising you, howls louder than ever.

Whereupon, some fat old lady remarks that " It 's strange how children take a dislike to anyone." " Oh, *they* know," replies another mysteriously. " It 's a wonderful thing," adds a third ; and then everybody looks sideways at you, convinced you are a scoundrel of the blackest dye ; and they glory in the beautiful idea that your true character, unguessed by your fellow-men, has been discovered by 'he untaught instinct of a little child.

(Idle Thoughts of an Idle Fellow.)

The Dwellers in the Elms.

IT was only a piece of broken glass. From its shape and colour, I should say it had, in its happier days, formed portion of a cheap scent-bottle. Lying isolated on the grass, shone upon by the early morning sun, it certainly appeared at its best. It attracted him.

He cocked his head, and looked at it with his right eye. Then he hopped round to the other side, and looked at it with his left eye. With either optic it seemed equally desirable.

That he was an inexperienced young rook goes without saying. An older bird would not have given a second glance to the thing. Indeed, one would have thought his own instinct might have told him that broken glass would be a mistake in a bird's nest.

But its glitter drew him too strongly for resistance. I am inclined to suspect that at some time, during the growth of his family tree, there must have occurred a *mésalliance*, perhaps worse. Possibly a strain of magpie blood?—one knows the character of magpies, or rather their lack of character—and such things have happened. But I will not pursue further so painful a train : I throw out the suggestion as a possible explanation, that is all.

He hopped nearer. Was it a sweet illusion, this flashing fragment of rainbow ; a beautiful vision to fade upon approach, typical of so much that is un-understandable in rook life ? He made a dart forward and tapped it with his beak. No, it was real,—as fine a lump of jagged green glass as any newly-married rook could desire, and to be had for the taking. *She* would be pleased with it. He was a well-meaning bird ; the mere upward inclination of his tail suggested earnest though possibly ill-directed endeavour.

He turned it over. It was an awkward thing to carry ; it had so very many corners. But he succeeded at last in getting it firmly between his beak, and in haste, lest some other bird should seek to dispute with him its possession, at once flew off with it.

A second rook, who had been watching the proceedings from the lime-tree, called to a third who was passing. Even with my limited knowledge of the language I found it easy to follow the conversation ; it was so obvious.

" Issachar ! "

" Hallo ! "

" What do you think ? Zebulun 's found a piece of broken bottle. He 's going to line his nest with it."

" No ! "

" God's truth. Look at him. There he goes ; he 's got it in his beak."

" Well, I 'm—— ! "

And they both burst into a laugh.

But Zebulun heeded them not. If he overheard, he probably put down the whole dialogue to jealousy. He made straight for his tree. By standing with my left cheek pressed close against the window-pane, I was able to follow him. He is building in what we

call the Paddock elms,—a suburb commenced only
last season, but rapidly growing. I wanted to see what
his wife would say.

At first she said nothing. He laid it carefully
down on the branch near the half-finished nest, and
she stretched up her head and looked at it.

Then she looked at him. For about a minute
neither spoke. I could see that the situation was
becoming strained.

When she did open her beak, it was with a
subdued tone, that had a vein of weariness running
through it.

" What is it ? " she asked.

He was evidently chilled by her manner. As I
have explained, he is an inexperienced young rook.
This is clearly his first wife, and he stands somewhat
in awe of her.

" Well, I don't exactly know what it 's *called*,"
he answered.

" Oh ! "

" No. But it 's pretty, isn't it ? " he added. He
moved it, trying to get it where the sun might reach it.
It was evident he was admitting to himself that, seen
in the shade, it lost much of its charm.

" Oh, yes ; very pretty," was the rejoinder ;
" perhaps you 'll tell me what you 're going to do
with it."

The question further discomforted him. It was
growing upon him that this thing was not going to be
the success he had anticipated. It would be necessary
to proceed warily.

" Of course it 's not a twig," he began.

" I see it isn't."

" No. You see, the nest is nearly all twigs as it is, and I thought—— "

" Oh, you did think."

" Yes, my dear. I thought—unless you are of opinion that it's too showy—I thought we might work it in somewhere."

Then she flared out.

" Oh, did you ? You thought that a good idea. An A1 prize idiot I seem to have married, I do. You 've been gone twenty minutes, and you bring me back an eight-cornered piece of broken glass, which you think we might ' work into ' the nest. You 'd like to see me sitting on it for a month, you would. You think it would make a nice bed for the children to lie on. You don't think you could manage to find a packet of mixed pins if you went down again, I suppose ? They 'd look pretty ' worked in ' somewhere, don't you think ? Here, get out of my way. I 'll finish this nest by myself." She always had been short with him.

She caught up the offending object—it was a fairly heavy lump of glass—and flung it out of the tree with all her force. I heard it crash through the cucumber frame. That makes the seventh pane of glass broken in that cucumber frame this week. The couple in the branch above are the worst. Their plan of building is the most extravagant, the most absurd, I ever heard of. They hoist up ten times as much material as they can possibly use ; you might think they were going to build a block and let it out in flats to the other rooks. Then what they don't want they fling down again. Suppose we built on such a principle. Suppose a human husband and wife were to start erecting their

D*

house in Piccadilly Circus, let us say ; and suppose the man spent all the day steadily carrying bricks up the ladder while his wife laid them, never asking her how many she wanted, whether she didn't think he had brought up sufficient, but just accumulating bricks in a senseless fashion, bringing up every brick he could find. And then suppose, when evening came, and looking round they found they had some twenty cartloads of bricks lying unused upon the scaffold, they were to begin flinging them down into Waterloo Place. They would get themselves into trouble ; somebody would be sure to speak to them about it. Yet that is precisely what those birds do, and nobody says a word to them. They are supposed to have a President. He lives by himself in the yew-tree outside the morning-room window.

What I want to know is what he is supposed to be good for. This is the sort of thing I want him to look into. I would like him to be worming underneath one evening when those two birds are tidying up ; perhaps he would do something then. I have done all I can. I have thrown stones at them that, in the course of nature, have returned to earth again, breaking more glass. I have blazed at them with a revolver ; but they have come to regard this proceeding as a mere expression of light-heartedness on my part, possibly confusing me with the Arab of the Desert, who, I am given to understand, expresses himself thus in moments of deep emotion. They merely retire to a safe distance to watch me, no doubt regarding me as a poor performer, inasmuch as I do not also dance and shout between each shot. I have no objection to their building there, if they only would build sensibly.

I want somebody to speak to them to whom they will pay attention.

You can hear them in the evening, discussing the matter of this surplus stock.

"Don't you work any more," he says, as he comes up with the last load ; "you 'll tire yourself."

"Well, I am feeling a bit done up," she answers, as she hops out of the nest and straightens her back.

"You 're a bit peckish, too, I expect," he adds sympathetically. "I know I am. We will have a scratch down, and be off."

"What about all this stuff ? " she asks, while titivating herself ; "we 'd better not leave it about, it looks so untidy."

"Oh, we 'll soon get rid of that," he answers. "I 'll have that down in a jiffy."

To help him, she seizes a stick and is about to drop it. He darts forward and snatches it from her.

"Don't waste that one," he cries ; "that 's a rare one, that is. You see me hit the old man with it."

And he does. What the gardener says, I will leave you to imagine.

Judged from its structure, the rook family is supposed to come next in intelligence to man himself. Judging from the intelligence displayed by certain human families with whom I have come in contact, I can quite believe it. That rooks talk I am positive. No one can spend half-an-hour watching a rookery without being convinced of this. Whether the talk be always wise and witty, I am not prepared to maintain ; but that there is a good deal of it is certain. A young French gentleman of my acquaintance, who visited England to study the language, told me that the impression made upon him by his first social evening in London was that of a parrot-house. Later on, when he came to comprehend, he, of course, recognised the brilliancy and depth of the average London drawing-room talk ; but that is how, not comprehending, it impressed him at first. Listening to the riot of a rookery is much the same experience. The conversation to us sounds meaningless ; the rooks themselves would probably describe it as sparkling.

(*Second Thoughts of an Idle Fellow.*)

On the Art of Making up One's Mind.

" Now, which would you advise, dear ? You see, with the red I shan't be able to wear my magenta hat."

" Well, then, why not have the grey ? "

" Yes, yes, I think the grey will be *more useful*."

" It 's a good material."

" Yes, and it 's a *pretty* grey. You know what I mean, dear ; not a *common* grey. Of course grey is always an *uninteresting* colour."

" It 's quiet."

" And then again, what I feel about the red is that it is so warm-looking. Red makes you *feel* warm even when you 're *not* warm. You know what I mean, dear."

" Well, then, why not have the red ? It suits you— red."

" No ; do you really think so ? "

" Well, when you 've got a colour, I mean, of course."

" Yes, that *is* the drawback to red. No, I think, on the whole, the grey is *safer*."

" Then you will take the grey, madam."

" Yes, I think I 'd better ; don't you, dear ? "

" I like it myself very much."

" And it is good wearing stuff. I shall have it

trimmed with—— Oh! you haven't cut it off,
have you?"

"I was just about to, madam."

"Well, don't for a moment. Just let me have
another look at the red. You see, dear, it has just
occurred to me—that chinchilla would look so well
on the red."

"So it would, dear."

"And, you see, I've *got* the chinchilla."

"Then have the red. Why not?"

"Well, there is the hat I'm thinking of."

"You haven't anything else you could wear with
that?"

"Nothing at all, and it would go so *beautifully*
with the grey. Yes, I think I'll have the grey. It's
always a safe colour,—grey."

"Fourteen yards I think you said, madam?"

"Yes, fourteen yards will be enough; because
I shall mix it with—one minute. You see, dear, if
I take the grey I shall have nothing to wear with my
black jacket."

"Won't it go with grey?"

"Not well—not so well as with red."

"I should have the red, then. You evidently
fancy it yourself."

"No, personally I prefer the grey. But then one
must think of *everything*, and—— Good gracious!
that's surely not the right time?"

"No, madam, it's ten minutes slow. We always
keep our clocks a little slow."

"And we were to have been at Madame Jannaway's
at a quarter past twelve. How long shopping does
take! Why, whatever time did we start?"

" Now, which would you advise, dear ? "

" About eleven, wasn't it ? "

" Half-past ten. I remember now ; because, you know, we said we 'd start at half-past nine. We 've been two hours already ! "

" And we don't seem to have done much, do we ? "

" Done literally nothing, and I meant to have done *so* much. I *must* go to Madame Jannaway's. Have you got my purse, dear ? Oh, it 's all right, I 've got it."

" Well, *now* you haven't decided whether you 're going to have the grey or the red."

" I 'm sure I don't know what I *do* want now. I had made up my mind a minute ago, and now it 's all gone again—oh, yes, I remember, the red. Yes, I 'll have the red. No, I don't mean the red ; I mean the grey."

" You were talking about the red last time, if you remember, dear."

" Oh, so I was ; you 're quite right. That 's the worst of shopping. Do you know, I get quite confused sometimes."

" Then you will decide on the red, madam ? "

" Yes, yes, I shan't do any better, shall I, dear ? What do *you* think ? You haven't got any other shades of red, have you ? This is such an *ugly* red."

The shopman reminds her that she has seen all the other reds, and that this is the particular shade she selected and admired.

" Oh, very well, she replies, with the air of one from whom all earthly cares are falling, " I must take that, then, I suppose. I can't be worried about it any longer. I 've wasted half the morning already."

Outside she recollects three insuperable objections

to the red, and four unanswerable arguments why she should have selected the grey. She wonders would they change it, if she went back and asked to see the shop-walker? Her friend, who wants her lunch, thinks not.

"That is what I hate about shopping," she says. "One never has time to really *think*."

(*Second Thoughts of an Idle Fellow.*)

The Music Hall of the Old Regime.

It was not until I was nearly seventeen that the idea occurred to me to visit a Music Hall again. Then, having regard to my double capacity of " Man About Town " and journalist (for I had written a letter to *The Era*, complaining of the way pit doors were made to open, and it had been inserted), I felt I had no longer any right to neglect acquaintanceship with so important a feature in the life of the people. Accordingly, one Saturday night, I wended my way to the " Pav." ; and there the first person that I ran against was my uncle. He laid a heavy hand upon my shoulder, and asked me, in severe tones, what I was doing there. I felt this to be an awkward question, for it would have been useless trying to make him understand my real motives (one's own relations are never sympathetic), and I was somewhat nonplussed for an answer, until the reflection occurred to me : What was *he* doing there ? This riddle I, in my turn, propounded to him, with the result that we entered into a treaty, by the terms of which it was agreed that no future reference should be made to the meeting by either of us— especially not in the presence of my aunt—and the compact was ratified according to the usual custom, my uncle paying the necessary expenses.

In those days we sat, some four or six of us, round

a little table, on which were placed our drinks. Now we have to balance them upon a narrow ledge ; and ladies, as they pass, dip the ends of their cloaks into them, and gentlemen stir them up for us with the ferrules of their umbrellas, or else sweep them off into our laps with their coat tails, saying as they do so, " Oh, I beg your pardon."

Also, in those days, there were " chairmen "— affable gentlemen, who would drink anything at any-body's expense, and drink any quantity of it, and never seem to get any fuller. I was introduced to a Music Hall chairman once, and when I said to him, " What is your drink ? " he took up the " List of beverages " that lay before him, and, opening it, waved his hand lightly across its entire contents, from clarets, past champagnes and spirits, down to liqueurs. " That's my drink, my boy," said he. There was nothing narrow-minded or exclusive about his tastes.

It was the chairman's duty to introduce the artists. " Ladies and gentlemen," he would shout, in a voice that united the musical characteristics of a fog-horn and a steam saw, " Miss 'Enerietta Montressor, the popular serio-comic will now happear." These announce-ments were invariably received with great applause by the chairman himself, and generally with chilling indifference by the rest of the audience.

It was also the privilege of the chairman to maintain order, and reprimand evil-doers. This he usually did very effectively, employing for the purpose language both fit and forcible. One chairman that I remember seemed, however, to be curiously deficient in the necessary qualities for this part of his duty. He was a mild and sleepy little man, and, unfortunately, he had to preside over an exceptionally rowdy audience at a small hall in the South-East district. On the night that I was present there occurred a great disturbance. "Joss Jessop, the Monarch of Mirth," a gentleman evidently high in local request, was, for some reason or other, not forthcoming, and in his place the management proposed to offer a female performer on the zithern, one Signorina Ballatino.

The little chairman made the announcement in a nervous, deprecatory tone, as if he were rather ashamed of it himself. "Ladies and gentlemen," he began,— the poor are staunch sticklers for etiquette : I overheard a small child explaining to her mother one night in Three Colts Street, Limehouse, that she could not get into the house because there was a " lady " on the doorstep, drunk,—" Signorina Ballatino, the world-renowned—— "

Here a voice from the gallery requested to know what had become of " Old Joss," and was greeted by loud cries of " 'Ear, 'ear."

The chairman, ignoring the interruption, continued :
" —— the world-renowned performer on the zither —— "

"On the whoter ? " came in tones of plaintive inquiry from the back of the hall.

" *Hon* the zither," retorted the chairman, waxing mildly indignant ; he meant zithern, but he called it a zither. "A hinstrument well known to anybody as 'as 'ad any learning."

This sally was received with much favour, and a gentleman who claimed to be acquainted with the family history of the interrupter begged the chairman to excuse that ill-bred person on the ground that his mother used to get drunk with the twopence a week and never sent him to school.

Cheered by this breath of popularity, our little president endeavoured to complete his introduction of the Signorina. He again repeated that she was the world-renowned performer on the zithern ; and, undeterred by the audible remark of a lady in the pit to the effect that she 'd " never 'eard on 'er," added :

" She will now, ladies and gentlemen, with your kind permission, give you examples of the—— "

" Blow yer zither ! " here cried out the gentleman who had started the agitation ; " we want Joss Jessop."

This was the signal for much cheering and shrill whistling, in the midst of which a wag with a piping voice suggested as a reason for the favourite's non-appearance that he had not been paid his last week's salary.

A temporary lull occurred at this point ; and the chairman, seizing the opportunity to complete his oft-impeded speech, suddenly remarked, " songs of the Sunny South " ; and immediately sat down and began hammering upon the table.

Then Signorina Ballatino, clothed in the costume of the Sunny South, where clothes are less essential than in these colder climes, skipped airily forward, and was most ungallantly greeted with a storm of groans and hisses. Her beloved instrument was unfeelingly alluded to as a pie-dish, and she was advised to take it back and get the penny on it. The chairman, addressed by his Christian name of " Jimmee," was told to lie down and let her sing him to sleep. Every time she attempted to start playing shouts were raised for Joss.

At length the chairman, overcoming his evident disinclination to take any sort of hand whatever in the game, rose and gently hinted at the desirability of silence. The suggestion not meeting with any support, he proceeded to adopt sterner measures. He addressed himself personally to the ringleader of the rioters, the man who had first championed the cause of the absent Joss. This person was a brawny individual, who, judging from appearances, followed in his business hours the calling of a coalheaver. "Yes, sir," said the chairman, pointing a finger towards him, where he sat in the front row of the gallery ; "you, sir, in the flannel shirt. I can see you. Will you allow this lady to give her entertainment ? "

"No," answered he of the coalheaving profession, in stentorian tones.

"Then, sir," said the little chairman, working himself up into a state suggestive of Jove about to launch a thunderbolt—"then, sir, all I can say is that you are no gentleman."

This was a little too much, or rather a good deal too little, for the Signorina Ballatino. She had hitherto been standing in a meek attitude of pathetic appeal, wearing a fixed smile of ineffable sweetness ; but she evidently felt that she could go a bit farther than that herself, even if she was a lady. Calling the chairman "an old messer," and telling him for Gawd's sake to shut up if that was all he could do for his living, she came down to the front, and took the case into her own hands.

She did not waste time on the rest of the audience. She went direct for that coalheaver, and thereupon ensued a slanging match the memory of which sends

a thrill of admiration through me even to this day.
It was a battle worthy of the gods. He was a heaver
of coals, quick and ready beyond his kind. During
many years sojourn East and South, in the course of

Took the case into her own hands.

many wanderings from Billingsgate to Limehouse Hole,
from Petticoat Lane to Whitechapel Road ; out of
eel-pie shop and penny gaff ; out of tavern and street,
and court and doss-house, he had gathered together

slang words and terms and phrases, and they came back to him now, and he stood up against her manfully.

But as well might the lamb stand up against the eagle, when the shadow of its wings falls across the green pastures, and the wind flies before its dark oncoming. At the end of two minutes he lay gasping, dazed, and speechless.

Then she began.

She announced her intention of " wiping down the bloomin' 'all " with him, and making it respectable ; and, metaphorically speaking, that is what she did. Her tongue hit him between the eyes, and knocked him down and trampled on him. It curled round and round him like a whip, and then it uncurled and wound the other way. It seized him by the scruff of his neck, and tossed him up into the air, and caught him as he descended, and flung him to the ground, and rolled him on it. It played round him like forked lightning, and blinded him. It danced and shrieked about him like a host of whirling fiends, and he tried to remember a prayer, and could not. It touched him lightly on the sole of his foot and the crown of his head, and his hair stood up straight, and his limbs grew stiff. The people sitting near him drew away, not feeling it safe to be near, and left him alone, surrounded by space, and language.

It was the most artistic piece of work of its kind that I have ever heard. Every phrase she flung at him seemed to have been woven on purpose to entangle him and to embrace in its choking folds his people and his gods, to strangle with its threads his every hope, ambition, and belief. Each term she put upon him clung to him like a garment, and fitted him without

a crease. The last name that she called him one felt
to be, until one heard the next, the one name that he
ought to have been christened by.

For five and three-quarter minutes by the clock
she spoke, and never for one instant did she pause or
falter ; and in the whole of that onslaught there was
only one weak spot.

That was when she offered to make a better man
than he was out of a Guy Fawkes and a lump of coal.
You felt that one lump of coal would not have been
sufficient.

At the end, she gathered herself together for one
supreme effort, and hurled at him an insult so bitter
with scorn, so sharp with insight into his career and
character, so heavy with prophetic curse, that strong
men drew and held their breath while it passed over
them, and women hid their faces and shivered.

Then she folded her arms, and stood silent ; and
the house, from floor to ceiling, rose and cheered her
until there was no more breath left in its lungs.

In that one night she stepped from oblivion into
success. She is now a famous " artiste."

But she does not call herself Signorina Ballatino,
and she does not play upon the zither. Her name
has a homelier sound, and her speciality is the delineation
of coster character.

(*John Ingerfield.*)

Wet to Stormy.

HOUSEBOATS then were not built to the scale of
Mississippi steamers, but this boat was a small one,
even for that primitive age. The man from whom
we hired it described it as "compact." The man to
whom, at the end of the first month, we tried to sub-let
it, characterised it as "poky." In our letters we
traversed this definition. In our hearts we agreed
with it.

At first, however, its size—or, rather, its lack of
size—was one of its chief charms in Ethelbertha's
eyes. The fact that if you got out of bed carelessly
you were certain to knock your head against the
ceiling, and that it was utterly impossible for any man
to put on his trousers except in the saloon, she regarded
as a capital joke.

That she herself had to take a looking-glass and go
upon the roof to do her back hair, she thought less
amusing.

Amenda accepted her new surroundings with her
usual philosophic indifference. On being informed
that what she had mistaken for a linen-press was her
bedroom, she remarked that there was one advantage
about it, and that was that she could not tumble out
of bed; seeing there was nowhere to tumble ; and on
being shown the kitchen, she observed that she should

like it for two things—one was that she could sit in the middle and reach everything without getting up ; the other, that nobody else could come into the apartment while she was there.

" You see, Amenda," explained Ethelbertha apologetically, " we shall really live outside."

" Yes, mum," answered Amenda, " I should say that would be the best place to do it."

If only we could have lived more outside, the life might have been pleasant enough, but the weather rendered it impossible, six days out of the seven, for us to do more than look out of the window and feel thankful that we had a roof over our heads.

I have known wet summers before and since. I have learnt by many bitter experiences the danger and foolishness of leaving the shelter of London any time between the first of May and the thirty-first of October. Indeed, the country is always associated in my mind with recollections of long, weary days passed in the pitiless rain, and sad evenings spent in other peoples' clothes. But never have I known, and never, I pray night and morning, may I know again, such a summer as the one we lived through (though none of us expected to) on that confounded houseboat.

In the morning we would be awakened by the rain's forcing its way through the window and wetting the bed, and would get up and mop out the saloon. After breakfast I would try to work, but the beating of the hail upon the roof just over my head would drive every idea out of my brain, and, after a wasted hour or two, I would fling down my pen and hunt up Ethelbertha, and we would put on our mackintoshes and take our umbrellas and go out for a row. At midday we would return and put on some dry clothes, and sit down to dinner.

In the afternoon the storm generally freshened up a bit, and we were kept pretty busy rushing about with towels and cloths, trying to prevent the water from coming into the rooms and swamping us. During

We would put on our mackintoshes and take our umbrellas and go out for a row.

tea-time the saloon was usually illuminated by forked lightning. The evenings were spent in bailing out the boat, after which we took it in turns to go into the kitchen and warm ourselves. At eight we supped, and from then until it was time to go to bed we sat wrapped up in rugs, listening to the roar of the thunder, and the howling of the wind, and the lashing of the waves, and wondering whether the boat would hold out through the night.

Friends would come down to spend the day with us—elderly, irritable people, fond of warmth and comfort ; people who did not, as a rule, hanker after jaunts, even under the most favourable conditions ; but who had been persuaded by our silly talk that a day on the river would be to them like a Saturday to Monday in Paradise.

They would arrive soaked, and we would shut them up in different bunks, and leave them to strip themselves and put on things of Ethelbertha's or of mine. But Ethel and I in those days were slim, so that stout, middle-aged people in our clothes neither looked well nor felt happy.

Upon their emerging we would take them into the saloon and try to entertain them by telling them what we had intended to do with them had the day been fine. But their answers were short, and occasionally snappy, and after a while the conversation would flag, and we would sit round reading last week's newspapers and coughing.

The moment their own clothes were dry (we lived in a perpetual atmosphere of steaming clothes) they would insist upon leaving us, which seemed to me discourteous after all that we had done for them, and would dress themselves once more and start off home, and get wet again before they got there.

We would generally receive a letter a few days afterwards, written by some relative, informing us that both patients were doing as well as could be expected, and promising to send us a card for the funeral in case of a relapse.

(Novel Notes.)

Vanity.

" 'Tis vanity that makes the world go round."
I don't believe any man ever existed without vanity,
and, if he did, he would be an extremely uncomfortable
person to have anything to do with. He would, of
course, be a very good man, and we should respect
him very much. He would be a very admirable man
—a man to be put under a glass case, and shown round
as a specimen—a man to be stuck upon a pedestal,
and copied, like a school exercise—a man to be
reverenced, but not a man to be loved, not a human
brother whose hand we should care to grip. Angels
may be very excellent sort of folk in their way, but we,
poor mortals, in our present state, would probably
find them precious slow company. Even mere good
people are rather depressing. It is in our faults and
failings, not in our virtues, that we touch one another,
and find sympathy. We differ widely enough in our
nobler qualities. It is in our follies that we are at
one. Some of us are pious, some of us are generous.
Some few of us are honest, comparatively speaking ;
and some, fewer still, may possibly be truthful. But
in vanity and kindred weaknesses we can all join hands.
Vanity is one of those touches of Nature that make
the whole world kin. From the Indian hunter, proud
of his belt of scalps, to the European general, swelling

beneath his row of stars and medals ; from the Chinee,
gleeful at the length of his pigtail, to the " professional
beauty," suffering tortures in order that her waist
may resemble a peg-top ; from the draggle-tailed
little Polly Stiggins, strutting through Seven Dials
with a tattered parasol over her head, to the princess,
sweeping through a drawing-room, with a train of
four yards long ; from 'Arry, winning by vulgar chaff
the loud laughter of
his pals, to the states-
man, whose ears are
tickled by the cheers
that greet his high-
sounding periods ;
from the dark-skinned
African, bartering his
rare oils and ivory
for a few glass beads to
hang about his neck,
to the Christian
maiden, selling her
white body for a score
of tiny stones and an
empty title to tack
before her name—all
march, and fight, and
bleed, and die be-
neath its tawdry flag.

Ay, ay, vanity is
truly the motive
power that moves
Humanity, and it is
flattery that greases

*The European general, swelling
beneath his row of stars
and medals.*

the wheels. If you want to win affection and respect in this world, you must flatter people. Flatter high and low, and rich and poor, and silly and wise. You will get on famously. Praise this man's virtues and that man's vices. Compliment everybody upon everything, and especially upon what they haven't got. Admire guys for their beauty, fools for their wit, and boors for their breeding. Your discernment and intelligence will be extolled to the skies.

Everyone can be got over by flattery. The belted earl—" belted earl " is the correct phrase, I believe. I don't know what it means, unless it be an earl that wears a belt instead of braces. Some men do. I don't like it myself. You have to keep the thing so tight, for it to be of any use, and that is uncomfortable. Anyhow, whatever particular kind of an earl a belted earl may be, he is, I assert, get-overable by flattery ; just as every other human being is, from a duchess to a cat's-meat man, from a ploughboy to a poet— and the poet far easier than the ploughboy, for butter sinks better into wheaten bread than into oaten cakes.

As for love, flattery is its very life blood. Fill a person with love for themselves, and what runs over will be your share, says a certain witty and truthful Frenchman, whose name I can't for the life of me remember. (Confound it, I never can remember names when I want to.) Tell a girl she is an angel, only more angelic than an angel; that she is a goddess, only more graceful, queenly, and heavenly than the average goddess ; that she is more fairy-like than Titania, more beautiful than Venus, more enchanting than Parthenopë ; more adorable, lovely, and radiant, in short, than any other woman that ever did live, does live, or could live, and you will make a very favourable impression upon her trusting little heart. Sweet innocent ! she will believe every word you say. It is so easy to deceive a woman—in this way.

Dear little souls, they hate flattery, so they tell you ; and, when you say, " Ah, darling, it isn't flattery in your case, it 's plain, sober truth ; you really are, without exaggeration, the most beautiful, the most good, the most charming, the most divine, the most perfect human creature that ever trod this earth," they will smile a quiet, approving smile, and, leaning against your manly shoulder, murmur that you are a dear good fellow after all.

By Jove, fancy a man trying to make love on strictly truthful principles, determining never to utter a word of mere compliment or hyperbole, but to scrupulously confine himself to exact fact ! Fancy his gazing rapturously into his mistress' eyes, and whispering softly to her that she wasn't, on the whole, bad looking, as girls went ! Fancy his holding up her little hand, and assuring her that it was of a light drab colour, shot with red ; and telling her, as he pressed her to his heart, that her nose, for a turned-up one, seemed rather pretty ; and that her eyes appeared to him, as far as he could judge, to be quite up to the average standard of such things !

A nice chance *he* would stand against the man who would tell her that her face was like a fresh blush rose, that her hair was a wandering sunbeam imprisoned by her smiles, and her eyes like two evening stars.

There are various ways of flattering, and, of course, you must adapt your style to your subject. Some

E

people like it laid on with a trowel, and this requires very little art. With sensible persons, however, it needs to be done very delicately, and more by suggestion than actual words. A good many like it wrapped up in the form of an insult, as—" Oh, you are a perfect fool you are. You would give your last sixpence to the first hungry-looking beggar you met ; " while others will swallow it only when administered through the medium of a third person, so that if C wishes to get at an A of this sort, he must confide to A's particular friend B that he thinks A a splendid fellow, and beg him, B, not to mention it, especially to A. Be careful that B is a reliable man, though, otherwise he won't.

Those fine, sturdy John Bulls, who " hate flatter y sir," " Never let anybody get over *me* by flattery," etc., etc., are very simply managed. Flatter them enough upon their absence of vanity, and you can do what you like with them.

After all, vanity is as much a virtue as a vice. It is easy to recite copy-book maxims against its sinfulness, but it is a passion that can move us to good as well as to evil. Ambition is only vanity ennobled. We want to win praise and admiration—or Fame as we prefer to name it—and so we write great books, and paint grand pictures, and sing sweet songs ; and toil with willing hands in study, loom, and laboratory.

(*Idle Thoughts of an Idle Fellow*.)

James : A Simple Soul.

SOMEBODY or other always had their head bumped whenever the ferry-boat arrived. It was a heavy and cumbersome machine, and the ferry-boy was not a good punter. He admitted this frankly, which was creditable of him. But he made no attempt to improve himself ; that is where he was wrong. His method was to arrange the punt before starting in a line with the point towards which he wished to proceed, and then to push hard, without ever looking behind him, until something suddenly stopped him. This was sometimes the bank, sometimes another boat, occasionally a steamer, from six to a dozen times a day our riparian dwelling. That he never succeeded in staving the houseboat in speaks highly for the man who built her.

One day he came down upon us with a tremendous crash. Amenda was walking along the passage at the moment, and the result to her was that she received a violent blow first on the left side of the head and then on the right.

She was accustomed to accept one bump as a matter of course, and to regard it as an intimation from the boy that he had come ; but this double knock annoyed her : so much "style" was out of place in a mere ferry-boy. Accordingly she went out to him in a state of high indignation.

"What do you think you are?" she cried, balancing accounts by boxing his ears first on one side and then on the other, "a torpedo! What are you doing here at all? What do you want?"

"I don't want nothin'," explained the boy, rubbing his head, "I've brought a gent down."

"A gent?" said Amenda looking round, but seeing no one. "What gent?"

"A stout gent in a straw 'at," answered the boy, staring round him bewilderedly.

"Well, where is he?" asked Amenda.

"I dunno," replied the boy in an awed voice; "'e was a-standin' there, at the other end of the punt, a-smokin' a cigar."

Just then a head appeared above the water, and a spent but infuriated swimmer struggled up between the houseboat and the bank.

"Oh, there 'e is!" cried the boy delightedly, evidently much relieved at this satisfactory solution of the mystery; "'e must ha' tumbled off the punt."

"You're quite right, my lad, that's just what he did do, and there's your fee for assisting him to do it." Saying which, my dripping friend, who had now scrambled upon deck, leant over, and following Amenda's excellent example, expressed his feelings upon the boy's head.

There was one comforting reflection about the transaction as a whole, and that was that the ferry-boy had at last received a fit and proper reward for his services. I had often felt inclined to give him something myself. I think he was, without exception, the most clumsy and stupid boy I have ever come across; and that is saying a good deal.

His mother undertook that for three-and-sixpence a week he should " make himself generally useful " to us for a couple of hours every morning.

Those were the old lady's very words, and I repeated them to Amenda when I introduced the boy to her.

" This is James, Amenda," I said ; " he will come down here every morning at seven, and bring us our milk and the letters, and from then till nine he will make himself generally useful."

Amenda took stock of him.

" It will be a change of occupation for him, sir, I should say, by the look of him," she remarked.

After that, whenever some more than usually stirring crash or blood-curdling bump would cause us to leap from our seats and cry : " What on earth has happened ? " Amenda would reply : " Oh, it 's only James, mum, making himself generally useful."

Whatever he lifted he let fall ; whatever he touched he upset ; whatever he came near—that was not a fixture—he knocked over : if it was a fixture, it knocked *him* over. This was not carelessness : it seemed to be a natural gift. Never in his life, I am convinced, had he carried a bucketful of anything anywhere without tumbling over it before he got there. One of his duties was to water the flowers on the roof. Fortunately—for the flowers—Nature, that summer, stood drinks with a lavishness sufficient to satisfy the most confirmed vegetable toper ; otherwise every plant on our boat would have died from drought. Never one drop of water did they receive from him. He was for ever taking them water, but he never arrived there with it. As a rule he upset the pail before he got it on to the boat at all, and this was the best thing that could happen, because then the water simply went back into the river, and did no harm to anyone. Sometimes, however, he would succeed in landing it, and then the chances were he would spill it over the deck or into the passage. Now and again, he would get halfway up the ladder before the accident occurred. Twice he nearly reached the top ; and once he actually did gain the roof. What happened there on that memorable occasion will never be known. The boy himself, when picked up, could explain nothing. It is supposed that he lost his head with the pride of the achievement, and essayed feats that neither his previous training nor his natural abilities justified him in attempting. However that may be, the fact remains that the main body of the water came down the kitchen chimney, and that the boy and the empty pail arrived together on deck before they knew they had started.

When he could find nothing else to damage, he would go out of his way to upset himself. He could not be sure of stepping from his own punt on to the boat with safety. As often as not, he would catch his foot in the chain or the punt-pole, and arrive on his chest.

Amenda used to condole with him.

" Your mother ought to be ashamed of herself," I heard her telling him one morning ; " she could never have taught you to walk. What you want is a go-cart."

He was a willing lad, but his stupidity was supernatural. A comet appeared in the sky that year, and everybody was talking about it. One day he said to me :—

" There 's a comet coming, ain't there, sir ? " He talked about it as though it were a circus.

" Coming ! " I answered, " it 's come. Haven't you seen it ? "

" No, sir."

" Oh, well, you have a look for it to-night. It's worth seeing."

" Yees, sir, I should like to see it. It's got a tail, ain't it, sir ? "

" Yes, a very fine tail."

" Yees, sir, they said it 'ad a tail. Where do you go to see it, sir ? "

" Go ! You don't want to go anywhere. You'll see it in your own garden at ten o'clock."

He thanked me, and, tumbling over a sack of potatoes, plunged head foremost into his punt and departed.

Next morning, I asked him if he had seen the comet.

" No, sir, I couldn't see it anywhere."

" Did you look ? "

" Yees, sir. I looked a long time."

" How on earth did you manage to miss it then ? " I exclaimed. " It was a clear enough night. Where did you look ? "

" In our garden, sir. Where you told me."

" Whereabouts in the garden ? " chimed in Amenda, who happened to be standing by ; " under the goose-berry bushes ? "

" Yees—everywhere."

That is what he had done : he had taken the stable lantern and searched the garden for it.

But the day when he broke even his own record for foolishness happened about three weeks later. MacShaughnassy was staying with us at the time, and on the Friday evening he mixed us a salad, according to a recipe given him by his aunt. On the Saturday morning, everybody was, of course, very ill. Everybody always is very ill after partaking of any dish prepared by MacShaughnassy. Some people attempt to explain this fact by talking glibly of "cause and effect." MacShaughnassy maintains that it is simply coincidence.

"How do you know," he says, "that you wouldn't have been ill if you hadn't eaten any ? You 're queer enough now, anyone can see, and I 'm very sorry for you ; but, for all that you can tell, if you hadn't eaten any of that stuff you might have been very much worse —perhaps dead. In all probability, it has saved your life." And for the rest of the day, he assumes toward you the attitude of a man who has dragged you from the grave.

The moment Jimmy arrived I seized hold of him.

"Jimmy," I said, "you must rush off to the chemist's immediately. Don't stop for anything. Tell him to give you something for colic—the result of vegetable poisoning. It must be something very strong, and enough for four. Don't forget, something to counteract the effects of vegetable poisoning. Hurry up, or it may be too late."

My excitement communicated itself to the boy. He tumbled back into his punt, and pushed off vigorously. I watched him land, and disappear in the direction of the village.

Half an hour passed, but Jimmy did not return. No one felt sufficiently energetic to go after him. We had only just strength enough to sit still and feebly abuse him. At the end of an hour we were all feeling very much better. At the end of an hour and a half we were glad he had not returned when he ought to have, and were only curious as to what had become of him.

In the evening, strolling through the village, we saw him sitting by the open door of his mother's cottage, with a shawl wrapped round him. He was looking worn and ill.

"Why, Jimmy," I said, "what's the matter? Why didn't you come back this morning?"

"I couldn't, sir," Jimmy answered, "I was so queer. Mother made me go to bed."

"You seemed all right in the morning," I said; "what's made you queer?"

"What Mr. Jones give me, sir: it upset me awful."

A light broke in upon me.

"What did you say, Jimmy, when you got to Mr. Jones's shop?" I asked.

"I told 'im what you said, sir, that 'e was to give me something to counteract the effects of vegetable poisoning. And that it was to be very strong, and enough for four."

"And what did he say?"

"'E said that was only your nonsense, sir, and that I'd better have enough for one to begin

Sitting by the open door of his mother's cottage, with a shawl wrapped round him.

E*

with ; and then 'e asked me if I 'd been eating green apples again."

" And you told him ? "

" Yees, sir, I told 'im I 'd 'ad a few, and 'e said it served me right, and that 'e 'oped it would be a warning to me. And then 'e put something fizzy in a glass and told me to drink it."

" And you drank it ? "

" Yees, sir."

" It never occurred to you, Jimmy, that there was nothing the matter with you—that you were never feeling better in your life, and that you did not require any medicine ? "

" No, sir."

" Did one single scintilla of thought of any kind occur to you in connection with the matter, Jimmy, from beginning to end ? "

" No, sir."

(Novel Notes.)

Cats and Dogs.

THEY are much superior to human beings as com-
panions. They do not quarrel or argue with you.
They never talk about themselves, but listen to you
while you talk about yourself, and keep up an appearance of being interested in the conversation. They
never make stupid remarks. They never observe to
Miss Brown across a dinner-table, that they always
understood she was very sweet on Mr. Jones (who has
just married Miss Robinson). They never mistake
your wife's cousin for her husband, and fancy that
you are the father-in-law. And they never ask a
young author with fourteen tragedies, sixteen comedies,
seven farces, and a couple of burlesques in his desk
why he doesn't write a play.

They never say unkind things. They never tell
us of our faults, "merely for our own good." They
do not, at inconvenient moments, mildly remind us
of our past follies and mistakes. They do not say,
"Oh yes, a lot of use *you* are, if you are ever really
wanted "—sarcastic like. They never inform us, like
our *inamoratas* sometimes do, that we are not nearly
so nice as we used to be. We are always the same to
them.

They are always glad to see us. They are with us
in all our humours. They are merry when we are glad,
sober when we feel solemn, sad when we are sorrowful.

"Hulloa! happy, and want a lark! Right you are; I'm your man. Here I am, frisking round you, leaping, barking, pirouetting, ready for any amount of fun and mischief. Look at my eyes, if you doubt me. What shall it be? A romp in the drawing-room, and never mind the furniture, or a scamper in the fresh, cool air, a scud across the fields, and down the hill, and won't we let old Gaffer Goggles's geese know what time o' day it is, neither. Whoop! come along."

Or you'd like to be quiet and think. Very well. Pussy can sit on the arm of the chair, and purr, and Montmorency will curl himself up on the rug, and blink at the fire, yet keeping one eye on you the while, in case you are seized with any desire in the direc- tion of rats.

And when we bury our face in our hands and wish we had never been born, they don't sit up very straight,

If it is a dog, he looks up at you with his big, true eyes, and says with them, " Well, you 've always got me, you know."

and observe that we have brought it all upon ourselves. They don't even hope it will be a warning to us. But they come up softly; and shove their heads against us. If it is a cat, she stands on your shoulder, rumples your hair, and says, " Lor', I am sorry for you, old man," as plain as words can speak; and if it is a dog, he looks up at you with his big, true eyes, and says with them, " Well, you 've always got me, you know. We 'll go through the world together, and always stand by each other, won't we ? "

He is very imprudent, a dog is. He never makes it his business to inquire whether you are in the right or in the wrong, never bothers as to whether you are going up or down upon life's ladder, never asks whether you are rich or poor, silly or wise, sinner or saint. You are his pal. That is enough for him, and, come luck or misfortune, good repute or bad, honour or shame, he is going to stick to you, to comfort you, guard you, give his life for you, if need be—foolish, brainless, soulless dog !

Ah ! old staunch friend, with your deep, clear eyes, and bright, quick glances, that take in all one has to say before one has time to speak it, do you know you are only an animal, and have no mind ? Do you know that that dull-eyed, gin-sodden lout, leaning against the post out there, is immeasurably your intellectual superior ? Do you know that every little-minded, selfish scoundrel, who lives by cheating and tricking, who never did a gentle deed, or said a kind word, who never had a thought that was not mean and low, or a desire that was not base, whose every action is a fraud, whose every utterance is a lie ; do you know that these crawling skulks (and there are millions of them in the world), do you know they are all as much superior to you as the sun is superior to rushlight, you honourable, brave-hearted, unselfish brute ? They are MEN, you know, and MEN are the greatest, and noblest, and wisest, and best Beings in the whole vast eternal Universe. Any man will tell you that.

Yes, poor doggie, you are very stupid, very stupid indeed, compared with us clever men, who understand all about politics and philosophy, and who know everything, in short, except what we are, and where we came from, and whither we are going, and what everything outside this tiny world and most things in it are.

(*Idle Thoughts of an Idle Fellow.*)

Advice to Edwin and Angelina.

LOVE is too pure a light to burn long among the noisome gases that we breathe, but before it is choked out we may use it as a torch to ignite the cosy fire of affection.

And, after all, that warming glow is more suited to our cold little back parlour of a world than is the burning spirit, love. Love should be the vestal fire of some mighty temple—some vast dim fane whose organ music is the rolling of the spheres. Affection will burn cheerily when the white flame of love is flickered out. Affection is a fire that can be fed from day to day, and be piled up ever higher as the winter years draw nigh. Old men and women can sit by it with their thin hands clasped, the little children can nestle down in front, the friend and neighbour has his welcome corner by its side, and even shaggy Fido and sleek Titty can toast their noses at the bars.

Let us heap the coals of kindness upon that fire. Throw on your pleasant words, your gentle pressures of the hand, your thoughtful and unselfish deeds. Fan it with good humour, patience, and forbearance. You can let the wind blow and the rain fall unheeded then, for your hearth will be warm and bright, and the faces round it will make sunshine in spite of the clouds without.

I am afraid, dear Edwin and Angelina, you expect too much from love. You think there is enough of your little hearts to feed this fierce, devouring passion for all your long lives. Ah, young folk! don't rely too much upon that unsteady flicker. It will dwindle and dwindle as the months roll on, and there is no replenishing the fuel. You will watch it die out in anger and disappointment. To each it will seem that it is the other who is growing colder. Edwin sees with bitterness that Angelina no longer runs to the gate to meet him, all smiles and blushes ; and, when he has a cough now, she doesn't begin to cry, and, putting her arms round his neck, say that she cannot live without him. The most she will probably do is to suggest a lozenge, and even that in a tone implying that it is the noise more than anything else she is anxious to get rid of.

Poor little Angelina, too, sheds silent tears, for Edwin has given up carrying her old handkerchief in the inside pocket of his waistcoat.

Both are astonished at the falling off in the other one, but neither sees their own change. If they did they would not suffer as they do They would look for the cause in the right quarter—in the littleness of poor human nature—join hands over their common failing, and start building their house anew on a more earthly and enduring foundation. But we are so blind to our own shortcomings, so wide awake to those of others. Everything that happens to us is always the other person's fault. Angelina would have gone on loving Edwin for ever and ever and ever, if only Edwin had not grown so strange and different. Edwin would have adored Angelina through eternity, if Angelina had only remained the same as when he first adored her.

It is a cheerless hour for you both, when the lamp of love has gone out, and the fire of affection is not yet lit, and you have to grope about in the cold raw dawn of life to kindle it. God grant it catches light before the day is too far spent. Many sit shivering by the dead coals till night comes.

(Idle Thoughts of an Idle Fellow.)

The Caution of Captain Goyles.

YEARS ago, when I was young and inexperienced, I hired a yacht. Three things had combined to lead me into this foolishness : I had had a stroke of unexpected luck ; Ethelbertha had expressed a yearning for sea air ; and the very next morning, in taking up casually at the club a copy of the *Sportsman*, I had come across the following advertisement :—

TO YACHTSMEN.—Unique Opportunity.—" Rogue," 28-ton Yawl.—Owner, called away suddenly on business, is willing to let this superbly-fitted " greyhound of the sea " for any period, short or long. Two cabins and saloon ; pianette, by Woffenkoff ; new copper. Terms, 10 guineas a week.—Apply Pertwee and Co., 3A Bucklersbury.

It had seemed to me like the answer to a prayer. " The new copper " did not interest me ; what little washing we might want could wait, I thought. But the " pianette by Woffenkoff " sounded alluring. I pictured Ethelbertha playing in the evening—something with a chorus, in which, perhaps, the crew, with a little training, might join—while our moving home bounded, " greyhound-like," over the silvery billows.

I took a cab and drove direct to 3A Bucklersbury. Mr. Pertwee was an unpretentious-looking gentleman, who had an unostentatious office on the third floor. He showed me a picture in water-colours of the *Rogue* flying before the wind. The deck was at an angle of 95° to the ocean. In the picture no human beings were represented on the deck; I suppose they had slipped off. Indeed, I do not see how anyone could have kept on, unless nailed. I pointed out this disadvantage to the agent, who, however, explained to me that the picture represented the *Rogue* doubling something or other on the well-known occasion of her winning the Medway Challenge Shield. Mr. Pertwee assumed that I knew all about the event, so that I did not like to ask any questions. Two specks near the frame of the picture, which at first I had taken for moths, represented, it appeared, the second and third winners in this celebrated race. A photograph of the yacht at anchor off Gravesend was less impressive, but suggested more stability. I took the thing for a fortnight. Mr. Pertwee asked me if I had a skipper in my eye. That I had not was also fortunate, because Mr. Pertwee felt sure I could not do better than keep on Mr. Goyles, at present in charge—an excellent skipper, so Mr. Pertwee assured me, a man who knew the sea as a man knows his own wife, and who had never lost a life.

It was still early in the day, and the yacht was lying off Harwich. I caught the ten forty-five from Liverpool Street, and by one o'clock was talking to Mr. Goyles on deck. He was a stout man, and had a fatherly way with him. I told him my idea, which was to take the outlying Dutch islands and then creep up to Norway. He said "Aye, aye, air," and appeared quite enthusiastic about the trip; said he should enjoy it himself. We came to the question of victualling, and he grew more enthusiastic. The amount of food suggested by Mr. Goyles, I confess, surprised me. Had we been living in the days of Drake and the Spanish Main, I should have feared he was arranging for something illegal. However, he laughed in his fatherly way, and assured me we were not overdoing it. Anything left over the crew would divide and take home with them—it seemed this was the custom. It appeared to me that I was providing for this crew for the winter, but I did not like to appear stingy, and said no more. The amount of drink required also surprised me. But Mr. Goyles was so cheerfully emphatic, and I was so inexperienced, that again I let him have his way. He also promised that even in this department he would see to it personally that nothing was wasted.

On Monday Ethelbertha and I put on all our clothes and started. I forget what Ethelbertha wore, but, whatever it may have been, it looked very fetching. My own costume was a dark blue, trimmed with a narrow white braid, which, I think, was rather effective.

Mr. Goyles met us on deck, and told us that lunch was ready. I must admit Goyles had secured the services of a very fair cook. The capabilities of the other members of the crew I had no opportunity of judging. Speaking of them in a state of rest, however, I can say of them they appeared to be a cheerful crew.

My idea had been that so soon as the men had finished their dinner we would weigh anchor, while I, smoking a cigar, with Ethelbertha by my side, would lean over the gunwale and watch the white cliffs of the Fatherland sink imperceptibly into the horizon. Ethelbertha and I carried out our part of the programme, and waited, with the deck to ourselves.

"They seem to be taking their time," said Ethelbertha.

"If, in the course of fourteen days," I said, "they eat half of what is on this yacht, they will want a fairly long time for every meal. We had better not hurry them, or they won't get through a quarter of it."

"They must have gone to sleep," said Ethelbertha, later on. "It will be tea-time soon."

They were certainly very quiet. I went for'ard, and hailed Captain Goyles down the ladder. I hailed him three times; then he came up slowly. He appeared to be a heavier and older man than when I had seen him last. He had a cold cigar in his mouth.

"When you are ready, Captain Goyles," I said, "we'll start."

Captain Goyles removed the cigar from his mouth.

"Not to-day we won't, sir," he replied, "*with* your permission."

"Why, what's the matter with to-day?" I said. I know sailors are a superstitious folk; I thought maybe a Monday might be considered unlucky.

"The day's all right," answered Captain Goyles, "it's the wind I'm a-thinking of. It don't look much like changing."

"But do we want it to change?" I asked. "It seems to me to be just where it should be, dead behind us."

"Aye, aye," said Captain Goyles, "dead's the right word to use, for dead we'd all be, bar Providence, if we was to put out in this. You see, sir," he explained, in answer to my look of surprise, " this is what we call a ' land wind,' that is, it 's a-blowing, as one might say, direct off the land."

" You see, sir, this is what we call a ' land wind,' that is, it 's a-blowing, as one might say, direct off the land."

When I came to think of it the man was right ; the wind was blowing off the land.

" It may change in the night," said Captain Goyles,

more hopefully; "anyhow, it's not violent, and she rides well."

Captain Goyles resumed his cigar, and I returned aft, and explained to Ethelbertha the reason for the delay. Ethelbertha, who appeared to be less high spirited than when we first boarded, wanted to know *why* we couldn't sail when the wind was off the land.

"If it was not blowing off the land," said Ethelbertha, "it would be blowing off the sea, and that would send us back into the shore again. It seems to me this is just the very wind we want."

I said: "That is your inexperience, love; it *seems* to be the very wind we want, but it is not. It's what we call a land wind, and a land wind is always very dangerous."

Ethelbertha wanted to know *why* a land wind was very dangerous.

Her argumentativeness annoyed me somewhat; maybe I was feeling a bit cross; the monotonous rolling heave of a small yacht at anchor depresses an ardent spirit.

"I can't explain it to you," I replied, which was true, "but to set sail in this wind would be the height of foolhardiness, and I care for you too much, dear, to expose you to unnecessary risks."

I thought this rather a neat conclusion, but Ethelbertha merely replied that she wished, under the circumstances, we hadn't come on board till Tuesday, and went below.

In the morning the wind veered round to the north; I was up early; and observed this to Captain Goyles.

"Aye, aye, sir," he remarked; "it's unfortunate, but it can't be helped."

" You don't think it possible for us to start to-day ? "
I hazarded.

He did not get angry with me, he only laughed.

" Well, sir," said he, " if you was a-wanting to go
to Ipswich, I should say as it couldn't be better for
us, but our destination being, as you see, the Dutch
coast—why there you are ! "

I broke the news to Ethelbertha, and we agreed
to spend the day on shore. Harwich is not a merry
town, towards evening you might call it dull. We
had some tea and watercress at Dovercourt, and
then returned to the quay to look for Captain Goyles
and the boat. We waited an hour for him. When
he came he was more cheerful than we were ; if he
had not told me himself that he never drank anything
but one glass of hot grog before turning in for the
night, I should have said he was drunk.

The next morning the wind was in the south,
which made Captain Goyles rather anxious, it appearing
that it was equally unsafe to move or to stop where
we were ; our only hope was it would change before
anything happened.

We passed another day at Harwich, and that night
and the next, the wind still continuing in the south,
we slept at the " King's Head." On Friday the wind
was blowing direct from the east. I met Captain
Goyles on the Quay, and suggested that, under these
circumstances, we might start. He appeared irritated
at my persistence.

" If you knew a bit more, sir," he said, " you'd
see for yourself that it's impossible. The wind's
a-blowing direct off the sea."

I said : " Captain Goyles, tell me what is this

thing I have hired? Is it a yacht or a house-boat?"

He seemed surprised at my question.

He said: "It's a yawl."

"What I mean is," I said, "can it be moved at all, or is it a fixture here? If it is a fixture," I continued, "tell me so frankly, then we will get some ivy in boxes and train over the port-holes, stick some flowers and an awning on deck, and make the thing look pretty. If, on the other hand, it can be moved—"

"Moved!" interrupted Captain Goyles. "You get the right wind behind the *Rogue*—"

I said: "What is the right wind?"

Captain Goyles looked puzzled.

"In the course of this week," I went on, "we have had wind from the north, from the south, from the east, from the west—with variations. If you can think of any other point of the compass from which it can blow, tell me, and I will wait for it. If not, and if that anchor has not grown into the bottom of the ocean, we will have it up to-day and see what happens."

He grasped the fact that I was determined.

"Very well, sir," he said, "you're master and I'm man. I've only got one child as is still dependent on me, thank God, and no doubt your executors will feel it their duty to do the right thing by the old woman."

His solemnity impressed me.

"Mr. Goyles," I said, "be honest with me. Is there any hope, in any weather, of getting away from this damned hole?"

Captain Goyles's kindly geniality returned to him. "You see, sir," he said, "this is a very peculiar coast. We'd be all right if we were once out, but getting away from it in a cockle-shell like that— well, to be frank, sir, it wants doing."

I left Captain Goyles with the assurance that he would watch the weather as a mother would her sleeping babe. I saw him again at twelve o'clock; he was watching it from the window of the "Chain and Anchor."

At five o'clock that evening a stroke of luck occurred; in the middle of the High Street I met a couple of yachting friends, who had had to put in by reason of a strained rudder. I told them my story, and they appeared less surprised than amused. Captain Goyles and the two men were still watching the weather. I ran into the "King's Head," and prepared Ethelbertha. The four of us crept quietly down to the quay, where we found our boat. Only the boy was on board; my two friends took charge of the yacht, and by six o'clock we were scudding merrily up the coast.

(*Three Men on the Bummel.*)

Too much Lover.

" I KNEW a girl," I said, " or, rather, a young married woman, who was cured of folly by the homœopathic method.   Her great trouble was that her husband had ceased to be her lover."

" It seems to me so sad," said the Old Maid. " Sometimes it is the woman's fault, sometimes the man's ; more often both.   The little courtesies, the fond words, the tender nothings that mean so much to those that love—it would cost so little not to forget them, and they would make life so much more beautiful."

" There is a line of common-sense running through all things," I replied ; " the secret of life consists in not diverging far from it on either side.   He had been the most devoted wooer, never happy out of her eyes ; but before they had been married a year she found to her astonishment that he could be content even away from her skirts, that he actually took pains to render himself agreeable to other women.   He would spend whole afternoons at his club, slip out for a walk occasionally by himself, shut himself up now and again in his study.   It went so far that one day he expressed a distinct desire to leave her for a week and go a-fishing with some other men.   She never complained—at least, not to him."

" That is where she was foolish," said the Girton Girl.   " Silence in such cases is a mistake.   The other party does not know what is the matter with you, and you yourself—your temper bottled up within—become more disagreeable every day."

"She confided her trouble to a friend," I explained.

"I so dislike people who do that," said the Woman of the World. "Emily never would speak to George ; she would come and complain about him to me, as if I were responsible for him : I wasn't even his mother. When she had finished, George would come along, and I had to listen to the whole thing over again from his point of view. I got so tired of it at last that I determined to stop it."

"How did you succeed ? " asked the Old Maid, who appeared to be interested in the recipe.

"I knew George was coming one afternoon," explained the Woman of the World, "so I persuaded Emily to wait in the conservatory. She thought I was going to give him good advice ; instead of that I sympathised with him and encouraged him to speak his mind freely, which he did. It made her so mad that she came out and told him what she thought of him. I left them at it. They were both of them the better for it ; and so was I."

"In my case," I said, "it came about differently. Her friend explained to him just what was happening. She pointed out to him how his neglect and indifference were slowly alienating from him his wife's affections. He argued the subject.

"'But a lover and a husband are not the same,' he contended ; 'the situation is entirely different. You run after somebody you want to overtake ; but when you have caught him up, you settle down quietly and walk beside him ; you don't continue shouting and waving your handkerchief after you have gained him.'

"Their mutual friend presented the problem differently.

"'You must hold what you have won,' she said, 'or it will slip away from you. By a certain course of conduct and behaviour you gained a sweet girl's regard ; show yourself other than you were, how can you expect her to think the same of you ? '

"'You mean,' he inquired, 'that I should talk and act as her husband exactly as I did when her lover ? '

"'Precisely,' said the friend ; 'why not ? '

"'It seems to me a mistake,' he grumbled.

"'Try it and see,' said the friend.

"'All right,' he said, 'I will.' And he went straight home and set to work."

"Was it too late," asked the Old Maid, "or did they come together again ? "

"For the next month," I answered, "they were together twenty-four hours of the day. And then it was the wife who suggested, like the poet in Gilbert's 'Patience,' the delight with which she would welcome an occasional afternoon off.

"He hung about her while she was dressing in the morning. Just as she had got her hair fixed he would kiss it passionately and it would come down again. All meal time he would hold her hand under the table and insist on feeding her with a fork. Before marriage he had behaved once or twice in this sort of way at picnics ; and after marriage, when at breakfast-time he had sat at the other end of the table reading the paper or his letters, she had reminded him of it reproachfully. The entire day he never left her side.

She could never read a book ; instead, he would read
to her aloud, generally Browning's poems or translations from Goethe. The Reading aloud was not an
accomplishment of his, but in their courting days
she had expressed herself pleased at his attempts,
and of this he took care, in his turn, to remind her.
It was his idea that if the game were played at all,
she should take a hand also. If he was to blither,
it was only fair that she should bleat back. As he
explained, for the future they would both be lovers
all their life long ; and no logical argument in reply
could she think of. If she tried to write a letter,
he would snatch away the paper her dear hands were
pressing and fall to kissing it—and, of course, smearing
it. When he wasn't giving her pins and needles by
sitting on her feet he was balancing himself on the arm
of her chair and occasionally falling over on top of her.
If she went shopping, he went with her and made himself
ridiculous at the dressmaker's. In society he took
no notice of anybody but of her, and was hurt if she
spoke to anybody but to him. Not that it was often,
during that month, that they did see any society ;
most invitations he refused for them both, reminding
her how once upon a time she had regarded an evening
alone with him as an entertainment superior to all
others. He called her ridiculous names, talked to her
in baby language ; while a dozen times a day it became
necessary for her to take down her back hair and do it
up afresh. At the end of a month, as I have said,
it was she who suggested a slight cessation of
affection."

   " Had I been in her place," said the Girton Girl,
" it would have been a separation I should have

suggested. I should have hated him for the rest of my life."

" For merely trying to agree with you ? " I said.

" For showing me I was a fool for ever having wanted his affection," replied the Girton Girl.

" You can generally," said the Philosopher, " make people ridiculous by taking them at their word."

(*Tea Table Talk.*)

Harris and the Maze.

HARRIS asked me if I 'd ever been in the maze at Hampton Court. He said he went in once to show somebody else the way. He had studied it up in a map, and it was so simple that it seemed foolish — hardly worth· the twopence charged for admission. Harris said he thought that map must have been got up as a practical joke, because it wasn't a bit like the real thing, and only misleading. It was a country cousin that Harris took in. He said :

" We 'll just go in here, so that you can say you 've been, but it 's very simple. It 's absurd to call it a maze. You keep on taking the first turning to the right. We 'll just walk round for ten minutes, and then go and get some lunch."

They met some people soon after they had got inside, who said they had been there for three-quarters of an hour, and had had about enough of it. Harris told them they could follow him, if they liked ; he was just going in, and then should turn round and come out again. They said it was very kind of him, and fell behind, and followed.

They picked up various other people who wanted to get it over, as they went along, until they had absorbed all the persons in the maze. People who had given up all hopes of ever getting either in or out, or of ever seeing their home and friends again, plucked up courage at the sight of Harris and his party, and joined the procession, blessing him. Harris said he should judge there must have been twenty people, following him, in all ; and one woman with a baby, who had been there all the morning, insisted on taking his arm, for fear of losing him.

Harris kept on turning to the right, but it seemed a long way, and his cousin said he supposed it was a very big maze.

" Oh, one of the largest in Europe," said Harris.

" Yes, it must be," replied the cousin, " because we 've walked a good two miles already."

Harris began to think it rather strange himself, but he held on until, at last, they passed the half of a penny bun on the ground that Harris's cousin swore he had noticed there seven minutes ago. Harris said : " Oh, impossible ! " but the woman with the baby said, " Not at all," as she herself had taken it from the child, and thrown it down there, just before she met Harris. She also added that she wished she never had met Harris, and expressed an opinion that he was an impostor. That made Harris mad, and he produced his map. and explained his theory.

" The map may be all right enough," said one of the party, " if you know whereabouts in it we are now."

Harris didn't know, and suggested that the best thing to do would be to go back to the entrance, and begin again. For the beginning again part of it there was not much enthusiasm ; but with regard to the advisability of going back to the entrance there was complete unanimity, and so they turned, and trailed after Harris again, in the opposite direction.

F

About ten minutes more passed, and then they found themselves in the centre.

Harris thought at first of pretending that that

They did not know where they were, and the map was once more consulted.

was what he had been aiming at ; but the crowd looked dangerous, and he decided to treat it as an accident.

Anyhow, they had got something to start from

then. They did know where they were, and the
map was once more consulted, and the thing seemed
simpler than ever, and off they started for the third
time.

And three minutes later they were back in the
centre again.

After that, they simply couldn't get anywhere
else. Whatever way they turned brought them back
to the middle. It became so regular at length, that
some of the people stopped there, and waited for the
others to take a walk round, and come back to them.
Harris drew out his map again, after a while, but
the sight of it only infuriated the mob, and they
told him to go and curl his hair with it. Harris said
that he couldn't help feeling that, to a certain extent,
he had become unpopular.

They all got crazy at last, and sang out for the
keeper, and the man came and climbed up the ladder
outside, and shouted out directions to them. But
all their heads were, by this time, in such a confused
whirl that they were incapable of grasping anything,
and so the man told them to stop where they
were, and he would come to them. They huddled
together, and waited ; and he climbed down, and
came in.

He was a young keeper, as luck would have it,
and new to the business ; and when he got in, he
couldn't find them, and he wandered about, trying
to get to them, and then *he* got lost. They caught
sight of him, every now and then, rushing about the
other side of the hedge, and he would see them, and
rush to get to them, and they would wait there for
about five minutes, and then he would reappear again

in exactly the same spot, and ask them where they had been.

They had to wait till one of the old keepers came back from his dinner before they got out.

Harris said he thought it was a very fine maze, so far as he was a judge ; and we agreed that we would try to get George to go into it, on our way back.

(Three Men in a Boat.)

Paul Talks with a Writer of Books.

MY talk with the stranger came about in this wise. One evening I had taken a walk to Victoria Park— a favourite haunt of mine in summer time. It was a fair and peaceful evening, and I fell a-wandering there in pleasant reverie, until the waning light hinted to me the question of time. I looked about me. Only one human being was in sight, a man with his back towards me, seated upon a bench overlooking the ornamental water. I drew nearer. He took no notice of me, and interested—though why, I could not say—I seated myself beside him at the other end of the bench. He was a handsome, distinguished-looking man, with wonderfully bright, clear eyes, and iron-grey hair and beard. I might have thought him a sea-captain, of whom many were always to be met with in that neighbourhood, but for his hands, which were crossed upon his stick, and which were white and delicate as a woman's. He turned his face and glanced at me. I fancied that his lips beneath the grey moustache smiled ; and instinctively I edged a little nearer to him.

" Please, sir," I said, after a while, " could you tell me the right time ? "

" Twenty minutes to eight," he answered, looking at his watch. And his voice drew me towards him even more than had his beautiful strong face. I thanked him, and we fell back into silence.

"Where do you live?" he turned and suddenly asked me.

"Oh, only over there," I answered, with a wave of my arm towards the chimney-fringed horizon behind us. "I needn't be in till half-past eight. I like this park so much," I added, "I often come and sit here of an evening."

"Why do you like to come and sit here?" he asked. "Tell me."

"Oh, I don't know," I answered; "I think."

I marvelled at myself. With strangers generally I was shy and silent; but the magic of his bright eyes seemed to have loosened my tongue.

I told him my name; that we lived in a street always full of ugly sounds, so that a gentleman could not think, not even in the evening time, when thought goes a-visiting.

"Mamma does not like the twilight time," I confided to him. "It always makes her cry. But then mamma is—not very young, you know, and has had a deal of trouble; and that makes a difference, I suppose."

He laid his hand upon mine. We were sitting nearer to each other now. "God made women weak to teach us men to be tender," he said. "But you, Paul, like this 'twilight time'?"

"Yes," I answered, "very much. Don't you?"

"And why do you like it?" he asked.

"Oh," I answered, "things come to you."

"What things?"

"Oh, fancies," I explained to him. "I am going to be an author when I grow up, and write books."

He took my hand in his and shook it gravely,

"I, too, am a writer of books," he said.

and then returned it to me. " I, too, am a writer of books," he said.

And then I knew what had drawn me to him.

So for the first time I understood the joy of talking "shop" with a fellow-craftsman. I told him my favourite authors—Scott, and Dumas, and Victor Hugo—and to my delight found they were his also, he agreeing with me that real stories are the best, stories in which people did things.

" I used to read silly stuff once," I confessed ; " Indian tales, and that sort of thing, you know. But mamma said I 'd never be able to write if I read that rubbish."

" You will find it so all through life, Paul," he replied. " The things that are nice are rarely good for us. And what do you read now ? "

" I am reading Marlowe's Plays and De Quincey's *Confessions* just now," I confided to him.

" And do you understand them ? "

" Fairly well," I answered. " Mamma says I 'll like them better as I go on. I want to learn to write very, very well indeed," I admitted to him ; " then I 'll be able to earn heaps of money."

He smiled. " So you don't believe in art for art's sake, Paul ? "

I was puzzled. " What does that mean ? " I asked.

" It means in our case, Paul," he answered, " writing books for the pleasure of writing books, without thinking of any reward—without desiring either money or fame."

It was a new idea to me. " Do many authors do that ? " I asked.

He laughed outright this time. It was a delightful

laugh. It rang through the quiet park, awaking echoes ; and caught by it, I laughed with him.

" Hush ! " he said, and he glanced round with a whimsical expression of fear, lest we might have been overheard. " Between ourselves, Paul," he continued, drawing me more closely towards him and whispering, " I don't think any of us do ; we talk about it. But I 'll tell you this, Paul, it is a trade secret, and you must remember it. No man ever made money or fame but by writing his very best. It may not be as good as somebody else's best, but it is his best. Remember that, Paul."

I promised I would.

" And you must not think merely of the money and the fame, Paul," he added the next moment, speaking more seriously. " Money and fame are very good things, and only hypocrites pretend to despise them. But if you write books thinking only of money you will be disappointed. It is earned easier in other ways. Tell me, that is not your only idea ? "

I pondered. " Mamma says it is a very noble calling, authorship," I remembered. " And that anyone ought to be proud and glad to be able to write books, because they give people happiness, and make them forget things ; and that one ought to be very good if one is going to be an author, so as to be worthy to help and teach others."

" And do you try to be good, Paul ? " he inquired.

" Yes," I answered ; " but it 's very hard to be quite good—until, of course, you 're grown up."

He smiled, but more to himself than to me. " Yes," he said, " I suppose it is difficult to be good until you are grown up. Perhaps we shall all of us be good when

F*

we 're quite grown up." Which, from a gentleman with a grey beard, appeared to me a puzzling observation.

" And what else does mamma say about literature ? " he asked. " Can you remember ? "

Again I pondered, and her words came back to me. " That he who can write a great book is greater than a king ; that the gift of being able to write is given to anybody in trust ; that an author should never forget he is God's servant."

He sat for a while without speaking, his chin resting on his folded hands, supported by his gold-topped cane. Then he turned and laid a hand upon my shoulder, and his clear, bright eyes were close to mine.

" Your mother is a wise lady, Paul," he said. " Remember her words always. In later life let them come back to you ; they will guide you better than the chatter of the clubs."

" And what modern authors do you read ? " he asked, after a silence. " Any of them—Thackeray, Bulwer Lytton, Dickens ? "

" I have read *The Last of the Barons*," I told him. " I like that. And I 've been to Barnet and seen the church ; and some of Mr. Dickens'."

" And what do you think of Mr. Dickens ? " he asked. But he did not seem very interested in the subject. He had picked up a few small stones, and was throwing them carefully into the water.

" I like him very much," I answered ; " he makes you laugh."

" Not always ? " he asked. He stopped his stone-throwing, and turned sharply towards me.

" Oh, no, not always," I admitted ; " but I like

the funny bits best.   I like so much where Mr. Pickwick
— —"

"Oh, damn Mr. Pickwick!" he said.

"Don't you like him ?" I asked.

"Oh yes, I like him well enough—or used to,"
he replied.   "I'm a bit tired of him, that's all.   Does
your mamma like Mr.—Mr. Dickens ?"

"Not the funny parts," I explained to him.   "She
thinks he is occasionally—— "

"I know," he interrupted, rather irritably I thought,
"a trifle vulgar."

It surprised me that he should have guessed her
exact words.   "I don't think mamma has much sense
of humour," I explained to him.   "Sometimes she
doesn't even see papa's jokes."

At that he laughed again.   "But she likes the
other parts," he inquired, "the parts where Mr. Dickens
isn't—vulgar ?"

"Oh yes," I answered.   "She says he can be so
beautiful and tender when he likes."

Twilight was deepening.   It occurred to me to
inquire of him again the time.

"Just over the quarter," he answered, looking
at his watch.

"I'm so sorry," I said.   "I must go now."

"So am I sorry, Paul," he answered.   "Perhaps
we shall meet again.   Good-bye."   Then as our hands
touched, "You have never asked me my name, Paul,"
he reminded me.

"Oh, haven't I ?" I answered.

"No, Paul," he replied, "and that makes me think
of your future with hope.   You are an egotist, Paul ;
and that is the beginning of all art."

And after that he would not tell me his name. " Perhaps next time we meet," he said. " Good-bye, Paul. Good luck to you ! "

So I went my way. Where the path winds out of sight I turned. He was still seated upon the bench, but his face was towards me, and he waved his hand to me. I answered with a wave of mine ; and then the intervening boughs and bushes gradually closed in around me. And across the rising mist there arose the hoarse, harsh cry, " All out ! All out ! "

(Paul Kelver.)

Swallow Street.

EVERY summer I suffer much from indignation. I love to watch the swallows building. They build beneath the eaves outside my study window. Such cheerful little chatter-boxes they are. Long after sunset, when all the other birds are sleeping, the swallows still are chattering softly. It sounds as if they were telling one another some pretty story, and often I am sure there must be humour in it, for every now and then one hears a little twittering laugh. I delight in having them there, so close to me. The fancy comes to me that one day, when my brain has grown more cunning, I, too, listening in the twilight, shall hear the stories that they tell.

One or two phrases already I have come to understand: "Once upon a time"—"Long, long ago"—"In a strange, far-off land." I hear these words so constantly, I am sure I have them right. I call it "Swallow Street," this row of six or seven nests. Two or three, like villas in their own grounds, stand alone, and others are semi-detached. It makes me angry that the sparrows will come and steal them. The sparrows will hang about deliberately waiting for a pair of swallows to finish their nest, and then, with a brutal laugh that makes my blood boil, drive the swallows away and take possession of it. And the swallows are so wonderfully patient.

"Never mind, old girl," says Tommy Swallow, after the first big cry is over, to Jenny Swallow, "let's try again."

And half an hour later, full of fresh plans, they are choosing another likely site, chattering cheerfully once more. I watched the building of a particular nest for nearly a fortnight one year ; and when, after two or three days' absence, I returned and found a pair of sparrows comfortably ensconced therein, I just felt mad. I saw Mrs. Sparrow looking out. Maybe my anger was working upon my imagination, but it seemed to me that she nodded to me :

"Nice little house, ain't it ? What I call well built."

Mr. Sparrow then flew up with a gaudy feather, dyed blue, which belonged to me. I recognised it. It had come out of the brush with which the girl breaks the china ornaments in our drawing-room. At any other time I should have been glad to see him flying off with the whole thing, handle included. But now I felt the theft of that one feather as an added injury. Mrs. Sparrow chirped with delight at sight of the gaudy monstrosity. Having got the house cheap, they were going to spend their small amount of energy upon internal decoration. That was their idea clearly, a "Liberty interior." She looked more like a Cockney sparrow than a country one—had been born and bred in Regent Street, no doubt.

"There's not much justice in this world," said I to myself ; "but there's going to be some introduced into this business—that is, if I can find a ladder."

I did find a ladder, and fortunately it was long enough.

Mr. and Mrs. Sparrow were out when I arrived, possibly on the hunt for cheap photo frames and Japanese fans. I did not want to make a mess. I removed the house neatly into a dust-pan, and wiped the street clear of every trace of it. I had just put back the ladder when Mrs. Sparrow returned with a piece of pink cotton-wool in her mouth. That was her idea of a colour scheme: apple-blossom pink and Reckett's blue side by side. She dropped her wool and sat on the water-spout, and tried to understand things.

"Number one, number two, number four; where the blazes"—sparrows are essentially common, and the women are as bad as the men—"is number three?"

Mr. Sparrow came up from behind, over the roof. He was carrying a piece of yellow-fluff, part of a lamp-shade, as far as I could judge.

"Move yourself," he said, "what's the sense of sitting there in the rain?"

"I went out just for a moment," replied Mrs. Sparrow; "I could not have been gone, no, not a couple of minutes. When I came back——"

"Oh, get indoors," said Mr. Sparrow, "talk about it there."

"It's what I'm telling you," continued Mrs. Sparrow, "if you would only listen. There isn't any door, there isn't any house——"

"Isn't any——" Mr. Sparrow, holding on to the rim of the spout, turned himself topsy-turvy and surveyed the street. From where I was standing behind the laurel bushes I could see nothing but his back. He stood up again, looking angry and flushed.

"What have you done with the house? Can't I turn my back a minute——"

"I ain't done nothing with it. As I keep on telling you, I had only just gone——"

"Oh, bother where you had gone. Where 's the darned house gone? that 's what I want to know."

They looked at one another. If ever astonishment was expressed in the attitude of a bird it was told by the tails of those two sparrows. They whispered wickedly together. The idea occurred to them that by force or cunning they might perhaps obtain possession of one of the other nests. But all the other nests were occupied, and even gentle Jenny Swallow, once in her own home with the children round about her, is not to be trifled with. Mr. Sparrow called at number two, put his head in at the door, and then returned to the waterspout.

"Lady says we don't live there," he explained to Mrs. Sparrow. There was silence for a while.

"Not what I call a classy street," commented Mrs. Sparrow.

"If it were not for that terrible tired feeling of mine," said Mr. Sparrow, "blame if I wouldn't build a house of my own."

"Perhaps," said Mrs. Sparrow, "—I have heard it said that a little bit of work, now and then, does you good."

"All sorts of wild ideas about in the air nowadays," said Mr. Sparrow, "it don't do to listen to everybody."

"And it don't do to sit still and do nothing neither," snapped Mrs. Sparrow. "I don't want to have to forget I 'm a lady, but—well, any man who was a man would see things for himself."

"Why did I ever marry ?" retorted Mr. Sparrow. They flew away together, quarrelling.

(*Idle Ideas in* 1905.)

Henry VIII. goes A-Wooing.

THERE are the ruins of an old priory in the grounds
of Ankerwyke House, which is close to Picnic Point,
and it was round about the grounds of this old priory
that Henry VIII. is said to have waited for and met
Anne Boleyn.　He also used to meet her at Hever Castle
in Kent, and also somewhere near St. Albans.　It
must have been difficult for the people of England in
those days to have found a spot where these thoughtless
young folk were *not* spooning.

Have you ever been in a house where there are a
couple courting ?　It is most trying.　You think you
will go and sit in the drawing-room, and you march
off there.　As you open the door, you hear a noise
as if somebody had suddenly recollected something,
and, when you get in, Emily is over by the window,
full of interest in the opposite side of the road, and
your friend, John Edward, is at the other end of the
room with his whole soul held in thrall by photographs
of other people's relatives.

" Oh ! " you say, pausing at the door, " I didn't
know anybody was here."

" Oh ! didn't you ? " says Emily, coldly, in a tone
which implies that she does not believe you.

You hang about for a bit, then you say :

" It 's very dark.　Why don't you light the
gas ? "

It was round about the grounds of this old priory that Henry VIII. is said to have waited for and met Anne Boleyn.

John Edward says, "Oh!" he hadn't noticed it; and Emily says that papa does not like the gas lit in the afternoon.

You tell them one or two items of news, and give them your views and opinions on the Irish question; but this does not appear to interest them. All they remark on any subject is, "Oh!" "Is it?" "Did he?" "Yes," and "You don't say so!" And, after ten minutes of such style of conversation, you edge up to the door, and slip out, and are surprised to find that the door immediately closes behind you, and shuts itself, without your having touched it.

Half an hour later, you think you will try a pipe in the conservatory. The only chair in the place is occupied by Emily; and John Edward, if the language of clothes can be relied upon, has evidently been sitting on the floor. They do not speak, but they give you a look that says all that can be said in a civilised community; and you back out promptly and shut the door behind you.

You are afraid to poke your nose into any room in the house now; so, after walking up and down the stairs for a while, you go and sit in your own bedroom. This becomes uninteresting, however, after a time, and so you put on your hat and stroll out into the garden. You walk down the path, and as you pass the summer-house you glance in, and there are those two young idiots, huddled up into one corner of it; and they see you, and are evidently under the idea that, for some wicked purpose of your own, you are following them about.

"Why don't they make a special room for this sort of thing, and make people keep to it?" you mutter ; and you rush back to the hall and get your umbrella and go out.

It must have been very much like this when that foolish boy Henry VIII. was courting his little Anne. People in Buckinghamshire would have come upon them unexpectedly when they were mooning round Windsor and Wraysbury, and have exclaimed, " Oh ! you here ! " and Henry would have blushed and said, " Yes ; he 'd just come over to see a man ; " and Anne would have said, " Oh, I 'm so glad to see you ! Isn't it funny ? I 've just met Mr. Henry VIII. in the lane, and he 's going the same way I am."

Then those people would have gone away and said to themselves : " Oh ! we 'd better get out of here while this billing and cooing is on. We 'll go down to Kent."

And they would go to Kent, and the first thing they would see in Kent when they got there would be Henry and Anne fooling round Hever Castle.

" Oh, drat this ! " they would have said. " Here, let 's go away. I can't stand any more of it. Let 's go to St. Albans—nice quiet place, St. Albans."

And when they reached St. Albans, there would be that wretched couple, kissing under the Abbey walls. Then these folks would go and be pirates until the marriage was over.

(*Three Men in a Boat.*)

Idle Thoughts on Memory.

Life altogether is but a crumbling ruin, when we turn to look behind: a shattered column here, where a massive portal stood; the broken shaft of a window to mark my lady's bower; and a mouldering heap of blackened stones where the glowing flames once leapt, and, over all, the tinted lichen and the ivy clinging green.

For everything looms pleasant through the softening haze of time. Even the sadness that is past seems sweet. Our boyish days look very merry to us now, all nutting, hoop, and ginger-bread. The snubbings and toothaches and the Latin verbs are all forgotten— the Latin verbs especially. And we fancy we were very happy when we were hobbledehoys, and loved; and we wish that we could love again. We never think of the heartaches, or the sleepless nights, or the hot dryness of our throats, when she said she could never be anything to us but a sister—as if any man wanted more sisters!

Yes, it is the brightness, not the darkness, that we see when we look back. The sunshine casts no shadows on the past. The road that we have traversed stretches fair behind us. We see not the sharp stones. We dwell but on the roses by the wayside, and the strong briars that stung us are, to our distant eyes, but gentle tendrils waving in the wind. God be thanked that it is so—that the ever-lengthening chain of memory has only pleasant links, and that the bitterness and sorrow of to-day are smiled at on the morrow.

It seems as though the brightest side of everything were also its highest and best, so that, as our little lives sink back behind us into the dark sea of forgetfulness, all that which is the lightest and the most gladsome is the last to sink, and stands upon the waters, long in sight, when the angry thoughts and smarting pain are buried deep below the waves and trouble us no more.

A friend came to me the other day, and urged me very eloquently to learn some wonderful system by which you never forgot anything. I don't know why he was so eager on the subject, unless it be that I occasionally borrow an umbrella, and have a knack of coming out, in the middle of a game of whist, with a mild, "Lor, I 've been thinking all along that clubs were trumps." I declined the suggestion, however, in spite of the advantages he so attractively set forth. I have no wish to remember everything. There are many things in most men's lives that had better be forgotten. There is that time, many years ago, when we did not act quite as honourably, quite as uprightly as we, perhaps, should have done—that unfortunate deviation from the path of strict probity we once committed and in which, more unfortunate still, we were found out—that act of folly, of meanness, of wrong. Ah! well, we paid the penalty, suffered the maddening hours of vain remorse, the hot agony of shame, the scorn, perhaps, of those we loved. Let us forget. Oh, Father Time, lift with your kindly hands those bitter memories from off our over-burdened hearts, for griefs are ever coming to us with the coming hours, and our little strength is only as the day.

Not that the past should be buried. The music of life would be mute if the chords of memory were snapped asunder. It is but the poisonous weeds, not the flowers, that we should root out from the garden of Mnemosyne. Do you remember Dickens's "Haunted Man," how he prayed for forgetfulness, and how, when his prayer was answered, he prayed for memory once more? We do not want all the ghosts laid. It is only the haggard, cruel-eyed spectres that we flee from. Let the gentle, kindly phantoms haunt us as they will; we are not afraid of them.

Ah, me! the world grows very full of ghosts as we grow older. We need not seek in dismal churchyards nor sleep in moated granges, to see their shadowy faces, and hear the rustling of their garments in the night. Every house, every room, every creaking chair has its own particular ghost. They haunt the empty chambers of our lives, they throng around us like dead leaves, whirled in the autumn wind. Some are living, some are dead. We know not. We clasped their hands once, loved them, quarrelled with them, laughed with them, told them our thoughts and hopes and aims, as they told us theirs, till it seemed our very hearts had joined in a grip that would defy the puny power of Death. They are gone now; lost to us for ever. Their eyes will never look into ours again, and their voices we shall never hear. Only their ghosts come to us, and talk with us. We see them, dim and shadowy, through our tears. We stretch our yearning hands to them, but they are air.

Ghosts! They are with us night and day. They

walk beside us in the busy street, under the glare of the sun. They sit by us in the twilight at home. We see their little faces looking from the windows of the old school-house. We meet them in the woods and lanes, where we shouted and played as boys. Hark! cannot you hear their low laughter from behind the blackberry bushes, and their distant whoops along the grassy glades? Down here, through the quiet fields, and by the wood, where the evening shadows are lurking, winds the path where we used to watch for her at sunset. Look, she is there now, in the dainty, white frock we knew so well, with the big bonnet dangling from her little hands, and the sunny brown hair all tangled. Five thousand miles away! Dead for all we know! What of that? She is beside us now, and we can look into her laughing eyes, and hear her voice. She will vanish at the stile by the wood, and we shall be alone; and the shadows will creep out across the fields, and the night wind will sweep past moaning. Ghosts! they are always with us, and always will be, while the sad old world keeps echoing to the sob of long good-byes, while the cruel ships sail away across the great seas, and the cold, green earth lies heavy on the hearts of those we loved.

But, oh, ghosts, the world would be sadder still without you. Come to us, and speak to us, oh! you ghosts of our old loves. Ghosts of playmates, and of sweethearts, and old friends, of all you laughing boys and girls, oh, come to us, and be with us, for the world is very lonely, and new friends and faces are not like the old, and we cannot love them, nay, nor laugh with them as we have loved and laughed with you. And when we walked together, oh, ghosts of our youth, the world was very gay and bright ; but now it has grown old, and we are growing weary, and only you can bring the brightness and the freshness back to us.

Memory is a rare ghost raiser. Like a haunted house, its walls are ever echoing to unseen feet. Through the broken casements we watch the flitting shadows of the dead, and the saddest shadows of them all are the shadows of our own dead selves.

(*Idle Thoughts of an Idle Fellow.*)

Paul's First Chum.

RAMBLING—" bummelling," as the Germans term it —was my bent. This my mother would have checked, but my father said—

" Don't molly-coddle him. Let him learn to be smart."

" I don't think the smart people are always the nicest," demurred my mother. " I don't call you at all ' smart,' Luke."

My father appeared surprised, but reflected.

" I should call myself smart—in a sense," he explained, after consideration.

" Perhaps you are right, dear," replied my mother ; " and of course boys are different from girls."

Sometimes I would wander Victoria Park way, which was then surrounded by many small cottages in leafy gardens, or even reach as far as Clapton, where old red-brick Georgian houses still stood behind high palings, and tall elms gave to the wide road on sunny afternoons an old-world air of peace. But such excursions were the exception, for, strange though it may read, the narrow, squalid streets had greater hold on me. Not the few main thoroughfares, filled ever with a dull, deep throbbing as of some tireless iron machine, where the endless human files, streaming ever up and down, crossing and re-crossing, seemed mere rushing chains of flesh and blood, working upon unseen wheels; but the dim, weary, lifeless streets—the dark, tortuous roots, as I fancied them, of that grim forest of entangled brick. Mystery lurked in their gloom; fear whispered from behind their silence. Dumb figures flitted to and fro, never pausing, never glancing right nor left. Far-off footsteps, rising swiftly into sound, as swiftly fading, echoed round their lonely corners. Dreading, yet drawn on, I would creep along their pavements as through some city of the dead, thinking of the eyes I saw not watching from the thousand windows: starting at each muffled sound penetrating the long, dreary walls, behind which that close-packed, writhing life lay hid.

One day there came a cry from behind a curtained window. I stood still for a moment and then ran; but before I could get far enough away I heard it again—a long, piercing cry, growing fiercer before it ceased—so that I ran faster still, not heeding where I went, till I found myself in a raw, unfinished street, ending in black waste land, bordering the river. I stopped, panting, wondering how I should find my way again. To recover myself and think I sat upon the doorstep of an empty house, and there came dancing down the road, with a curious half-running, half-hopping step—something like a water wagtail's—a child, a boy about my own age, who, after eyeing me strangely, sat down beside me.

We watched each other for a few minutes, and I noticed that his mouth kept opening and shutting, though he said nothing. Suddenly, edging closer to me, he spoke in a thick whisper. It sounded as though his mouth were full of wool.

"Wot 'appens to yer when yer dead?"

" If you 're good, you go to heaven ; if you 're bad, you go to hell."

" Long way off, both of 'em, ain't they ? "

" Yes. Millions of miles."

" They can't come after yer ? Can't fetch yer back again ? "

" No, never."

The doorstep that we occupied was the last. A yard beyond began the black waste of mud. From the other end of the street, now growing dark, he never took his staring eyes for an instant.

" Ever seen a stiff 'un—a dead 'un ? "

" No."

" I 'ave—stuck a pin into 'im. 'E never felt it. Don't feel anything when yer dead, do yer ? "

All the while he kept swaying his body to and fro, twisting his arms and legs and making faces. Comical figures made of gingerbread, with quaintly curved limbs, and grinning features, were to be bought then in bakers' shops ; he made me hungry, reminding me of such.

" Of course not. When you are dead you 're not there, you know. Our bodies are but senseless clay."

I was glad I remembered that line. I tried to think of the next one, which was about food for worms, but it evaded me.

" I like you," he said, and making a fist he gave me a punch in the chest. It was the token of palship among the youth of that neighbourhood, and gravely I returned it, meaning it ; for friendship with children is an affair of the instant, or not at all, and I knew him for my first chum.

He wormed himself up.

" Yer won't tell ? " he said.

I had no notion what I was not to tell, but our compact demanded that I should agree.

" Say ' I swear.' "

" I swear."

The heroes of my favourite fiction bound themselves by such-like secret oaths. Here evidently was a comrade after my own heart.

" Good-bye, cockey."

But he turned again, and taking from his pocket an old knife, thrust it into my hand. Then with that extraordinary hopping movement of his ran off across the mud.

I stood watching him, wondering where he could be going. He stumbled a little further, where the mud began to get softer and deeper, but struggling up again, went hopping on towards the river.

I shouted to him, but he never looked back. At every few yards he would sink down almost to his knees in the black mud, but wrenching himself free, would flounder forward. Then still some distance from the river, he fell upon his face, and did not rise again. I saw his arms beating feebler and feebler as he sank till at last the oily slime closed over him, and I could detect nothing but a faint heaving underneath the mud. And after a time even that ceased.

It was late before I reached home, and fortunately my father and mother were still out. I did not tell anyone what I had seen, having sworn not to ; and as time went on the incident haunted me less and less until it became subservient to my will. But of my fancy for those silent, lifeless streets it cured me for

the time.   From behind their still walls I could hear
that long cry ;   down their narrow vistas see that
writhing figure, like some animated gingerbread,
hopping, springing, falling.

(Paul Kelver.)

Should we Say What we Think?

A MAD friend of mine will have it that the characteristic of the age is Make-Believe. He argues that all social intercourse is founded on make-believe. A servant enters to say that Mr. and Mrs. Bore are in the drawing-room.

"Oh, damn!" says the man.

"Hush!" says the woman. "Shut the door, Susan. How often am I to tell you never to leave the door open?"

The man creeps upstairs on tiptoe and shuts himself in his study. The woman does things before a looking-glass, waits till she

Mr. and Mrs. Bore are in the drawing-room.

feels she is sufficiently mistress of herself not to show her feelings, and then enters the drawing-room with outstretched hands and the look of one welcoming an angel's visit. She says how delighted she is to see the Bores—how good it was of them to come. Why did they not bring more Bores with them? Where is naughty Bore junior? Why does he never come to see her now? She will have to be really angry with him. And sweet little Flossie Bore? Too young to pay calls! Nonsense. An "At Home" day is not worth having where all the Bores are not.

The Bores, who had hoped that she was out—who have only called because the etiquette book told them that they must call at least four times in the season, explain how they have been trying and trying to come.

"This afternoon," recounts Mrs. Bore, "we were determined to come. ' John, dear,' I said this morning, ' I shall go and see dear Mrs. Bounder this afternoon, no matter what happens.' "

The idea conveyed is that the Prince of Wales, on calling at the Bores, was told that he could not come in. He might call again in the evening or come some other day. That afternoon the Bores were going to enjoy themselves in their own way ; they were going to see Mrs. Bounder.

"And how is Mr. Bounder ? " demands Mrs. Bore.

Mrs. Bounder remains mute for a moment, straining her ears. She can hear him creeping past the door on his way downstairs. She hears the front door softly opened and closed-to. She wakes, as from a dream. She has been thinking of the sorrow that will fall on Bounder when he returns home later and learns what he has missed.

G

And thus it is, not only with the Bores and Bounders, but even with us who are not Bores or Bounders. Society in all ranks is founded on the make-believe that everybody is charming ; that we are delighted to see everybody ; that everybody is delighted to see us ; that it is so good of everybody to come ; that we are desolate at the thought that they really must go now.

Which would we rather do—stop and finish our cigar or hasten into the drawing-room to hear Miss Screecher sing ? Can you ask us ? We tumble over each other in our hurry. Miss Screecher would really rather not sing ; but if we insist—— We do insist. Miss Screecher, with pretty reluctance, consents. We are careful not to look at one another. We sit with our eyes fixed on the ceiling. Miss Screecher finishes, and rises.

" But it was so short," we say, so soon as we can be heard above the applause. Is Miss Screecher quite sure that was the whole of it ? Or has she been playing tricks upon us, the naughty lady, defrauding us of a verse ? Miss Screecher assures us that the fault is the composer's. But she knows another. At this hint, our faces lighten again with gladness. We clamour for more.

Our host's wine is always the most extraordinary we have ever tasted. No, not another glass ; we dare not—doctor's orders, very strict. Our host's cigars ! We did not know they made such cigars in this workaday world. No, we really could not smoke another. Well, if he will be so pressing, may we put it in our pocket ? The truth is, we are not used to high smoking. Our hostess's coffee ! Would she confide to us her secret ? The baby ! We hardly trust ourselves to speak. The usual baby—we have seen it. As a rule, to be candid, we never could detect much beauty in babies—have always held the usual gush about them to be insincere. But this baby ! We are almost on the point of asking them where they got it. It is just the kind we wanted for ourselves. Little Janet's recitation : " A Visit to the Dentist ! " Hitherto the amateur reciter has not appealed to us. But this is genius, surely. She ought to be trained for the stage. Her mother does not altogether approve of the stage. We plead for the stage—that it may not be deprived of such talent.

Every bride is beautiful. Every bride looks charming in a simple costume of—for further particulars see local papers. Every marriage is a cause for universal rejoicing. With our wine-glass in our hand we picture the ideal life we know to be in store for them. How can it be otherwise ? She, the daughter of her mother. (Cheers.) He—well, we all know him. (More cheers.) Also involuntary guffaw from ill-regulated young man at end of table, promptly suppressed.

We carry our make-believe even into our religion. We sit in church, and in voices swelling with pride, mention to the Almighty, at stated intervals, that we are miserable worms—that there is no good in us. This sort of thing, we gather, is expected of us ; it does us no harm, and is supposed to please.

(Idle Ideas in 1905.)

Noel Hasluck.

"HASLUCK," exclaimed my father, with sudden vehemence, "is little better than a thief; I told him so."

"What did he say?" asked my mother.

"Laughed, and said that was better than some people." My father laughed himself.

I wish to do the memory of Noel Hasluck no injustice. Ever was he a kind friend to me, not only then, but in later years, when, having come to learn that kindness is rarer in the world than I had dreamt, I was glad of it. Added to which, if only for Barbara's sake, I would prefer to write of him throughout in terms of praise. Yet even were his good-tempered, thick-skinned ghost—and unless it were good-tempered and thick-skinned it would be no true ghost of old Noel Hasluck—to be reading over my shoulder the words as I write them down, I think it would agree with me, I do not think it would be offended with me—for ever in his life he was an admirer and a lover of the truth, being one of those good fighters capable of respecting even his foe, his enemy against whom from ten to four, occasionally a little later, he fought right valiantly—for saying that of all the men who go down into the City each day in cab or 'bus or train, he was perhaps one of the most unprincipled; and whether that be saying much or little I leave to those with more knowledge to decide.

To do others, as it was his conviction, right or wrong, that they would do him if ever he gave them half a chance, was his notion of " business "; and in most of his transactions he was successful. " I play a game," he would argue, " where cheating is the rule. Nine out of every ten men round the table are sharpers like myself, and the tenth man is a fool who has no business to be there. We prey upon each other, and the cutest of us is the winner."

" But the innocent people, lured by your fine promises," I ventured once to suggest to him, " the widows and the orphans ? "

" My dear lad," he said, with a laugh, laying his fat hand upon my shoulder, " I remember one of your widows writing me a pathetic letter about some shares she had taken in a silver company of mine. Lord knows where the mine is now—somewhere in Spain, I think. It looked as though all her savings were gone. She had an only son, and it was nearly all they possessed in the world, etc., etc.—you know the sort of thing. Well, I did what I 've often been numskull enough to do in similar cases, wrote and offered to buy her out at par. A week later she answered, thanking me, but saying it did not matter. There had occurred a momentary rise, and she had sold out at a profit— to her own brother-in-law, as I discovered, happening to come across the transfers. You can find widows and orphans round the Monte Carlo gambling-tables, if you like to look for them ; they are no more deserving of consideration than the rest of the crowd. Besides, if it comes to that, I 'm an orphan myself," and he laughed again, one of his deep, hearty, honest laughs. No one ever possessed a laugh more suggestive in its every cadence of simple, transparent honesty. He used to say himself it was worth thousands to him.

Better, from the moralist's point of view, had such a man been an out-and-out rogue. Then might one have pointed, crying, " Behold ! dishonesty, as you will observe in the person of our awful example, to be hated needs but to be seen." But the duty of the chronicler is to bear witness to what he knows, leaving Truth with the whole case before her to sum up and direct the verdict. In the City old Hasluck had a bad reputation, and deserved it ; in Stoke Newington—then a green suburb, containing many fine old houses standing in great wooded gardens—he was loved and respected. In his business he was a man void of all moral sense, without bowels of compassion for any living thing ; in retirement a man with a strong sense of duty and a fine regard for the rights and feelings of others, never happier than when planning to help or give pleasure. In his office he would have robbed his own mother ; at home he would have spent his last penny to add to her happiness or comfort. I make no attempt to explain. I only know that such men do exist, and that Hasluck was one of them. One avoids difficulty by dismissing them as a product of our curiously complex civilisation—a convenient phrase ; let us hope the recording angel may be equally impressed by it.

(Paul Kelver.)

The Thing that Spoilt the Picture.

IT was a glorious day, and the lock was crowded ; and, as is a common practice up the river, a speculative photographer was taking a picture of us all as we lay upon the rising waters.

I did not catch what was going on at first, and was, therefore, extremely surprised at noticing George hurriedly smooth out his trousers, ruffle up his hair, and stick his cap on in a rakish manner at the back of his head, and then, assuming an expression of mingled affability and sadness, sit down in a graceful attitude, and try to hide his feet.

My first idea was that he had suddenly caught sight of some girl he knew, and I looked about to see who it was. Everybody in the lock seemed to have been suddenly struck wooden. They were all standing or sitting about in the most quaint and curious attitudes I have ever seen off a Japanese fan. All the girls were smiling. Oh, they did look so sweet ! And all the fellows were frowning, and looking stern and noble.

And then, at last, the truth flashed across me, and I wondered if I should be in time. Ours was the first boat, and it would be unkind of me to spoil the man's picture, I thought.

So I faced round quickly, and took up a position in the prow, where I leant with careless grace upon the hitcher, in an attitude suggestive of agility and strength. I arranged my hair with a curl over the forehead, and threw an air of tender wistfulness into my expression, mingled with a touch of cynicism, which I am told suits me.

As we stood, waiting for the eventful moment, I heard someone behind call out :

" Hi ! look at your nose."

I could not turn round to see what was the matter, and whose nose it was that was to be looked at. I stole a side-glance at George's nose ! It was all right—at all events, there was nothing wrong with it that could be altered. I squinted down at my own, and that seemed all that could be expected also.

" Look at your nose, you stupid ass ! " came the same voice again, louder.

And then another voice cried :

" Push your nose out, can't you, you—you two with the dog ! "

Neither George nor I dared to turn round. The man's hand was on the cap, and the picture might be taken at any moment. Was it us they were calling to ? What was the matter with our noses ? Why were they to be pushed out !

But now the whole lock started yelling, and a stentorian voice from the back shouted :

" Look at your boat, sir ; you in the red and black caps. It 's your two corpses that will get taken in that photo, if you ain't quick."

We looked then, and saw that the nose of our boat had got fixed under the woodwork of the lock, while the in-coming water was rising all around it, and tilting it up. In another moment we should be over. Quick as thought, we each seized an oar, and a vigorous blow against the side of the lock with the butt-ends released the boat, and sent us sprawling on our backs.

We did not come out well in that photograph, George and I. Of course, as was to be expected, our luck ordained it, that the man should set his wretched machine in motion at the precise moment that we were both lying on our backs with a wild expression of " Where am I ? and what is it ? " on our faces, and our four feet waving madly in the air.

Our feet were undoubtedly the leading article in that photograph. Indeed, very little else was to be seen. They filled up the foreground entirely. Behind them, you caught glimpses of the other boats, and bits of the surrounding scenery ; but everything and everybody else in the lock looked so utterly insignificant and paltry compared with our feet that all the other people felt quite ashamed of themselves, and refused to subscribe to the picture.

The owner of one steam launch, who had bespoke six copies, rescinded the order on seeing the negative. He said he would take them if anybody could show him his launch, but nobody could. It was somewhere behind George's right foot.

There was a good deal of unpleasantness over the business. The photographer thought we ought to take a dozen copies each, seeing that the photo was about nine-tenths us, but we declined. We said we had no objection to being photo'd full-length, but we preferred to be taken the right way up.

(*Three Men in a Boat.*)

G*

The Polite Art of Buying Boots.

"IT is not a brilliant publication," I remarked, handing the book back to George ; " it is not a book that personally I would recommend to any German about to visit England ; I think it would get him disliked. But I have read books published in London for the use of English travellers abroad every whit as foolish. Some educated idiot, misunderstanding seven languages, would appear to go about writing these books for the misinformation and false guidance of modern Europe."

" You cannot deny," said George, " that these books are in large request. They are bought by the thousand, I know. In every town in Europe there must be people going about talking this sort of thing."

" Maybe," I replied ; " but fortunately nobody understands them. I have noticed, myself, men standing on railway platforms and at street corners reading aloud from such books. Nobody knows what language they are speaking ; nobody has the slightest knowledge of what they are saying. This is, perhaps, as well ; were they understood they would probably be assaulted."

George said : " Maybe you are right ; my idea is to see what would happen if they were understood. My proposal is to get to London early on Wednesday morning, and spend an hour or two going about and shopping with the aid of this book. There are one or two little things I want—a hat and a pair of bedroom slippers, among other articles. I want to try this sort of talk where I can properly judge its effect. I want to see how the foreigner feels when he is talked to in this way."

It struck me as a sporting idea. In my enthusiasm I offered to accompany him, and wait outside the shop. I said I thought that Harris would like to be in it, too—or rather outside.

George said that was not quite his scheme. His proposal was that Harris and I should accompany him into the shop. With Harris, who looks formidable, to support him, and myself at the door to call the police if necessary, he said he was willing to adventure the thing.

We walked round to Harris's, and put the proposal before him. He examined the book, especially the chapters dealing with the purchase of shoes and hats. He said :

" If George talks to any bootmaker or any hatter the things that are put down here, it is not support he will want ; it is carrying to the hospital that he will need."

That made George angry.

" You talk," said George, " as though I were a foolhardy boy without any sense. I shall select from the more polite and less irritating speeches ; the grosser insults I shall avoid."

This being clearly understood, Harris gave in his adhesion ; and our start was fixed for early Wednesday morning.

We arrived at Waterloo a little after nine, and at

once proceeded to put George's experiment into operation. Opening the book at the chapter entitled "At the Cab Rank," we walked up to a hansom, raised our hats, and wished the driver " Good-morning."

This man was not to be outdone in politeness by any foreigner, real or imitation. Calling to a friend named "Charles" to "hold the steed," he sprang

He welcomed us to England.

from his box, and returned to us a bow that would have done credit to Mr. Turveydrop himself. Speaking apparently in the name of the nation, he welcomed us to England, adding a regret that Her Majesty was not at the moment in London.

We could not reply to him in kind. Nothing of this sort had been anticipated by the book. We

called him " coachman," at which he again bowed
to the pavement, and asked him if he would have
the goodness to drive us to the Westminster Bridge road.

He laid his hand upon his heart, and said the
pleasure would be his.

Taking the third sentence in the chapter, George
asked him what his fare would be.

The question, as introducing a sordid element
into the conversation, seemed to hurt his feelings.
He said he never took money from distinguished
strangers ; he suggested a souvenir—a diamond scarf
pin, a gold snuff-box, some little trifle of that sort
by which he could remember us.

As a small crowd had collected, and as the joke
was drifting rather too far in the cabman's direction,
we climbed in without further parley, and were driven
away amid cheers. We stopped the cab at a boot
shop a little past Astley's Theatre that looked the
sort of place we wanted. It was one of those overfed
shops that the moment their shutters are taken down
in the morning disgorge their goods all round them.
Boxes of boots stood piled on the pavement or in the
gutter opposite. Boots hung in festoons about its
doors and windows. Its sun-blind was as some grimy
vine, bearing bunches of black and brown boots.
Inside, the shop was a bower of boots. The man,
when we entered, was busy with a chisel and hammer
opening a new crate full of boots.

George raised his hat, and said " Good-morning."

The man did not even turn round. He struck me
from the first as a disagreeable man. He grunted
something which might have been " Good-morning,"
or might not, and went on with his work.

George said : " I have been recommended to your shop by my friend, Mr. X."

In response, the man should have said : " Mr. X. is a most worthy gentleman ; it will give me the greatest pleasure to serve any friend of his."

What he did say was : " Don't know him : never heard of him."

This was disconcerting. The book gave three or four methods of buying boots ; George had carefully selected the one centred round " Mr. X." as being of all the most courtly. You talked a good deal with the shopkeeper about this " Mr. X," and then, when by this means friendship and understanding had been established, you slid naturally and gracefully into the immediate object of your coming, namely, your desire for boots, " cheap and good." This gross, material man cared, apparently, nothing for the niceties of retail dealing. It was necessary with such an one to come to business with brutal directness. George abandoned " Mr. X," and turning back to a previous page, took a sentence at random. It was not a happy selection ; it was a speech that would have been superfluous made to any bootmaker. Under the present circumstances, threatened and stifled as we were on every side by boots, it possessed the dignity of positive imbecility. It ran :—" One has told me that you have here boots for sale."

For the first time the man put down his hammer and chisel, and looked at us. He spoke slowly, in a thick and husky voice. He said :

" What d 'ye think I keep boots for—to smell 'em ? "

He was one of those men that begin quietly and

grow more angry as they proceed, their wrongs apparently working within them like yeast.

"What d'ye think I am," he continued, "a boot collector? What d'ye think I'm running this shop for—my health? D'ye think I love the boots, and can't bear to part with a pair? D'ye think I hang 'em about here to look at 'em? Ain't there enough of 'em? Where d'ye think you are—in an international exhibition of boots? What d'ye think these boots are—a historical collection? Did you ever hear of a man keeping a boot shop and not selling boots? D'ye think I decorate the shop with 'em to make it look pretty? What d'ye take me for—a prize idiot?"

I have always maintained that these conversation books are never of any real use. What we wanted was some English equivalent for the well-known German idiom: "Behalten Sie Ihr Haar auf."

Nothing of the sort was to be found in the book from beginning to end. However, I will do George the credit to admit he chose the very best sentence that was to be found therein and applied it. He said:

"I will come again, when, perhaps, you will have some more boots to show me. Till then, adieu!"

(*Three Men on the Bummel.*)

The Good Fisherman.

I AM not a good fisherman myself. I devoted a considerable amount of attention to the subject at one time, and was getting on, as I thought, fairly well; but the old hands told me that I should never be any real good at it, and advised me to give it up. They said that I was an extremely neat thrower, and that I seemed to have plenty of gumption for the thing, and quite enough constitutional laziness. But they were sure I should never make anything of a fisherman. I had not got sufficient imagination.

They said that as a poet, or a shilling shocker, or a reporter, or anything of that kind, I might be satisfactory, but that, to gain any position as a Thames angler, would require more play of fancy, more power of invention than I appeared to possess.

Some people are under the impression that all that is required to make a good fisherman is the ability to tell lies easily and without blushing ; but this is a mistake. Mere bald fabrication is useless ; the veriest tyro can manage that. It is in the circumstantial detail, the embellishing touches of probability, the general air of scrupulous—almost of pedantic—veracity, that the experienced angler is seen.

Anybody can come in and say, "Oh, I. caught fifteen dozen perch yesterday evening ; " or " Last Monday I landed a gudgeon, weighing eighteen pounds, and measuring three feet from the tip to the tail."

There is no art, no skill, required for that sort of thing. It shows pluck, but that is all.

No ; your accomplished angler would scorn to tell a lie, that way. His method is a study in itself.

He comes in quietly with his hat on, appropriates the most comfortable chair, lights his pipe, and commences to puff in silence. He lets the youngsters brag away for a while, and then, during a momentary lull, he removes the pipe from his mouth, and remarks, as he knocks the ashes out against the bars :

" Well, I had a haul on Tuesday evening that it 's not much good my telling anybody about."

" Oh ! why 's that ? " they ask.

" Because I don't expect anybody would believe me if I did," replies the old fellow calmly, and without even a tinge of bitterness in his tone, as he refills his pipe, and requests the landlord to bring him three of Scotch, cold.

There is a pause after this, nobody feeling sufficiently sure of himself to contradict the old gentleman. So he has to go on by himself without any encouragement.

" No," he continues thoughtfully ; " I shouldn't

believe it myself if anybody told it to me, but it 's a fact, for all that. I had been sitting there all the afternoon and had caught literally nothing—except a few dozen dace and a score of jack ; and I was just about giving it up as a bad job when I suddenly felt a rather smart pull at the line. I thought it was another little one, and I went to jerk it up. Hang me, if I could move the rod ! It took me half-an-hour— half-an-hour, sir !—to land that fish ; and every moment I thought the line was going to snap ! I reached him at last, and what do you think it was ? A sturgeon ! a forty pound sturgeon ! taken on a line, sir ! Yes, you may well look surprised—I 'll have another three of Scotch, landlord, please."

And then he goes on to tell of the astonishment of everybody who saw it ; and what his wife said, when he got home, and of what Joe Buggles thought about it.

I asked the landlord of an inn up the river once, if it did not injure him, sometimes, listening to the tales that the fishermen about there told him ; and he said :

"Oh, no ; not now, sir. It did used to knock me over a bit at first, but, lor love you ! me and the missus we listens to 'em all day now. It 's what you 're used to, you know. It 's what you 're used to."

(*Three Men in a Boat.*)

An Evening at the Play.

BUT the most marvellous feat, to my thinking, ever accomplished by Barbara was the bearing off of my father and mother to witness " A Voice from the Grave, or the Power of Love. New and Original Drama in five acts and thirteen tableaux."

They had been bred in a narrow creed, both my father and my mother. That Puritan blood flowed in their veins that throughout our land has drowned much harmless joyousness ; yet those who know of it only from hearsay do foolishly to speak ill of it. If ever earnest times should come again, not how to enjoy but how to live being the question, Fate demanding of us to show not what we have, but what we are, we may regret that they are fewer among us than formerly, those who trained themselves to despise all pleasure, because in pleasure they saw the subtlest foe to principle and duty. No graceful growth, this Puritanism, for its roots are in the hard, stern facts of life ; but it is strong, and from it has sprung all that is worth preserving in the Anglo-Saxon character. Its men feared and its women loved God, and if their words were harsh their hearts were tender. If they shut out the sunshine from their lives, it was that their eyes might see better the glory lying beyond ; and if their view be correct, that earth's threescore years and ten are but a preparation for eternity, then who shall call them even foolish for turning away their thoughts from its allurements ?

" Still, I think I should like to have a look at one, just to see what it is like," argued my father ; " one cannot judge of a thing that one knows nothing about."

I imagine that it was his first argument rather than his second that convinced my mother.

" That is true," she answered. " I remember how shocked my poor father was when he found me one night at the bedroom window reading Sir Walter Scott by the light of the moon."

" What about the boy ? " said my father, for I had been included in the invitation.

" We will all be wicked together," said my mother.

So an evening or two later the four of us stood at the corner of Pigott Street waiting for the 'bus.

" It is a close evening," said my father, " let 's go the whole hog and ride outside."

In those days for a lady to ride outside a 'bus was as in these days for a lady to smoke in public. Surely my mother's guardian angel must have betaken himself off in a huff.

" Will you keep close behind and see to my skirt ? " answered my mother, commencing preparations. If you will remember that these were the days of crinolines, that the " knife-boards " of omnibuses were then approached by a perpendicular ladder, the rungs two feet apart, you will understand the necessity for such precaution.

Which of us was the most excited throughout that long ride it would be difficult to say. Barbara, feeling keenly her responsibility as prompter and leader of the dread enterprise, sat anxious, as she explained to us afterwards, hoping there would be nothing shocking in the play, nothing to belie its innocent title; pleased with her success so far, yet still fearful of failure, doubtful till the last moment lest we should suddenly repent, and stopping the 'bus, flee from the wrath to come. My father was the youngest of us all. Compared with him I was sober and contained. He fidgeted—people marked upon it. He hummed. But for the stern eye of a thin young man sitting next to him trying to read a paper, I believe he would have broken out into song. Every minute he would lean across to inquire of my mother: "How are you feeling—all right?" To which my mother would reply with a nod and a smile. She sat very silent herself, clasping and unclasping her hands. As for myself, I remember feeling so sorry for the crowds that passed us on their way home. It was sad to think of the long, dull evening that lay before them. I wondered how they could face it.

Our seats were in the front row of the upper circle. The lights were low and the house only half full when we reached them.

"It seems very orderly and—and respectable," whispered my mother. There seemed a touch of disappointment in her tone.

"We are rather early," replied Barbara; "it will be livelier when the band comes in and they turn up the gas."

But even when this happened my mother was not content. "There is so little room for the actors," she complained.

It was explained to her that the green curtain would go up, that the stage lay behind.

So we waited, my mother sitting stiffly on the extreme edge of her seat, holding me tightly by the hand ; I believe with some vague idea of flight, should out of that vault-scented gloom the devil suddenly appear to claim us for his own. But before the curtain was quite up she had forgotten him.

You poor folk that go to the theatre a dozen times a year, perhaps oftener, what do you know of plays ? You see no drama, you see but middle-aged Mr. Brown, churchwarden, payer of taxes, foolishly pretending to be a brigand ; Miss Jones, daughter of old Jones, the chemist, making believe to be a haughty princess. How can you, a grown man, waste money on a seat to witness such tomfoolery ? What we saw was something very different. A young and beautiful girl— true, not a lady by birth, being merely the daughter of an honest yeoman, but one equal in all the essentials of womanhood to the noblest in the land—suffered before our very eyes an amount of misfortune that, had one not seen it for oneself, one could never have believed Fate could have accumulated upon the head of any single individual. Beside her woes our own poor troubles sank into insignificance. We had used to grieve, as my mother in a whisper reminded my father, if now and again we had not been able to afford meat for dinner. This poor creature, driven from her wretched attic, compelled to wander through the snow without so much as an umbrella to protect her, had not even a crust to eat ; and yet never lost her faith in Providence. It was a lesson, as my mother remarked afterwards, that she would never forget. And virtue had been triumphant, let shallow critics say what they will. Had we not proved it with our own senses ? The villain—I think his Christian name, if one can apply the word " Christian " in connection with such a fiend, was Jasper—had never really loved the heroine. He was incapable of love. My mother had felt this before he had been on the stage five minutes, and my father—in spite of protests from callous people behind who appeared to be utterly indifferent to what was going on under their very noses—had agreed with her. What he was in love with was her fortune— the fortune that had been left to her by her uncle in Australia, but about which nobody but the villain knew anything. Had she swerved a hair's breadth from the course of almost supernatural rectitude, had her love for the hero ever weakened, her belief in him—in spite of damning evidence to the contrary— for a moment wavered, then wickedness might have triumphed. How at times, knowing all the facts but helpless to interfere, we trembled, lest, deceived by the cruel lies the villain told her, she should yield to importunity ! How we thrilled when, in language eloquent though rude, she flung his false love back into his teeth ! Yet still we feared. We knew well that it was not the hero who had done the murder. " Poor dear," as Amy would have called him, he was quite incapable of doing anything requiring one-half as much smartness. We knew that it was not he, poor innocent lamb ! who had betrayed the lady with the French accent ; we had heard her on the subject, and had formed a very shrewd conjecture. But appearances, we could not help admitting, were terribly to his disfavour. The circumstantial evidence against him would have hanged an archbishop. Could she in face of it still retain her faith ? There were moments when my mother restrained with difficulty her desire to rise and explain.

Between the acts Barbara would whisper to her that she was not to mind, because it was only a play, and that everything would be sure to come right in the 'end.

" I know, my dear," my mother would answer, laughing, " it is very foolish of me ; I forget. Paul, when you see me getting excited, you must remind me."

But of what use was I in such case ?

I, who only by holding on to the arms of my seat could keep myself from swarming down on to the stage to fling myself between this noble damsel and her persecutor—this fair-haired, creamy angel, in whose presence for the time being I had forgotten even Barbara ?

The end came at last. The uncle from Australia was not dead. The villain—bungler as well as knave— had killed the wrong man—somebody of no importance whatever. As a matter of fact, the comic man himself was the uncle from Australia—had been so all along. My mother had had a suspicion of this from the very first. She told us so three times—to make up, I suppose, for not having mentioned it before. How we cheered and laughed, in spite of the tears in our eyes !

By pure accident it happened to be the first night of the piece, and the author, in response to much shouting and whistling, came before the curtain. He was fat, and looked commonplace, but I deemed him a genius, and my mother said he had a good face, and

waved her handkerchief wildly, while my father
shouted "Bravo!" long after everybody else had
finished; and people round about muttered "Packed
house," which I didn't understand at the time, but
came to later.

And stranger still, it happened to be before that
very same curtain that many years later I myself
stepped forth to make my first bow as a playwright.
I saw the house but dimly, for on such occasion one's
vision is apt to be clouded. All that I clearly saw
was in the front row of the second circle—a sweet face
laughing, though the tears were in her eyes; and she
waved to me a handkerchief. And on one side of her
stood a gallant gentleman with merry eyes, who shouted
"Bravo!" and on the other
a dreamy-looking lad, but he
appeared disappointed, having
expected better work from me.
And the fourth face I could
not see, for it was turned away
from me.

Barbara, determined on
completeness, insisted
upon supper. In those
days res-
pectability
fed at
home, but
one resort
possible
there was:
an eating-
house with

*The villain—bungler as well as knave—had killed
the wrong man.*

some pretence to gaiety behind St. Clement Danes, and to that she led us. It was a long, narrow room, divided into wooden compartments after the old coffee-house plan, a gangway down the centre. Now we should call it a dismal hole, and closing the door, hasten away. But to Adam, Eve in her Sunday fig-leaves was a stylishly dressed woman ; and to my eyes, with its gilded mirrors and its flaring gas, the place seemed a palace.

Barbara ordered oysters, a fish that familiarity with its empty shell had made me curious concerning. Truly, no spot on the globe is so rich in oyster shells as the East End of London. A stranger might be led to the impression (erroneous) that the customary lunch of the East End labourer consisted of oysters. How they collect there in such quantities is a mystery, though Washburn, to whom I once presented the problem, found no difficulty in solving it to his own satisfaction : " To the rich man the oyster ; to the poor man the shell. Thus are the Creator's gifts divided among all His creatures, none being sent empty away." For drink the others had stout, and I had ginger beer. The waiter, who called me " Sir," advised against this mixture, but among us all the dominating sentiment by this time was that nothing really mattered very much. Afterwards my father called for a cigar and boldly lighted it, though my mother looked anxious, and fortunately, perhaps, it would not draw. And then it came out that he himself had once written a play.

" You never told me of that," complained my mother.

" It was a long while ago," replied my father ; " nothing came of it."

"It might have been a success," said my mother ; "you always had a gift for writing."

"I must look it over again," said my father. "I had quite forgotten it, I have an impression it wasn't at all bad."

"It can be of much help," said my mother, "a good play ; it makes one think."

We put Barbara into a cab, and rode home ourselves inside a 'bus. My mother was tired, so my father slipped his arm round her, telling her to lean against him, and soon she fell asleep with her head upon his shoulder. A coarse-looking wench sat opposite, her man's arm round her likewise, and she also fell asleep, her powdered face against his coat.

"They can do with a bit of nursing, can't they ? " said the man, with a grin, to the conductor.

"Ah, they 're just kids," agreed the conductor sympathetically, "that 's what they are, all of 'em, just kids."

(*Paul Kelver.*)

Man and his Relations.

" WHAT woman suffers from," said the Philosopher, " is over-praise.   It has turned her head."

" You admit, then, that she has a head ? " demanded the Girton Girl.

" It has always been a theory of mine," returned the Philosopher, " that by Nature she was intended to possess one.   It is her admirers who have always represented her as brainless."

" Why is it that the brainy girl invariably has straight hair ? " asked the Woman of the World.

" Because she doesn't curl it," explained the Girton Girl.   She spoke somewhat snappishly, it seemed to me.

" I never thought of that," murmured the Woman of the World.

" When I was younger even than I am now," said the Minor Poet, " I thought a good deal of marriage— very young men do.   My wife, I told myself, must be a woman of mind.   Yet, curiously, of all the women I have ever loved, no single one has been remarkable for intellect—present company, as usual, of course, excepted."

" Why is it," sighed the Philosopher, " that in the most serious business of our life, marriage, serious considerations count for next to nothing ?   A dimpled chin can, and often does, secure for a girl the best of husbands ; while virtue and understanding combined cannot be relied upon to obtain for her even one of the worst."

"I think the explanation is," replied the Minor Poet, "that as regards, let us say, the most natural business of our life, marriage, our natural instincts alone are brought into play. Marriage—clothe the naked fact in what flowers of rhetoric we will—has to do with the purely animal part of our being. The man is drawn towards it by his primeval desires; the woman by her inborn craving towards mother-hood."

The thin, white hands of the Old Maid fluttered, troubled, where they lay upon her lap. "Why should we seek to explain away all the beautiful things of life?" she said. She spoke with a heat unusual to her. "The blushing lad, so timid, so devotional, worshipping as at the shrine of some mystic saint; the young girl moving spellbound among dreams! They think of nothing but one another."

"Tracing a mountain stream to its sombre source need not mar its music for us as it murmurs through the valley," expounded the Philosopher. "The hidden law of our being feeds each leaf of our life as sap runs through the tree. The transient blossom, the ripened fruit, is but its changing outward form."

"I hate going to the roots of things," said the Woman of the World. "Poor, dear papa was so fond of doing that. He would explain to us the genesis of oysters just when we were enjoying them. Poor mamma could never bring herself to touch them after that. While in the middle of dessert he would stop to argue with my uncle Paul whether pig's blood or bullock's was the best for grape vines."

"There is a time for everything," agreed the Philosopher. "With the lover, penning poetry to the wondrous red and white upon his mistress' cheek, we do not discuss the subject of pigment in the blood, its cause and probable duration. Nevertheless, the subject is interesting."

"We men and women," continued the Minor Poet, "we are Nature's favourites, her hope, for whom she has made sacrifice, putting aside so many of her own convictions, telling herself she is old-fashioned. She has let us go from her to the strange school where they laugh at all her notions. We have learnt new, strange ideas that bewilder the good dame. Yet, returning home, it is curious to notice how little, in the few essential things of life, we differ from her other children, who have never wandered from her side. Our vocabulary has been extended and elaborated, yet face to face with the realities of existence it is unavailing. Clasping the living, standing beside the dead, our language still is but a cry. Our wants have grown more complicated ; the ten-course banquet, with all that it involves, has substituted itself for the handful of fruit and nuts gathered without labour ; the stalled ox and a world of trouble for the dinner of herbs and leisure therewith. Are we so far removed thereby above our little brother, who, having swallowed his simple, succulent worm, mounts a neighbouring twig and with easy digestion carols thanks to God ? The square brick box about which we move, hampered at every step by wooden lumber, decked with many rags and strips of coloured paper, cumbered with odds and ends of melted flint and moulded clay, has replaced the cheap, convenient cave. We clothe ourselves in the skins of other animals instead of allowing our own to develop into a natural protection.   We hang about us bits of stone and metal, but underneath it all we are little two-legged animals, struggling with the rest to live and breed.   Beneath each hedgerow in the springtime we can read our own romances in the making—the first faint stirring of the blood, the roving eye, the sudden marvellous discovery of the indispensable She, the wooing, the denial, hope, coquetry, despair, contention, rivalry, hate, jealousy, love, bitterness, victory, and death.   Our comedies, our tragedies, are being played upon each blade of grass. In fur and feather we run epitomised."

(*Tea Table Talk.*)

His First Engagement.

A DELIGHTFUL dreaminess was stealing over me. Everything and everybody appeared to be a long way off, but, whether because of this or in spite of it, exceedingly attractive. Never had I noticed the Signora so bewitching ; in a motherly sort of way even the third-floor front was good to look upon ; Mrs. Peedles I could almost have believed to be the real Flora MacDonald sitting in front of me. But the vision of Miss Rosina Sellars made literally my head to swim. Never before had I dared to cast upon female loveliness the satisfying gaze with which I now boldly regarded her every movement. Evidently she noticed it, for she turned away her eyes. I had heard that exceptionally strong-minded people merely by concentrating their will could make other ordinary people do just whatever 'they, the exceptionally strong-minded people, wished. I willed that Miss Rosina Sellars should turn her eyes again towards me. Victory crowned my efforts. Evidently I was one of these exceptionally strong-minded persons. Slowly her eyes came round and met mine with a smile—a helpless, pathetic smile that said, so I read it : " You know no woman can resist you : be merciful ! "

Inflamed by the brutal lust of conquest I suppose I must have willed still further, for the next thing I remember is sitting with Miss Sellars on the sofa, holding her hand, the while the O'Kelly sang a sentimental ballad, only one line of which comes back to me! "For the angels must have told him, and he knows I love him now," much stress upon the "now." The others had their backs towards us. Miss Sellars, with a look that pierced my heart, dropped her somewhat large head upon my shoulder, leaving, as I observed the next day, a patch of powder on my coat.

Miss Sellars observed that one of the saddest things in the world was unrequited love.

I replied gallantly, "Whateryou know about it?"

"Ah, you men, you men," murmured Miss Sellars; "you 're all alike."

This suggested a personal aspersion on my character. "Not allerus," I murmured.

"You don't know what love is," said Miss Sellars. "You 're not old enough."

The O'Kelly had passed on to Sullivan's "Sweethearts," then in its first popularity.

> "Oh, love for a year—a week—a day!
> But oh for the love that loves al-wa-ay!"

Miss Sellars' languishing eyes were fixed upon me; Miss Sellars' red lips pouted and twitched; Miss Sellars' white bosom rose and fell. Never, so it seemed to me, had so large an amount of beauty been concentrated in one being.

"Yeserdo," I said. "I love you."

I stooped to kiss the red lips, but something was in my way. It turned out to be a cold cigar. Miss Sellars thoughtfully removed it, and threw it away. Our lips met. Her large arms closed about my neck and held me tight.

H

" Well, I 'm sure ! " came the voice of Mrs. Peedles, as from afar. " Nice goings-on ! "

I have a vague remembrance of a somewhat heated discussion in which everybody but myself appeared to be taking extreme interest—of Miss Sellars in her most ladylike and chilling tones defending me against the charge of " being no gentleman," which Mrs. Peedles was explaining nobody had said I wasn't. The argument seemed to be of the circular order. No gentleman had ever kissed Miss Sellars who had not every right to do so, nor ever would. To kiss Miss Sellars without such right was to declare himself no gentleman. Miss Sellars appealed to me to clear my character from the aspersion of being no gentleman. I was trying to understand the situation when Jarman, seizing me somewhat roughly by the arm, suggested my going to bed. Miss Sellars, seizing my other arm, suggested my refusing to go to bed. So far I was with Miss Sellars—I didn't want to go to bed and said so. My desire to sit up longer was proof positive to Miss Sellars that I was a gentleman, but to no one else. The argument shifted, the question being now as to whether Miss Sellars were a lady. To prove the point it was, according to Miss Sellars, necessary that I should repeat I loved her. I did repeat it, adding, with a faint remembrance of my own fiction, that if a life's devotion was likely to be of the slightest further proof, my heart's blood was at her service. This cleared the air, Mrs. Peedles observing that under such circumstances it only remained for her to withdraw everything she had said ; to which Miss Sellars replied graciously that she had always known Mrs. Peedles to be a good sort at bottom.

Nevertheless, gaiety was gone from among us, and for this, in some way I could not understand, I appeared to be responsible. Jarman was distinctly sulky. The O'Kelly, suddenly thinking of the time, went to the door and discovered that the two cabs were waiting. The third floor recollected that work had to be finished. I myself felt sleepy.

I found getting into bed a difficulty owing to the strange behaviour of the room.

Our host and hostess departed, Jarman again suggested bed, and this time I agreed with him. After a slight misunderstanding with the door, I found myself upon the stairs. I had never noticed before that they were quite perpendicular. Adapting myself to the changed conditions, I climbed them with the help of my hands. I accomplished the last flight somewhat quickly, and feeling tired, sat down the moment I was within my room. Jarman knocked at the door. I told him to come in ; but he didn't. It occurred to me that the reason was I was sitting on the floor with my back against the door. The discovery amused me exceedingly, and I laughed ; and Jarman, baffled, descended to his own floor. I found getting into bed a difficulty owing to the strange behaviour of the room. It spun round and round. Now the bed was just in front of me, now it was behind me. I managed at last to catch it before it could get past me, and holding on by the ironwork, frustrated its efforts to throw me out again on to the floor.

But it was some time before I went to sleep, and over my intervening experiences I draw a veil.

(Paul Kelver.)

A Charming Woman.

" Not *the* Mr. ——, *really ?*"

In her deep brown eyes there lurked pleased surprise, struggling with wonder. She looked from myself to the friend who introduced us with a bewitching smile of incredulity, tempered by hope.

He assured her, adding laughingly, " The only genuine and original," and left us.

" I 've always thought of you as a staid, middle-aged man," she said, with a delicious little laugh, then added in

" I 've always thought of you as a staid, middle-aged man."

low soft tones, " I 'm so very pleased to meet you, really."

The words were conventional, but her voice crept round one like a warm caress.

"Come and talk to me," she said, seating herself upon a small settee, and making room for me.

I sat down awkwardly beside her, my head buzzing just a little as with one glass too many of champagne. I was in my literary childhood. One small book and a few essays and criticisms, scattered through various obscure periodicals had been as yet my only contributions to current literature. The sudden discovery that I was *the* Mr. Anybody, and that charming women thought of me, and were delighted to meet me, was a brain-disturbing thought.

"And it was really you who wrote that clever book ? " she continued, " and all those brilliant things in the magazines and journals. Oh, it must be delightful to be clever."

She gave breath to a little sigh of vain regret that went to my heart. To console her I commenced a laboured compliment, but she stopped me with her fan. On after reflection I was glad she had—it would have been one of those things better expressed otherwise.

"I know what you are going to say," she laughed, "but don't. Besides, from you I should not know quite how to take it. You can be so satirical."

I tried to look as though I could be, but in her case would not.

She let her ungloved hand rest for an instant upon mine. Had she left it there for two, I should have gone down on my knees before her, or have stood on

my head at her feet—have made a fool of myself in
some way or another before the whole room full. She
timed it to a nicety.

"I don't want *you* to pay me compliments," she
said, "I want us to be friends. Of course, in years,
I 'm old enough to be your mother." (By the register
I should say she might have been thirty-two, but
looked twenty-six. I was twenty-three, and I fear
foolish for my age.) "But you know the world, and
you 're so different to the other people one meets.
Society is so hollow and artificial; don't you find it
so ? You don't know how I long sometimes to get
away from it, to know someone to whom I could show
my real self, who would understand me. You 'll
come and see me sometimes—I 'm always at home on
Wednesdays—and let me talk to you, won't you,
and you must tell me all your clever thoughts."

It occurred to me that, maybe, she would like to
hear a few of them there and then, but before I had
got well started a hollow Society man came up and
suggested supper, and she was compelled to leave me.
As she disappeared, however, in the throng, she looked
back over her shoulder with a glance half pathetic,
half comic, that I understood. It said, "Pity me,
I 've got to be bored by this vapid, shallow creature,"
and I did.

I sought her through all the rooms before I went.
I wished to assure her of my sympathy and support.
I learned, however, from the butler that she had
left early, in company with the hollow Society man.

A fortnight later I ran against a young literary
friend in Regent Street, and we lunched together at
the Monico.

"I met such a charming woman last night," he said, "a Mrs. Clifton Courtenay, a delightful woman."

"Oh, do *you* know her?" I exclaimed. "Oh, we're very old friends. She's always wanting me to go and see her. I really must."

"Oh, I didn't know *you* knew her," he answered. Somehow, the fact of my knowing her seemed to lessen her importance in his eyes. But soon he recovered his enthusiasm for her.

"A wonderfully clever woman," he continued. "I'm afraid I disappointed her a little though." He said this, however, with a laugh that contradicted his words. "She would not believe I was *the* Mr. Smith. She imagined from my book that I was quite an old man."

I could see nothing in my friend's book myself to suggest that the author was, of necessity, anything over eighteen. The mistake appeared to me to display want of acumen, but it had evidently pleased him greatly.

"I felt sorry for her," he went on, "chained to that bloodless, artificial society in which she lives. 'You can't tell,' she said to me, 'how I long to meet someone to whom I can show my real self—who would understand me.' I'm going to see her on Wednesday."

I went with him. My conversation with her was not as confidential as I had anticipated, owing to there being some eighty other people present in a room intended for the accommodation of eight; but after surging round for an hour in hot and aimless misery— as very young men at such gatherings do, knowing as a rule only the man who has brought them, and being unable to find him—I contrived to get a few words with her.

She greeted me with a smile, in the light of which I at once forgot my past discomfort, and let her fingers rest, with delicious pressure, for a moment upon mine.

" How good of you to keep your promise," she said. " These people have been tiring me so. Sit here, and tell me all you have been doing."

She listened for about ten seconds, and then interrupted me with—

" And that clever friend of yours that you came with. I met him at dear Lady Lennon's last week. Has *he* written anything ? "

I explained to her that he had.

" Tell me about it," she said. " I get so little time for reading, and then I only care to read the books that help me," and she gave me a grateful look more eloquent than words.

I described the work to her, and wishing to do my friend justice I even recited a few of the passages upon which, as I knew, he especially prided himself.

One sentence in particular seemed to lay hold of her. " A good woman's arms round a man's neck is a lifebelt thrown out to him from heaven."

" How beautiful ! " she murmured. " Say it again."

I said it again, and she repeated it after me.

Then a noisy old lady swooped down upon her, and I drifted away into a corner, where I tried to look as if I were enjoying myself, and failed.

Later on, feeling it time to go, I sought my friend, and found him talking to her in a corner. I approached and waited. They were discussing the latest East End murder. A drunken woman had been killed by her

H*

husband, a hard-working artisan, who had been maddened by the ruin of his home.

"Ah," she was saying, "what power a woman has to drag a man down or lift him up. I never read a case in which a woman is concerned without thinking of those beautiful lines of yours : 'A good woman's arms round a man's neck is a lifebelt thrown out to him from heaven.'"

(*Sketches in Lavender.*)

George gets up too Early.

GEORGE said that the same kind of thing, only worse, had happened to him some eighteen months ago, when he was lodging by himself in the house of a certain Mrs. Gippings. He said his watch went wrong one evening, and stopped at a quarter-past eight. He did not know this at the time because, for some reason or other, he forgot to wind it up when he went to bed (an unusual occurrence with him), and hung it up over his pillow without ever looking at the thing.

It was in the winter when this happened, very near the shortest day, and a week of fog into the bargain, so the fact that it was still very dark when George awoke in the morning was no guide to him as to the time. He reached up, and hauled down his watch. It was a quarter-past eight.

" Angels and ministers of grace defend us ! " exclaimed George ; " and here have I got to be in the City by nine. Why didn't somebody call me ? Oh, this is a shame ! " And he flung the watch down, and sprang out of bed, and had a cold bath, and washed himself, and dressed himself, and shaved himself in cold water because there was not time to wait for the hot, and then rushed and had another look at the watch.

Whether the shaking it had received in being thrown down on the bed had started it, or how it was, George could not say, but certain it was that from a quarter-past eight it had begun to go, and now pointed to twenty minutes to nine.

George snatched it up, and rushed downstairs. In the sitting-room, all was dark and silent : there was no fire, no breakfast. George said it was a wicked shame of Mrs. G., and he made up his mind to tell her what he thought of her when he came home in the evening. Then he dashed on his great-coat and hat, and, seizing his umbrella, made for the front door. The door was not even unbolted. George anathematized Mrs. G. for a lazy old woman, and thought it was very strange that people could not get up at a decent, respectable time, unlocked and unbolted the door, and ran out.

He ran hard for a quarter of a mile, and at the end of that distance it began to be borne in upon him as a strange and curious thing that there were so few people about, and that there were no shops open. It was certainly a very dark and foggy morning, but still it seemed an unusual course to stop all business on that account. *He* had to go to business : why should other people stop in bed merely because it was dark and foggy !

At length he reached Holborn. Not a shutter was down ! not a bus was about ! There were three men in sight, one of whom was a policeman ; a market-cart full of cabbages, and a dilapidated looking cab. George pulled out his watch and looked at it : it was five minutes to nine ! He stood still and counted his pulse. He stooped down and felt his legs. Then, with his watch still in his hand, he went up to the policeman, and asked him if he knew what the time was.

" What 's the time ? " said the man, eyeing George up and down with evident suspicion ; " why, if you listen you will hear it strike."

George listened, and a neighbouring clock immediately obliged.

" But it 's only gone three ! " said George in an injured tone, when it had finished.

" Well, and how many did you want it to go ? " replied the constable.

" Why, nine," said George, showing his watch.

" Do you know where you live ? " said the guardian of public order, severely.

George thought, and gave the address.

" Oh ! that 's where it is, is it ? " replied the man ; " well, you take my advice and go there quietly, and take that watch of yours with you ; and don't let 's have any more of it."

And George went home again, musing as he walked along, and let himself in.

At first, when he got in, he determined to undress and go to bed again ; but when he thought of the re-dressing and re-washing, and the having of another bath, he determined he would not, but would sit up and go to sleep in the easy-chair.

But he could not get to sleep : he never felt more wakeful in his life ; so he lit the lamp and got out the chess-board, and played himself a game of chess. But even that did not enliven him : it seemed slow somehow ; so he gave up chess and tried to read. He did not seem able to take any sort of interest in reading either, so he put on his coat again and went out for a walk.

It was horribly lonesome and dismal, and all the

policemen he met regarded him with undisguised suspicion, and turned their lanterns on him and followed him about, and this had such an effect upon him at last that he began to feel as if he really had done something, and he got to slinking down the by-streets and hiding in dark doorways when he heard the regulation flip-flop approaching.

Turned their lanterns on him and followed him about.

Of course, this conduct made the force only more distrustful of him than ever, and they would come and rout him out and ask him what he was doing there ; and when he answered, " Nothing," he had merely come out for a stroll (it was then four o'clock in the morning), they looked as though they did not believe him, and two plain-clothes constables came home with him to see if he really did live where he had said he did. They saw him go in with his key, and then they took up a position opposite and watched the house.

He thought he would light the fire when he got inside, and make himself some breakfast, just to pass away the time ; but he did not seem able to handle anything from a scuttleful of coals to a teaspoon without dropping it or falling over it, and making such a noise that he was in mortal fear that it would wake Mrs. G. up, and that she would think it was burglars and open the window and call "Police!" and then those two detectives would rush in and handcuff him, and march him off to the police-court.

He was in a morbidly nervous state by this time, and he pictured the trial, and his trying to explain the circumstances to the jury, and nobody believing him, and his being sentenced to twenty years' penal servitude, and his mother dying of a broken heart. So he gave up trying to get breakfast, and wrapped himself up in his overcoat and sat in the easy-chair till Mrs. G. came down at half-past seven.

He said he had never got up too early since that morning : it had been such a warning to him.

(Three Men in a Boat.)

How to Go to Bed in Germany.

WE went to bed after our wash. To the *blasé* English bed-goer, accustomed all his life to the same old hackneyed style of bed night after night, there is something very pleasantly piquant about the experience of trying to sleep in a German bed. He does not know it is a bed at first. He thinks that someone has been going round the room, collecting all the sacks and cushions and anti-macassars and such articles that he has happened to find about, and has piled them up on a wooden tray ready for moving. He rings for the chambermaid, and explains to her that she has shown him into the wrong room. He wanted a bedroom.

She says : "This *is* a bedroom."

He says : "Where 's the bed ? "

" There ! " she says, pointing to the box on which the sacks and anti-macassars and cushions lie piled.

" That ! " he cries. " How am I going to sleep in that ? "

The chambermaid does not know how he is going to sleep there, never having seen a gentleman go to sleep anywhere, and not knowing how they set about it ; but suggests that he might try lying down flat, and shutting his eyes.

" But it is not long enough," he says.

The chambermaid thinks he will be able to manage, if he tucks his legs up.

He sees that he will not get anything better, and that he must put up with it.

" Oh, very well ! " he says. " Look sharp and get it made, then."

She says : " It is made."

He turns and regards the girl sternly. Is she taking advantage of his being a lonely stranger, far from home and friends, to mock him ? He goes over to what she calls the bed, and snatching off the top-most sack from the pile and holding it up, says :

" Perhaps you will tell me what this is, then ? "

" That," says the girl ; " that 's the bed ! "

He is somewhat nonplussed at the unexpected reply.

" Oh ! " he says. " Oh ! the bed, is it ?   I thought it was a pincushion ! Well, if it is the bed, then what is it doing out here, on the top of everything else ? You think that because I 'm only a man, I don't understand a bed ! "

" That 's the proper place for it," responds the chambermaid.

" What ! on top ? "

" Yes, sir."

" Well, then, where are the clothes ? "

" Underneath, sir."

" Look here, my good girl," he says ; " you don't understand me, or I don't understand you, one or the other. When I go to sleep, I lie on a bed and pull the clothes over me. I don't want to lie on the clothes, and cover myself with the bed. This isn't a comic ballet, you know ! "

The girl assures him that there is no mistake about the matter at all. There is the bed, made according to German notions of how a bed should be made. He can make the best of it and try to go to sleep upon it, or he can be sulky and go to sleep on the floor.

He is very much surprised. It looks to him the sort of bed that a man would make for himself on coming home late from a party. But it is no use arguing the matter with the girl.

" All right," he says ; " bring me a pillow, and I 'll risk it ! "

The chambermaid explains that there are two pillows on the bed already, indicating, as she does so, two flat cushions, each one a yard square, placed one on top of the other at each end of the mixture.

" These ! " exclaims the weary traveller, beginning to feel that he does not want to go to bed at all. " These are not pillows ! I want something to put my head on ; not a thing that comes down to the middle of my back ! Don't tell me that I 've got to sleep on these things ! "

But the girl does tell him so, and also implies that she has something else to do than to stand there all day talking bed-gossip with him.

" Well, just show me how to start," he says, " which way you get into it, and then I won't keep you any longer ; I 'll puzzle out the rest for myself."

She explains the trick to him and leaves, and he undresses and crawls in.

The pillows give him a good deal of worry. He does not know whether he is meant to sit on them or merely to lean up against them. In experimenting upon this point, he bumps his head against the top board of the bedstead. At this, he says, "Oh!" and shoots himself down to the bottom of the bed. Here all his ten toes simultaneously come into sharp contact with the board at the bottom.

Nothing irritates a man more than being rapped over the toes, especially if he feels that he has done nothing to deserve it. He says, "Oh, damn!" this time, and spasmodically doubles up his legs, thus giving his knees a violent blow against the board at the side of the bed. (The German bedstead, be it remembered, is built in the form of a shallow, open box, and the victim is thus completely surrounded by solid pieces of wood with sharp edges. I do not know what species of wood it is that is employed. It is extremely hard, and gives forth a curious musical sound when struck sharply with a bone.)

After this he lies perfectly still for a while, wondering where he is going to be hit next. Finding that nothing happens, he begins to regain confidence, and ventures to gently feel around with his left leg and take stock of his position.

For clothes, he has only a very thin blanket and sheet, and beneath these he feels decidedly chilly. The bed is warm enough, so far as it goes, but there is not enough of it. He draws it up round his chin, and then his feet begin to freeze. He pushes it down over his feet, and then all the top part of him shivers.

He tries to roll up into a ball, so as to get the whole of himself underneath it, but does not succeed ; there is always some of him left outside in the cold.

He reflects that a " boneless wonder " or a " man serpent " would be comfortable enough in this bed, and wishes that he had been brought up as a con- tortionist.　If he could only tie his legs round his neck, and tuck his head in under his arm, all would yet be well.

Never having been taught to do any really useful tricks such as these, however, he has to be content to remain spread out, warming a bit of himself at a time.

It is, perhaps, foolish of him, amid so many real troubles, to allow a mere æsthetical consideration to worry him, but as he lies there on his back, looking down at himself, the sight that he presents to himself considerably annoys him.　The puffed-up bed, resting on the middle of him, gives him the appearance of a man suffering from some monstrous swelling, or else of some exceptionally well-developed frog that has been turned up the wrong way and does not know how to get on to its legs again.

Another vexation that he has to contend with is, that every time he moves a limb or breathes extra hard, the bed (which is only of down) tumbles off on to the floor.

You cannot lean out of a German bed to pick up anything off the floor, owing to its box-like formation ; so he has to scramble out after it, and of course every time he does this he barks both his shins twice against the sides of the bed.

When he has performed this feat for about the tenth

time, he concludes that it was madness for him, a mere amateur at the business, to think that he could manage a complicated, tricky bed of this sort, that must take even an experienced man all he knows to sleep in it ; and gets out and camps on the floor.

(Diary of a Pilgrimage.)

Does Art Elevate?

"I AM contending," said the Minor Poet, "that what we choose to call civilisation has done little beyond pandering to our animal desires. The noble savage of to-day flings aside his clear spring water to snatch at the missionary's gin. He will even discard his feathers, which at least were picturesque, for a chimney-pot hat innocent of nap. Plaid trousers and cheap champagne follow in due course. Where is the advancement? Civilisation provides us with more luxuries for our bodies. That I grant you. Has it brought us any real improvement that could not have been arrived at sooner by other roads?"

"It has given us Art," said the Girton Girl.

"When you say 'us,'" replied the Minor Poet, "I presume you are referring to the one person in half a million to whom Art is anything more than a name. Dismissing the countless hordes who have absolutely never heard the word, and confining attention to the few thousands scattered about Europe and America who prate of it, how many of even these do you think it really influences, entering into their lives, refining, broadening them? Watch the faces of the thin but conscientious crowd streaming wearily through our miles of picture galleries and art museums; gaping, with guide-book in hand, at ruined temple or cathedral tower; striving, with the spirit of the martyr, to feel enthusiasm for Old Masters at which, left to themselves, they would enjoy a good laugh—for chipped statues which, uninstructed, they would have mistaken for the damaged stock of a suburban tea-garden. Not more than one in twelve enjoys what he is looking at, and he by no means is bound to be the best of the dozen. Nero was a genuine lover of Art ; and in modern times August the Strong, of Saxony, ' the man of sin,' as Carlyle calls him, has left undeniable proof behind him that he was a connoisseur of the first water. One recalls names even still more recent. Are we so sure that Art *does* elevate ? "

" You are talking for the sake of talking," told him the Girton Girl.

" One can talk for the sake of thinking also," reminded her the Minor Poet. " The argument is one that has to be faced. But admitting that Art has been of service to mankind on the whole, that it possesses one-tenth of the soul-forming properties claimed for it in the advertisements—which I take to be a generous estimate—its effect upon the world at large still remains infinitesimal."

" It works down," maintained the Girton Girl. " From the few it spreads to the many."

" The process appears to be somewhat slow," answered the Minor Poet. " The result, for whatever it may be worth, we might have obtained sooner by doing away with the middleman."

" What middleman ? " demanded the Girton Girl.

" The artist," explained the Minor Poet ; " the man who has turned the whole thing into a business, the shopman who sells emotions over the counter. A Corot, a Turner is, after all, but a poor apology compared with a walk in spring through the Black Forest or the view from Hampstead Heath on a November afternoon. Had we been less occupied acquiring ' the advantages of civilisation,' working upward through the weary centuries to the city slum, the corrugated-iron-roofed-farm, we might have found time to learn to love the beauty of the world. As it is, we have been so busy ' civilising ' ourselves that we have forgotten to live. We are like an old lady I once shared a carriage with across the Simplon Pass."

" By the way," I remarked, " one is going to be saved all that bother in the future. They have nearly completed the new railway line. One will be able to go from Domo d'Orsola to Brieg in a little over the two hours. They tell me the tunnelling is wonderful."

" It will be very charming," sighed the Minor Poet. " I am looking forward to a future when, thanks to ' civilisation,' travel will be done away with altogether. We shall be sewn up in a sack and shot there. At the time I speak of we still had to be content with the road winding through some of the most magnificent scenery in Switzerland. I rather enjoyed the drive myself, but my companion was quite unable to appreciate it. Not because she did not care for scenery. As she explained to me, she was passionately fond of it. But her luggage claimed all her attention. There were seventeen pieces of it altogether, and every time the ancient vehicle lurched or swayed, which on the average was once every thirty seconds, she was in terror lest one or more of them should be jerked out. Half her day was taken up in counting them and rearranging them, and the only view in which she was interested was the cloud of dust behind us. One bonnet-box did contrive during the course of the journey to make its escape, after which she sat with her arms round as many of the remaining sixteen articles as she could encompass, and sighed."

" I knew an Italian countess," said the Woman of the World ; " she had been at school with mamma. She never would go half a mile out of her way for scenery. ' Why should I ? ' she would say. ' What are the painters for ? If there is anything good, let them bring it to me and I will look at it.' She said she preferred the picture to the real thing, it was so much more artistic. In the landscape, itself, she complained, there was sure to be a chimney in the distance, or a restaurant in the foreground, that spoilt the whole effect. The artist left it out. If necessary, he could put in a cow or a pretty girl to help the thing. The actual cow, if it happened to be there at all, would probably be standing the wrong way round ; the girl, in all likelihood, would be fat and plain, or be wearing the wrong hat. The artist knew precisely the sort of girl that ought to be there, and saw to it that she was there, with just the right sort of hat. She said she had found it so all through life—the poster was always an improvement on the play."

" It is rapidly coming to that," answered the Minor Poet. " Nature, as a well-known painter once put it, is not ' creeping up ' fast enough to keep pace with our ideals. In advanced Germany they improve the water-falls and ornament the rocks. In Paris they paint the babies' faces."

" You can hardly lay the blame for that upon civilisation," pleaded the Girton Girl. " The ancient Briton had a pretty taste in woads."

" Man's first feeble steps upon the upward path of art," assented the Minor Poet, " culminating in the rouge-pot and the hair-dye."

(Tea Table Talk.)

Sailing ! Sailing !

SAILING is a thing that wants knowledge and practice —though, as a boy, I did not think so. I had an idea it came natural to a body, like rounders and touch. I knew another boy who held this view likewise, and so, one windy day, we thought we would try the sport. We were stopping down at Yarmouth, and we decided we would go for a trip up the Yare. We hired a sailing boat at the yard by the bridge, and started off.

"It's rather a rough day," said the man to us, as we put off : "better take in a reef and luff sharp when you get round the bend."

We said we would make a point of it, and left him with a cheery "Good-morning," wondering to ourselves how you "luffed," and where we were to get a "reef" from, and what we were to do with it when we had got it.

We rowed until we were out of sight of the town, and then, with a wide stretch of water in front of us, and the wind blowing a perfect hurricane across it, we felt that the time had come to commence operations.

Hector—I think that was his name—went on pulling while I unrolled the sail. It seemed a complicated job, but I accomplished it at length, and then came the question, which was the top end ?

By a sort of natural instinct, we, of course, eventually decided that the bottom was the top, and set to work to fix it upside down. But it was a long time before we could get it up, either that way or any other way. The impression on the mind of the sail seemed to be that we were playing at funerals, and that I was the corpse and itself was the winding-sheet.

When it found that this was not the idea, it hit me over the head with the boom, and refused to do anything.

"Wet it," said Hector; "drop it over and get it wet."

He said people in ships always wetted the sails before they put them up. So I wetted it; but that only made matters worse than they were before. A dry sail clinging to your legs and wrapping itself round your head is not pleasant, but, when the sail is sopping wet, it becomes quite vexing.

We did get the thing up at last, the two of us together. We fixed it, not exactly upside down— more sideways like—and we tied it up to the mast with the painter, which we cut off for the purpose.

That the boat did not upset I simply state as a fact. Why it did not upset I am unable to offer any reason. I have often thought about the matter since, but I have never succeeded in arriving at any satisfactory explanation of the phenomenon.

Possibly the result may have been brought about by the natural obstinacy of all things in this world. The boat may possibly have come to the conclusion, judging from a cursory view of our behaviour, that we had come out for a morning's suicide, and had thereupon determined to disappoint us. That is the only suggestion I can offer.

By clinging like grim death to the gunwale, we just managed to keep inside the boat, but it was exhausting work. Hector said that pirates and other seafaring people generally lashed the rudder to something or other, and hauled in the main top-jib, during severe squalls, and thought we ought to try to do something of the kind ; but I was for letting her have her head to the wind.

As my advice was by far the easiest to follow, we ended by adopting it, and contrived to embrace the gunwale and give her her head.

The boat travelled up stream for about a mile at a pace I have never sailed at since, and don't want to again. Then, at a bend, she heeled over till half her sail was under water. Then she righted herself by a miracle and flew for a long low bank of soft mud.

That mud-bank saved us. The boat ploughed its way into the middle of it and then stuck. Finding that we were once more able to move according to our ideas, instead of being pitched and thrown about like peas in a bladder, we crept forward, and cut down the sail.

We had had enough sailing. We did not want to overdo the thing and get a surfeit of it. We had had a sail—a good all-round exciting, interesting sail—and now we thought we would have a row, just for a change like.

We took the sculls and tried to push the boat off the mud, and, in doing so, we broke one of the sculls. After that we proceeded with great caution, but they were a wretched old pair, and the second one cracked almost easier than the first, and left us helpless.

The mud stretched out for about a hundred yards in front of us, and behind us was the water. The only thing to be done was to sit and wait until someone came by.

It was not the sort of day to attract people out on the river, and it was three hours before a soul came in sight. It was an old fisherman who, with immense difficulty, at last rescued us, and we were towed back in an ignominious fashion to the boatyard.

What between tipping the man who had brought us home, and paying for the broken sculls, and for having been out four hours and a half, it cost us a pretty considerable number of weeks' pocket-money, that sail. But we learned experience, and they say that is always cheap at any price.

(*Three Men in a Boat.*)

Paul is Invited to a Marriage Feast.

My place at breakfast was to the left of the maternal Sellars, the Signora next to me, and the O'Kelly opposite. Uncle Gutton faced the bride and bridegroom. The disillusioned Joseph was hidden from me by flowers, so that his voice, raised from time to time, fell upon my ears, embellished with the mysterious significance of the unseen oracle.

For the first quarter of an hour or so the meal proceeded almost in silence. The maternal Sellars, when not engaged in whispered argument with the perspiring waiter, was furtively occupied in working sums upon the tablecloth by aid of a blunt pencil. The Signora, strangely unlike her usual self, was not in talkative mood.

"It was so kind of them to invite me," said the Signora, speaking low. "But I feel I ought not to have come."

"Why not?" I asked.

"I'm not fit to be here," murmured the Signora in a broken voice. "What right have I at wedding breakfasts? Of course, for dear Willie it is different; he is married."

The O'Kelly, who never, when the Signora was present, seemed to care much for conversation in which she was unable to participate, took advantage of his neighbour's being somewhat deaf to lapse into abstraction. Jarman essayed a few witticisms of a general character, of which nobody took any notice. The professional admirers of the Lady 'Ortensia, seated together at a corner of the table, appeared to be enjoying a small joke among themselves. Occasionally one or another of them would laugh nervously. But for the most part the only sounds to be heard were the clatter of the knives and forks, the energetic shuffling of the waiter, and a curious hissing noise as of escaping gas, caused by Uncle Gutton drinking champagne.

With the cutting, or rather, the smashing into a hundred fragments, of the wedding-cake—a work that taxed the united strength of bride and bridegroom to the utmost—the atmosphere lost something of its sombreness. The company, warmed by food, displayed indications of being nearly done, commenced to simmer. The maternal Sellars, putting away with her blunt pencil considerations of material nature, embraced the table with a smile.

" But it is a sad thing," sighed the maternal Sellars the next moment, with a shake of her huge head, " when your daughter marries, and goes away and leaves you."

" Damned sight sadder," commented Uncle Gutton, " when she don't go off, but hangs on home year after year and expects you to keep her."

I credit Uncle Gutton with intending this as an aside for the exclusive benefit of the maternal Sellars ; but his voice was not of the timbre that lends itself to secrecy. One of the bridesmaids, a plain, elderly girl, bending over her plate, flushed scarlet. I concluded her to be Miss Gutton.

"It doesn't seem to me," said Aunt Gutton from the other end of the table, "that gentlemen are as keen on marrying nowadays as they used to be."

"Got to know a bit about it, I expect," sounded the small, shrill voice of the unseen Joseph.

"To my thinking," exclaimed a hatchet-faced gentleman, "one of the evils crying most loudly for redress at the present moment is the utterly needless and monstrous expense of legal proceedings." He spoke rapidly and with warmth. "Take divorce. At present, what is it ? The rich man's luxury."

Conversation appeared to be drifting in a direction unsuitable to the occasion ; but Jarman was fortunately there to seize the helm.

"The plain fact of the matter is," said Jarman, "girls have gone up in value. Time was, so I 've heard, when they used to be given away with a useful bit of household linen, maybe a chair or two. Nowadays— well, it 's only chaps wallowing in wealth, like Clapper there, as can afford a really first-class article."

Mr. Clapper, not a gentleman in other respects of exceptional brilliancy, possessed one quality that popularity-seekers might have envied him : the ability to explode on the slightest provocation into a laugh instinct with all the characteristics of genuine delight.

"Give and take," observed the maternal Sellars so soon as Mr. Clapper's roar had died away ; "that 's what you 've got to do when you 're married."

"Give a deal more than you bargained for and take what you don't want—that sums it up," came the bitter voice of the unseen.

"Oh, do be quiet, Joe," advised the stout young

I

lady, from which I concluded she had once been the lean young lady. "You talk enough for a man."

"Can't I open my mouth?" demanded the indignant oracle.

"You look less foolish when you keep it shut," returned the stout young lady.

"We'll show them how to get on," observed the Lady 'Ortensia to her bridegroom, with a smile.

Mr. Clapper responded with a gurgle.

"When me and the old girl there fixed things up," said Uncle Gutton, "we didn't talk no nonsense, and we didn't start with no misunderstandings. 'I'm not a duke,' I says——"

"Had she been mistaking you for one?" inquired Minikin.

Mr. Clapper commented, not tactfully, with an appreciative laugh. I feared for a moment lest Uncle Gutton's little eyes should leave his head.

"Not being a natural-born, one-eyed fool," replied Uncle Gutton, glaring at the unabashed Minikin, "she did not. 'I'm not a duke,' I says, and *she* had sense enough to know I was talking sarcastic-like. 'I'm not offering you a life of luxury and ease. I'm offering you myself, just what you see, and nothing more.'"

"She took it?" asked Minikin, who was mopping up his gravy with his bread.

"She accepted me, sir," returned Uncle Gutton in a voice that would have awed anyone but Minikin. "Can you give me any good reason for her not doing so?"

"No need to get mad with me," explained Minikin.

" I am not blaming the poor woman. We all have our moments of despair."

The unfortunate Clapper again exploded. Uncle Gutton rose to his feet. The ready Jarman saved the situation.

" 'Ear, 'ear ! " cried Jarman, banging the table with the handles of two knives. " Silence for Uncle Gutton ! 'E 's going to propose a toast. 'Ear, 'ear ! "

Mrs. Clapper seconding his efforts, the whole table broke into applause.

" What, as a matter of fact, I did get up to say—— " began Uncle Gutton.

" Good old Uncle Gutton ! " persisted the determined Jarman. " Bride and bridegroom—long life to 'em ! "

Uncle Gutton, evidently pleased, allowed his indignation against Minikin to evaporate.

" Well," said Uncle Gutton, " if you think I 'm the one to do it—— "

The response was unmistakable. In our enthusiasm we broke two glasses and upset a cruet ; a small, thin lady was unfortunate enough to shed her chignon. Thus encouraged Uncle Gutton launched himself upon his task. Personally I should have been better pleased had Fate not interposed to assign to him the duty.

Starting with a somewhat uninstructive history of his own career, he suddenly, and for no reason at all obvious, branched off into fierce censure of the Adulteration Act. Reminded of the time by the maternal Sellars, he got in his first sensible remark by observing that with such questions, he took it, the present company was not particularly interested,

and directed himself to the main argument. To his,
Uncle Gutton's foresight, wisdom, and instinctive
understanding of humanity, Mr. Clapper, it appeared,
owed his present happiness.   Uncle Gutton it was who
had divined from the outset the sort of husband the
fair Rosina would come eventually to desire—a plain,
simple, hard-working, level-headed sort of chap, with
no hity-tity nonsense about him : such an one, in
short, as Mr. Clapper himself—(at this Mr. Clapper
expressed approval by a lengthy laugh)—a gentleman,
who, so far as Uncle Gutton's knowledge went, had
but one fault : a silly habit of laughing when there was
nothing whatever to laugh at ; of which, it was to be
hoped, the cares and responsibilities of married life
would cure him.   (To the rest of the discourse Mr.
Clapper listened with a gravity painfully maintained.)
There had been moments, Uncle Gutton was compelled
to admit, when the fair Rosina had shown inclination
to make a fool of herself—to desire in place of honest
worth mere painted baubles.   He used the term in no
offensive sense.   Speaking for himself, what a man
wanted beyond his weekly newspaper, he, Uncle Gutton,
was unable to understand ; but if there were fools in
the world who wanted to read rubbish written by other
fools, then the other fools would, of course, write it ;
Uncle Gutton did not blame them.   He mentioned
no names, but what he would say was a plain man for
a sensible girl, and no painted baubles.

The waiter here entering with a message from the
cabman to the effect that if he was to catch the twelve-
twenty-five from Charing Cross, it was about full time
he started, Uncle Gutton was compelled to bring his
speech to a premature conclusion.   The bride and

bridegroom were hustled into their clothes. There followed much female embracing and male hand-shaking. The rice having been forgotten, the waiter was almost thrown downstairs, with directions to at once procure some. There appearing danger of his not returning in time, the resourceful Jarman suggested cold semolina pudding, as a substitute. But the idea was discouraged by the bride. A slipper of remarkable antiquity, discovered on the floor and regarded as a gift from Providence, was flung from the window by brother George, with admirable aim, and alighted on the roof of the cab. The waiter, on his return, not being able to find it, seemed surprised.

(*Paul Kelver.*)

Talk about the Weather.

THE weather forecast prophesied " rain, cold, wet to fine" (whatever more than usually ghastly thing in weather that may be), " occasional local thunderstorms, east wind, with general depression over the Midland Counties (London and Channel). Bar. falling."

I do think that, of all the silly, irritating tomfoolishness by which we are plagued, this " weatherforecast" fraud is about the most aggravating. It " forecasts" precisely what happened yesterday or the day before, and precisely the opposite of what is going to happen to-day.

I remember a holiday of mine being completely ruined one late autumn by our paying attention to the weather report of the local newspaper. " Heavy showers, with thunderstorms, may be expected to-day," it would say on Monday, and so we would give up our picnic, and stop indoors all day, waiting for the rain. And people would pass the house, going off in wagonettes and coaches as jolly and merry as could be, the sun shining out, and not a cloud to be seen.

" Ah!" we said, as we stood looking out at them through the window, " won't they come home soaked!"

And we chuckled to think how wet they were going to get, and came back and stirred the fire, and got our books, and arranged our specimens of seaweed and cockle shells. By twelve o'clock, with the sun pouring into the room, the heat became quite oppressive, and we wondered when those heavy showers and occasional thunderstorms were going to begin.

"Ah! they'll come in the afternoon, you'll find," we said to each other. "Oh, *won't* those people get wet. What a lark!"

At one o'clock, the landlady would come in to ask if we weren't going out, as it seemed such a lovely day.

"No, no," we replied, with a knowing chuckle, "not we. *We* don't mean to get wet—no, no."

And when the afternoon was nearly gone, and still there was no sign of rain, we tried to cheer ourselves up with the idea that it would come down all at once, just as the people had started for home, and were out of the reach of any shelter, and that they would thus get more drenched than ever. But not a drop ever fell, and it finished a grand day, and a lovely night after it.

The next morning we would read that it was going to be a "warm, fine to set-fair day; much heat;" and we would dress ourselves in flimsy things, and go out, and, half-an-hour after we had started, it would commence to rain hard, and a bitterly cold wind would spring up, and both would keep on steadily for the whole day, and we would come home with colds and rheumatism all over us, and go to bed.

The weather is a thing that is beyond me altogether. I never can understand it. The barometer is useless: it is as misleading as the newspaper forecast.

There was one hanging up in a hotel at Oxford

at which I was staying last spring, and, when I got there, it was pointing to "set-fair." It was simply pouring with rain outside, and had been all day; and I couldn't quite make matters out. I tapped the barometer, and it jumped up and pointed, to "very dry." The Boots stopped as he was passing, and said he expected it meant to-morrow. I fancied that maybe it was thinking of the week before last, but Boots said, No, he thought not.

I tapped it again the next morning, and it went up still higher, and the rain came down faster than ever. On Wednesday I went and hit it again, and the pointer went round towards "set fair," "very dry," and "much heat," until it was stopped by the peg, and couldn't go any further. It tried its best, but the instrument was built so that it couldn't prophesy fine weather any harder than it did without breaking itself. It evidently wanted to go on, and prognosticate drought, and water famine, and sunstroke, and simooms, and such things, but the peg prevented it, and it had to be content with pointing to the mere commonplace "very dry."

Meanwhile, the rain came down in a steady torrent, and the lower part of the town was under water, owing to the river having overflowed.

Boots said it was evident that we were going to have a prolonged spell of grand weather *some time*, and read out a poem which was printed over the top of the oracle, about

> "Long foretold, long last;
> Short notice, soon past."

The fine weather never came that summer. I

expect that machine must have been referring to the following spring.

Then there are those new style of barometers, the long straight ones. I never can make head or tail of those. There is one side for 10 a.m. yesterday, and one side for 10 a.m. to-day ; but you can't always get there as early as ten, you know. It rises or falls for rain and fine, with much or less wind, and one end is " Nly " and the other " Ely " (what 's Ely got to do with it ?), and if you tap it, it doesn't tell you anything. And you 've got to correct it to sea-level, and reduce it to Fahrenheit, and even then I don't know the answer.

(Three Men in a Boat.)

1*

Silhouettes.

I FEAR I must be of a somewhat gruesome turn of mind. My sympathies are always with the melancholy side of life and nature. I love the chill October days,

The black tide gurgles softly round worm-eaten piles.

when the brown leaves lie thick and sodden underneath your feet, and a low sound as of stifled sobbing is heard in the damp woods— the evenings in late autumn time, when the white mist creeps across the fields, making it seem as though old Earth, feeling the night air cold to its poor bones, were drawing ghostly bedclothes round its withered limbs. I like the twilight of the long grey street, sad with the wailing cry of the distant muffin man. One thinks of him, as, strangely mitred, he glides by through the gloom, jangling his harsh bell, as the High Priest of the pale spirit of Indigestion, summoning the devout to come forth and worship. I find a sweetness in the aching dreariness of Sabbath afternoons in genteel suburbs—in the evil-laden desolateness of waste places by the river, when the yellow fog is stealing inland across the ooze and mud, and the black tide gurgles softly round worm-eaten piles.

I love the bleak moor, when the thin long line of the winding road lies white on the darkening heath, while overhead some belated bird, vexed with itself for being out so late, scurries across the dusky sky, screaming angrily. I love the lonely, sullen lake, hidden away in mountain solitudes. I suppose it was my childhood's surroundings that instilled in me this affection for sombre hues. One of my earliest recollections is of a dreary marshland by the sea. By day, the water stood there in wide, shallow pools. But when one looked in the evening they were pools of blood that lay there.

It was a wild, dismal stretch of coast. One day, I found myself there all alone—I forget how it came about—and, oh, how small I felt amid the sky and the sea and the sandhills! I ran, and ran, and ran, but I never seemed to move; and then I cried, and screamed, louder and louder, and the circling seagulls screamed back mockingly at me. It was an "unken" spot, as they say up North.

In the far back days of the building of the world, a long, high ridge of stones had been reared up by the sea, dividing the swampy grassland from the sand. Some of these stones—"pebbles" so they called them round about—were as big as a man, and many as big as a fair-sized house ; and when the sea was angry— and very prone he was to anger by that lonely shore, and very quick to wrath ; often have I known him sink to sleep with a peaceful smile on his rippling waves, to wake in fierce fury before the night was spent— he would snatch up giant handfuls of these pebbles and fling and toss them here and there, till the noise of their rolling and crashing could be heard by the watchers in the village afar off.

"Old Nick's playing at marbles to-night," they would say to one another, pausing to listen. And then the women would close tight their doors, and try not to hear the sound.

Far out to sea, by where the muddy mouth of the river yawned wide, there rose ever a thin white line of surf, and underneath those crested waves there dwelt a very fearsome thing, called the Bar. I grew to hate and be afraid of this mysterious Bar, for I heard it spoken of always with bated breath, and I knew that it was very cruel to fisher folk, and hurt them so sometimes that they would cry whole days and nights together with the pain, or would sit with white, scared faces, rocking themselves to and fro.

Once when I was playing among the sandhills, there came by a tall, grey woman, bending beneath a load of driftwood. She paused when nearly opposite to me, and, facing seaward, fixed her eyes upon the breaking surf above the Bar. "Ah, how I hate the sight of your white teeth ! " she muttered ; then turned and passed on.

Another morning, walking through the village, I heard a low wailing come from one of the cottages, while a little further on a group of women were gathered in the roadway, talking. " Ay," said one of them, " I thought the Bar was looking hungry last night."

So, putting one and the other together, I concluded that the " Bar " must be an ogre, such as a body reads of in books, who lived in a coral castle deep below the river's mouth, and fed upon the fishermen as he caught them going down to the sea or coming home.

From my bedroom window, on moonlight nights, I could watch the silvery foam, marking the spot beneath where he lay hid ; and I would stand on tip-toe, peering out, until at length I would come to fancy I could see his hideous form floating below the waters. Then, as the little white-sailed boats stole by him, tremblingly, I used to tremble too, lest he should suddenly open his grim jaws and gulp them down ; and when they had all safely reached the dark, soft sea beyond, I would steal back to the bedside, and pray to God to make the Bar good, so that he would give up eating the poor fishermen.

Another incident connected with that coast lives in my mind. It was the morning after a great storm —great even for that stormy coast—and the passion-worn waters were still heaving with the memory of a fury that was dead. Old Nick had scattered his marbles far and wide, and there were rents and fissures in the pebbly wall such as the oldest fisherman had never known before. Some of the hugest stones lay tossed a hundred yards away, and the waters had dug pits here and there along the ridge so deep that a tall man might stand in some of them, and yet his head not reach the level of the sand.

Round one of these holes a small crowd was pressing

eagerly, while one man, standing in the hollow, was lifting the few remaining stones off something that lay there at the bottom. I pushed my way between the straggling legs of a big fisher lad, and peered over with the rest. A ray of sunlight streamed down into the pit, and the thing at the bottom gleamed white. Sprawling there among the black pebbles it looked like a huge spider. One by one the last stones were lifted away, and the thing was left bare, and then the crowd looked at one another and shivered.

" Wonder how he got there," said a woman at length ; " somebody must ha' helped him."

" Some foreign chap, no doubt," said the man who had lifted off the stones ; " washed ashore and buried here by the sea."

" What, six foot below the water-mark, wi' all they stones atop of him ? " said another.

" That 's no foreign chap," cried a grizzled old woman, pressing forward. " What 's that that 's aside him ? "

Some one jumped down and took it from the stone where it lay glistening, and handed it up to her, and she clutched it in her skinny hand. It was a gold earring, such as fishermen sometimes wear. But this was a somewhat large one, and of rather unusual shape.

" That 's young Abram Parsons, I tell 'ee, as lies down there," cried the old creature, wildly. " I ought to know. I gave him the pair o' these forty year ago."

It may be only an idea of mine, born of after brooding upon the scene. I am inclined to think it must be so, for I was only a child at the time, and would hardly have noticed such a thing. But it seems to my remembrance that as the old crone ceased, another woman in the crowd raised her eyes slowly, and fixed them on a withered, ancient man, who leant upon a stick, and that for a moment, unnoticed by the rest, these two stood looking strangely at each other.

(*John Ingerfield.*)

Learning the Bagpipes.

It must be disheartening work, learning a musical instrument. You would think that Society, for its own sake, would do all it could to assist a man to acquire the art of playing a musical instrument. But it doesn't !

I knew a young fellow once, who was studying to play the bagpipes, and you would be surprised at the amount of opposition he had to contend with. Why, not even from the members of his own family did he receive what you would call active encouragement. His father was dead against the business from the beginning, and spoke quite unfeelingly on the subject.

My friend used to get up early in the morning to practise, but he had to give that idea up, because of his sister. She was somewhat religiously inclined, and she said it seemed such an awful thing to begin the day like that.

So he sat up at night instead, and played after the family had gone to bed, but that did not do, as it got the house such a bad name. People, going home late, would stop outside to listen, and then put it about all over the town, the next morning, that a fearful murder had been committed at Mr. Jefferson's the night before ; and would describe how they had heard the victim's shrieks and the brutal oaths and curses of the murderer, followed by the prayer for mercy, and the last dying gurgle of the corpse.

So they let him practise in the day-time, in the back-kitchen with all the doors shut ; but his more successful passages could generally be heard in the sitting-room, in spite of these precautions, and would affect his mother almost to tears.

She said it put her in mind of her poor father (he had been swallowed by a shark, poor man, while bathing off the coast of New Guinea—where the connection came in, she could not explain).

Then they knocked up a little place for him at the bottom of the garden, about quarter of a mile from the house, and made him take the machine down there when he wanted to work it ; and sometimes a visitor would come to the house who knew nothing of the matter, and they would forget to tell him all about it, and caution him, and he would go out for a stroll round the garden and suddenly get within earshot of those bagpipes, without being prepared for it, or knowing what it was. If he were a man of strong mind, it only

There is, it must be confessed, something very sad about the early efforts of an amateur in bagpipes.

gave him fits ; but a person of mere average intellect it usually sent mad.

There is, it must be confessed, something very sad about the early efforts of an amateur in bagpipes. I have felt that myself when listening to my young friend. They appear to be a trying instrument to perform upon. You have to get enough breath for the whole tune before you start—at least, so I gathered from watching Jefferson.

He would begin magnificently with a wild, full, come-to-the-battle sort of a note, that quite roused you. But he would get more and more piano as he went on, and the last verse generally collapsed in the middle with a splutter and a hiss.

You want to be in good health to play the bagpipes.

(*Three Men in a Boat.*)

Choosing a Profession.

A COFFEE-SHOP becomes a bit of a desert towards three o'clock; and, after a while, young Tidelman, for that was his name, got to putting down his book and chatting to me. His father was dead; which, judging from what he told me about the old man, must have been a bit of luck for everybody; and his mother, it turned out, had come from my own village in Suffolk; and that constituted a sort of bond between us, seeing I had known all her people pretty intimately. He was earning good money at a dairy, where his work was scouring milk-cans; and his Christian name—which was the only thing Christian about him, and that, somehow or other, didn't seem to fit him—was Joseph.

One afternoon he came into the shop looking as if he had lost a shilling and found sixpence, as the saying is; and instead of drinking water as usual, sent the girl out for a pint of ale. The moment it came he drank off half of it at a gulp, and then sat staring out of the window.

"What's up?" I says. "Got the shove?"

"Yes," he answers; "but, as it happens, it's a shove up. I've been taken off the yard and put on the walk, with a rise of two bob a week." Then he took another pull at the beer and looked more savage then ever.

"Well," I says, "that ain't the sort of thing to be humpy about."

"Yes it is," he snaps back; "it means that if I don't take precious good care I'll drift into being a blooming milkman, spending my life yelling 'Milk ahoi!' and spooning smutty-faced servant-gals across area railings."

"Oh!" I says, "and what may you prefer to spoon—duchesses?"

"Yes," he answers sulky-like; "duchesses are right enough—some of 'em."

"So are servant-gals," I says, "some of 'em. Your hat's feeling a bit small for you this morning, ain't it?"

"Hat's all right," says he; "it's the world as I'm complaining of—beastly place; there's nothing to do in it."

"Oh!" I says; "some of us find there's a bit too much." I'd been up since five that morning myself; and his own work, which was scouring milk-cans for twelve hours a day, didn't strike me as suggesting a life of leisured ease.

"I don't mean that," he says. "I mean things worth doing."

"Well, what do you want to do," I says, "that this world ain't big enough for?"

"It ain't the size of it," he says; "it's the dulness of it. Things used to be different in the old days."

"How do you know?" I says.

"You can read about it," he answers.

"Oh," I says, "and what do they know about it—these gents that sit down and write about it for their living ! You show me a book cracking up the old times, writ by a chap as lived in 'em, and I 'll believe you. Till then I 'll stick to my opinion that the old days were much the same as these days, and maybe a trifle worse."

" From a Sunday School point of view, perhaps yes," says he ; " but there 's no gainsaying—— "

" No what ? " I says.

" No gainsaying," repeats he ; " it 's a common word in literatoor."

" Maybe," says I, " but this happens to be ' The Blue Posts Coffee House,' established in the year 1863. We will use modern English here, if you don't mind." One had to take him down like that at times. He was the sort of boy as would talk poetry to you if you weren't firm with him.

" Well, then, there 's no denying the fact," says he, " if you prefer it that way, that in the old days there was more opportunity for adventure."

" What about Australia ? " says I.

" Australia ! " retorts he ; " what would I do there ? Be a shepherd, like you see in the picture, wear ribbons, and play the flute ? "

" There 's not much of that sort of shepherding over there," says I, " unless I 've been deceived ; but if Australia ain't sufficiently uncivilised for you, what about Africa ? "

" What 's the good of Africa ? " replies he ; " you don't read advertisements in the *Clerkenwell News* : ' Young men wanted as explorers.' I 'd drift into a barber's shop at Capetown more likely than anything else."

" What about the gold diggings ? " I suggests.

I like to see a youngster with the spirit of adventure in him. It shows grit as a rule.

"Played out," says he. "You are employed by a company, wages ten dollars a week, and a pension for your old age. Everything's played out," he continues. "Men ain't wanted nowadays. There's only room for clerks, and intelligent artisans, and shopboys."

"Go for a soldier," says I; "there's excitement for you."

"That would have been all right," says he, "in the days when there was real fighting."

"There's a good bit of it going about nowadays," I says. "We are generally at it, on and off, between shouting about the blessings of peace."

"Not the sort of fighting I mean," replies he; "I want to do something myself, not be one of a row."

"Well," I says, "I give you up. You've dropped into the wrong world it seems to me. We don't seem able to cater for you here."

"I've come a bit too late," he answers; "that's the mistake I've made. Two hundred years ago there were lots of things a fellow might have done."

"Yes, I know what's in your mind," I says, "pirates."

"Yes, pirates would be all right," says he; "they got plenty of sea-air and exercise, and didn't need to join a blooming funeral club."

"You've got ideas above your station," I says. "You work hard, and one day you'll have a milk-shop of your own, and be walking out with a pretty housemaid on your arm, feeling as if you were the Prince of Wales himself."

"Stow it!" he says; "it makes me shiver for fear it might come true. I'm not cut out for a respectable cove, and I won't be one neither, if I can help it!"

"Yes, I know what's in your mind," I says, "pirates."

"What do you mean to be then? " I says; "we've all got to be something, until we're stiff 'uns."

"Well," he says, quite cool-like, "I think I shall be a burglar."

I dropped into the seat opposite and stared at him. If any other lad had said it I should have known it was only foolishness, but he was just the sort to mean it.

"It's the only calling I can think of," says he, "that has got any element of excitement left in it."

"You call seven years at Portland 'excitement,' do you?" says I, thinking of the argument most likely to tell upon him.

"What's the difference," answers he, "between Portland and the ordinary labouring man's life, except that at Portland you never need fear being out of work?" He was a rare one to argue. "Besides," says he, "it's only the fools as gets copped. Look at that diamond robbery in Bond Street, two years ago. Fifty thousand pounds worth of jewels stolen, and never a clue to this day! Look at the Dublin Bank robbery," says he, his eyes all alight, and his face flushed like a girl's. "Three thousand pounds in golden sovereigns walked away with in broad daylight, and never so much as the flick of a coat-tail seen. Those are the sort of men I'm thinking of, not the bricklayer out of work, who smashes a window and gets ten years for breaking open a cheesemonger's till with nine and fourpence ha'penny in it."

"Yes," says I, "and are you forgetting the chap who was nabbed at Birmingham only last week? He wasn't exactly an amatoor. How long do you think he'll get?"

"A man like that deserves what he gets," answers he; "couldn't hit a policeman at six yards."

"You bloodthirsty young scoundrel," I says; "do you mean you wouldn't stick at murder?"

"It's all in the game," says he, not in the least

put out. " I take my risks, he takes his. It 's no more murder than soldiering is."

" It 's taking a human creature's life," I says.

" Well," he says, " what of it ? There 's plenty more where he comes from."

I tried reasoning with him from time to time, but he wasn't a sort of boy to be moved from a purpose. His mother was the only argument that had any weight with him. I believe so long as she had lived he would have kept straight ; that was the only soft spot in him. But unfortunately she died a couple of years later, and then I lost sight of Joe altogether. I made enquiries, but no one could tell me anything. He had just disappeared, that 's all.

(*Observations of Henry and Others.*)

In Rain Time.

WE rowed on all that day through the rain, and very melancholy work it was. We pretended, at first, that we enjoyed it. We said it was a change, and that we liked to see the river under all its different aspects. We said we could not expect to have it all sunshine, nor should we wish it. We told each other that Nature was beautiful, even in her tears.

Indeed, Harris and I were quite enthusiastic about the business, for the first few hours. And we sang a song about a gipsy's life, and how delightful a gipsy's existence was !—free to storm and sunshine, and to every wind•that blew !—and how he enjoyed the rain, and what a lot of good it did him ; and how he laughed at people who didn't like it.

George took the fun more soberly, and stuck to the umbrella.

We hoisted the cover before we had lunch, and kept it up all the afternoon, just leaving a little space in the bow, from which one of us could paddle and keep a look-out. In this way we made nine miles, and pulled up for the night a little below Day's Lock.

I cannot honestly say that we had a merry evening. The rain poured down with quiet persistency. Everything in the boat was damp and clammy. Supper was not a success. Cold veal pie, when you don't feel hungry, is apt to cloy. I felt I wanted whitebait and a cutlet ; Harris babbled of soles and white-sauce, and passed the remains of his pie to Montmorency, who declined it, and, apparently insulted by the offer, went and sat over at the other end of the boat by himself.

George requested that we would not talk about these things, at all events until he had finished his cold boiled beef without mustard.

We played penny nap after supper. We played for about an hour and a half, by the end of which time George had won fourpence—George always is lucky at cards—and Harris and I had lost exactly twopence each.

We thought we would give up gambling then. As Harris said, it breeds an unhealthy excitement when carried too far. George offered to go on and give us our revenge ; but Harris and I decided not to battle any further against Fate.

After that, we mixed ourselves some toddy, and sat round and talked. George told us about a man he had known, who had come up the river two years ago, and who had slept out in a damp boat on just such another night as that was, and it had given him rheumatic fever, and nothing was able to save him, and he had died in great agony ten days afterwards. George said he was quite a young man, and was engaged to be married. He said it was one of the saddest things he had ever known.

And that put Harris in mind of a friend of his, who had been in the Volunteers, and who had slept out under canvas one wet night down at Aldershot, "on just such another night as this," said Harris ; and he had woke up in the morning a cripple for life. Harris said he would introduce us both to the man when we got back to town ; it would make our hearts bleed to see him.

This naturally led to some pleasant chat about sciatica, fevers, chills, lung diseases, and bronchitis. After that, we went to bed.

(*Three Men in a Boat.*)

To What End ?

" CHRISTIANITY," continued the Minor Poet, " gave merely an added force to impulses the germs of which were present in the infant race. The printing-press, teaching us to think in communities, has nonplussed to a certain extent the aims of the individual as opposed to those of humanity. Without prejudice, without sentiment, cast your eye back over the panorama of the human race. What is the picture that presents itself ? Scattered here and there over the wild voiceless desert, first the holes and the caves, next the rude-built huts, the wigwams, the lake dwellings of primitive man. Lonely, solitary, followed by his dam and brood, he creeps through the tall grass, ever with watchful, terror-haunted eyes satisfies his few desires ; communicates, by means of a few grunts and signs, his tiny store of knowledge to his offspring ; then, crawling beneath a stone, or into some tangled corner of the jungle, dies and disappears. We look again. A thousand centuries have flashed and faded. The surface of the earth is flecked with strange quivering patches : here, where the sun shines on the wood and sea, close together, almost touching one another ; there, among the shadows, far apart. The Tribe has formed itself. The whole tiny mass moves forward, halts, runs backward, stirred always by one common impulse. Man has learnt the secret of combination, of mutual help. The City rises. From its stone centre spreads its power ; the Nation leaps to life ; civilisation springs from leisure ; no longer is each man's life devoted to his mere animal necessities. The artificer, the thinker—his fellows shall protect him. Socrates dreams, Phidias carves the marble, while Pericles maintains the law and Leonidas holds the Barbarian at bay. Europe annexes piece by piece the dark places of the earth, gives to them her laws. The Empire swallows the small State ; Russia stretches her arm round Asia. In London we toast the union of the English-speaking peoples ; in Berlin and Vienna we rub a salamander to the *deutscher Bund ;* in Paris we whisper of a communion of the Latin races. In great things so in small. The stores, the huge Emporium displaces the small shopkeeper ; the Trust amalgamates a hundred firms ; the Union speaks for the worker. The limits of country, of language, are found too narrow for the new ideas. German, American, or English—let what yard of coloured cotton you choose float from the mizzenmast, the business of the human race is their captain. One hundred and fifty years ago old Sam Johnson waited in a patron's anteroom ; to-day the entire world invites him to growl his table-talk, the while it takes its dish of tea. The poet, the novelist, speak in twenty languages. Nationality—it is the County Council of the future. The world's high roads run turnpike-free from pole to pole. One would be blind not to see the goal towards which we are rushing. At the outside it is but a generation or two off. It is one huge murmuring Hive— one universal Hive just the size of the round earth. The bees have been before us ; they have solved the riddle towards which we in darkness have been groping.

The Old Maid shuddered visibly. " What a terrible idea ! " she said.

" To us," replied the Minor Poet ; " not to those who will come after us. The child dreads manhood. To Abraham, roaming the world with his flocks, the life of your modern City man, chained to his office from ten to four, would have seemed little better than penal servitude."

" My sympathies are with the Abrahamitical ideal," observed the Philosopher.

" Mine also," agreed the Minor Poet. " But neither you nor I represent the tendency of the age. We are its curiosities. We, and such as we, serve as the brake regulating the rate of progress. The genus of the species shows itself moving in the direction of the organised community—all life welded together, controlled by one central idea. The individual worker is drawn into the factory. Chippendale to-day would have been employed sketching designs ; the chair would have been put together by fifty workers, each one trained to perfection in his own particular department. Why does the hotel, with its five hundred servants, its catering for three thousand mouths, work smoothly, while the desirable family residence, with its two or three domestics, remains the scene of waste, confusion, and dispute ? We are losing the talent of living alone ; the instinct of living in communities is driving it out."

" So much the worse for the community," was the comment of the Philosopher. " Man, as Ibsen has said, will always be at his greatest when he stands alone. To return to our friend Abraham, surely he, wandering in the wilderness, talking with his God, was nearer the ideal than the modern citizen, thinking with his morning paper, applauding silly shibboleths from a theatre pit, guffawing at coarse jests, one of a music-hall crowd ? In the community it is the lowest always leads. You spoke just now of all the world inviting Samuel Johnson to its dish of tea. How many read him as compared to the number of subscribers to the *Ha'penny Joker ?* This ' thinking in communities,' as it is termed, to what does it lead ? To mafficking and Dreyfus scandals. What crowd ever evolved a noble idea ? If Socrates and Galileo, Confucius and Christ had ' thought in communities,' the world would indeed be the ant-hill you appear to regard as its destiny."

(Tea Table Talk.)

At Ober-Ammergau.

WE ourselves saw the play yesterday and are now discussing it. I am explaining to B. the difficulty I experience in writing an account of it for my diary. I tell him that I really do not know what to say about it.

" Give them the history of the Passion Play," he suggests, " how it came to be played."

" Oh, but so many people have done that already," I say again.

" So much the better for you," is his reply. " Having previously heard precisely the same story from half a dozen other sources, the public will be tempted to believe you when you repeat the account. Tell them that during the Thirty Years' War a terrible plague (as if half a dozen different armies, marching up and down their country, fighting each other about the Lord only knows what, and living on them while doing it, was not plague enough) swept over Bavaria, devastating each town and hamlet. Of all the highland villages, Ober-Ammergau by means of a strictly enforced quarantine alone kept, for a while, the black foe at bay. No soul was allowed to leave the village ; no living thing to enter it.

" But one dark night Caspar Schuchler, an inhabitant of Ober-Ammergau, who had been away working in the plague-stricken neighbouring village of Eschenlohe,

K

creeping low on his belly, passed the drowsy sentinels, and gained his home, and saw what for many a day he had been hungering for—a sight of his wife and bairns. It was a selfish act to do, and he and his fellow-villagers paid dearly for it.   Three days after he had entered his house he and all his family lay dead, and the plague was raging through the valley, and nothing seemed able to stay its course.

" When human means fail, we feel it is only fair to give Heaven a chance.   The good people who dwelt by the side of the Ammer vowed that, if the plague left them, they would, every ten years, perform a Passion Play.   The celestial powers seem to have at once closed with this offer.   The plague disappeared as if by magic, and every recurring tenth year since, the Ober-Ammergauites have kept their promise and played their Passion Play.   They act it to this day as a pious observance. Before each performance all the characters gather together on the stage around their pastor, and, kneeling, pray for a blessing upon the work then about to commence.   The profits that are made, after paying the performers a wage that just compensates them for their loss of time—wood-carver Maier, who plays the Christ, only receives about fifty pounds for the whole of the thirty or so performances given during the season, to say nothing of the winter's rehearsals—is put aside, part for the temporal benefit of the community, and the rest for the benefit of the Church.   From Burgomaster down to shepherd lad, from the Mary and the Jesus down to the meanest super, all work for the love of their religion, not for money.   Each one feels that he is helping forward the cause of Christianity."

"And I could also speak," I add, "of grand old Daisenberger, the gentle, simple old priest, ' the father of the valley,' who now lies in silence among his children that he loved so well. It was he, you know, that shaped the rude burlesque of a coarser age into the impressive reverential drama that we saw yesterday. That is a portrait of him over the bed. What a plain, homely, good face it is! How pleasant, how helpful it is to come across a good face now and then! I do not mean a sainted face, suggestive of stained glass and marble tombs, but a rugged human face that has had the grit, and rain, and sunshine of life rubbed into it, and that has gained its expression not by looking up with longing at the stars, but by looking down with eyes full of laughter and love at the human things around it."

"Yes," assented B. "You can put in that if you like. There is no harm in it. And then you can go on to speak of the play itself, and give your impressions concerning it. Never mind their being silly. They will be all the better for that. Silly remarks are generally more interesting than sensible ones."

"But what is the use of saying anything about it at all?" I urge. "The merest schoolboy must know all about the Ober-Ammergau Passion Play by this time."

"What has that to do with you?" answers B. "You are not writing for cultured schoolboys. You are writing for mere simple men and women. They will be glad of a little information on the subject, and then when the schoolboy comes home for his holiday they will be able, so far as this topic, at all events, is concerned, to converse with him on his own level and not appear stupid.

"Come," he says, kindly, trying to lead me on, "what did you think about it?"

"Well," I reply, after musing for a while, "I think that a play of eighteen acts and some forty scenes, which commences at eight o'clock in the morning, and continues, with an interval of an hour and a half for dinner, until six o'clock in the evening, is too long. I think the piece wants cutting. About a third of it is impressive and moving, and what the earnest student of the drama at home is for ever demanding that a play should be—namely, elevating; but I consider that the other two-thirds are tiresome."

"Quite so," answers B. "But then we must remember that the performance is not intended as an entertainment, but as a religious service. To criticise any part of it as uninteresting, is like saying that half the Bible might very well have been omitted, and that the whole story could have been told in a third of the space."

"And now, as to the right or wrong of the performance as a whole. Do you see any objection to the play from a religious point of view?"

"No," I reply, "I do not; nor do I understand how anybody else, and least of all a really believing Christian, can either. To argue as some do, that Christianity should be treated as a sacred mystery, is to argue against the whole scheme of Christianity. It was Christ himself that rent the veil of the Temple, and brought religion down into the streets and market-places of the world. Christ was a common man. He lived a common life, among common men and women,

He died a common death. His own methods of teaching were what a Saturday reviewer, had he to deal with the case, would undoubtedly term vulgar. The roots of Christianity are planted deep down in the very soil of life, amid all that is commonplace, and mean, and petty, and everyday. Its strength lies in its simplicity, its homely humanness. It has spread itself through the world by speaking to the hearts, rather than to the heads of men. If it is still to live and grow, it must be helped along by such methods as these peasant players of Ober-Ammergau employ, not by high-class essays and the learned discussions of the cultured.

" The crowded audience that sat beside us in the theatre yesterday saw Christ of Nazareth nearer than any book, however inspired, could bring him to them ; clearer than any words, however eloquent, could show him. They saw the sorrow of his patient face. They heard his deep tones calling to them. They saw him in the hour of his so-called triumph, wending his way through the narrow streets of Jerusalem, the multitude that thronged round him waving their branches of green palms and shouting loud hosannas.

" What a poor scene of triumph !—a poor-clad, pale-faced man, mounted upon the back of a shuffling, unwilling little grey donkey, passing slowly through the byways of a city, busy upon other things. Beside him, a little band of worn, anxious men, clad in threadbare garments—fishermen, petty clerks, and the like ; and, following, a noisy rabble, shouting, as crowds in all lands and in all times shout, and as dogs bark, they know not why—because others are shouting, or barking. And that scene marks the highest triumph

won while he lived on earth by the village carpenter
of Galilee, about whom the world has been fighting and
thinking and talking so hard for the last eighteen
hundred years.

"They were present at the parting of Mary and
Jesus by Bethany, and it will be many a day before
the memory of that scene ceases to vibrate in their
hearts. It is the scene that brings the humanness
of the great tragedy most closely home to us. Jesus
is going to face sorrow and death at Jerusalem. Mary's
instinct tells her that this is so, and she pleads to him
to stay.

"Poor Mary! To others he is the Christ, the
Saviour of mankind, setting forth upon his mighty
mission to redeem the world. To loving Mary Mother,
he is her son : the baby she has suckled at her breast,
the little one she has crooned to sleep upon her lap,
whose little cheek has lain against her heart, whose
little feet have made sweet music through the poor home
at Bethany : he is her boy, her child ; she would wrap
her mother's arms around him, and hold him safe against
all the world, against even heaven itself.

"Never, in any human drama, have I witnessed
a more moving scene than this. Never has the voice
of any actress (and I have seen some of the greatest,
if any great ones are living) stirred my heart as did
the voice of Rosa Lang, the Burgomaster's daughter.
It was not the voice of one woman, it was the voice
of Motherdom, gathered together from all the world
over.

"Oliver Wendell Holmes, in *The Autocrat of the
Breakfast Table*, I think, confesses to having been
bewitched at different times by two women's voices,

and adds that both these voices belonged to German
women. I am not surprised at either statement of
the good doctor's. I am sure if a man did fall in love
with a voice, he would find, on tracing it to its source,
that it was the voice of some homely-looking German
woman. I have never heard such exquisite soul-
drawing music in my life, as I have more than once
heard float from the lips of some sweet-faced German
Fraulein when she opened her mouth to speak. The
voice has been so pure, so clear, so deep, so full of soft
caressing tenderness, so strong to comfort, so gentle
to soothe, it has seemed like one of those harmonies
musicians tell us that they dream of, but can never
chain to earth.

"As I sat in the theatre, listening to the wondrous
tones of this mountain peasant-woman, rising and falling
like the murmur of a sea, filling the vast sky-covered
building with their yearning notes, stirring like a great
wind stirs Æolian strings, the thousands of trembling
hearts around her, it seemed to me that I was indeed
listening to the voice of the 'mother of the world,'
of mother Nature herself.

"They saw him, as they had often seen him in
pictures, sitting for the last time with his disciples
at supper. But yesterday they saw him, not a mute,
moveless figure, posed in conventional, meaningless
attitude, but a living, loving man, sitting in fellowship
with the dear friends that against all the world had
believed in him, and had followed his poor fortunes,
talking with them for the last sweet time, comforting
them.

"They heard him bless the bread and wine that
they themselves to this day take in remembrance of him.

" They saw his agony in the Garden of Gethsemane, the human shrinking from the cup of pain. They saw the false friend, Judas, betray him with a kiss. Alas! poor Judas! He loved Jesus, in a way, like the rest did. It was only his fear of poverty that made him betray his Master. He was so poor—he wanted the money so badly! We cry out in horror against Judas. Let us pray rather that we are never tempted to do a shameful action for a few pieces of silver. The fear of poverty ever did, and ever will, make scamps of men. We would like to be faithful, and noble, and just, only really times are so bad that we cannot afford it! As Becky Sharp says, it is so easy to be good and noble on five thousand a year, so very hard if it be on the mere five. If Judas had only been a well-to-do man, he might have been Saint Judas this day, instead of cursed Judas. He was not bad. He had only one failing—the failing that makes the difference between a saint and a villain, all the world over—he was a coward; he was afraid of being poor.

" They saw him, pale and silent, dragged now before the priests of his own countrymen, and now before the Roman Governor, while the voice of the people —the people who had cried ' Hosanna ' to him— shouted ' Crucify him! crucify him! ' They saw him bleeding from the crown of thorns. They saw him, still followed by the barking mob, sink beneath the burden of his cross. They saw the woman wipe the bloody sweat from off his face. They saw the last, long, silent look between the mother and the son, as, journeying upward to his death, he passed her in the narrow way through which he once had ridden in brief-lived triumph. They heard her low sob as she turned away, leaning on Mary Magdalen. They saw him nailed upon the cross between the thieves. They saw the blood start from his side. They heard his last cry to his God. They saw him rise victorious over death!

" Few believing Christians among the vast audience but must have passed out from that strange playhouse with their belief and love strengthened. The God of the Christian, for his sake, became a man, and lived and suffered and died as a man ; and, as a man, living, suffering, dying among other men, he had that day seen him.

" The unbeliever, also, passes out into the village street full of food for thought. The rude sermon preached in this hillside temple has shown to him, clearer than he could have seen before, the secret wherein lies the strength of Christianity ; the reason why, of all the faiths that Nature has taught to her children to help them in their need, to satisfy the hunger of their souls, this faith, born by the Sea of Galilee, has spread the farthest over the world, and struck its note the deepest into human life. Not by his doctrines, not even by his promises, has Christ laid hold upon the hearts of men, but by the story of his life."

(*Diary of a Pilgrimage.*)

K*

Humour and " The Penny-a-Liner."

To my literary labours I found it necessary to add
journalism. I lacked Dan's magnificent assurance.
Fate never befriends the nervous. Had I burst into
the editorial sanctum, the editor most surely would
have been out ; if in, would have been a man of short
ways, would have seen to it that I went out, quickly.
But the idea was not to be thought of ; Robert Macaire
himself in my one coat would have been diffident,
apologetic. I joined the ranks of the penny-a-liners—
to be literally exact, three-halfpence-a-liners. In
company with half-a-dozen other shabby outsiders—
some of them young men like myself seeking to climb ;
others, old men who had sunk—I attended inquests,
police courts ; flew after fire-engines ; rejoiced in
street-accidents ; yearned for murders. Somewhat
vulture-like we lived precariously upon the mis-
fortunes of others. We made occasional half-crowns
by providing the public with scandal, occasional crowns
by keeping our information to ourselves.

" I think, gentlemen," would explain our spokesman
in a hoarse whisper, on returning to the table, " I
think the corpse's brother-in-law is anxious that the
affair, if possible, should be kept out of the papers."

The closeness and attention with which we would
follow that particular case, the fulness and completeness

of our notes, would be quite remarkable.   Our spokesman would rise, drift carelessly away, to return five
minutes later, wiping his mouth.

"Not a very interesting case, gentlemen, I don't
think.   Shall we say five shillings apiece ?"   Sometimes a sense of the dignity of our calling would induce
us to stand out for ten.

And here also my sense of humour came to my aid ;
gave me perhaps
an undue advantage
over my competitors.
Twelve good men
and true had been
asked to say how a
Lascar sailor had met
his death.   It was
perfectly clear how
he had met his death.
A plumber, working
on the roof of a
small   two - storied
house, had slipped
and fallen on him.
The plumber had
escaped with a few
bruises ; the unfortu-
nate sailor had been
picked up dead.
Some blame attached
to the plumber.   His
mate, an excellent
witness, told us the
whole story.

Others, old men who had sunk.

"I was fixing a gas-pipe on the first floor," said the man. "The prisoner was on the roof."

"We won't call him the 'prisoner,'" interrupted the coroner, "at least, not yet. Refer to him, if you please, as the 'last witness.'"

"The last witness," corrected himself the man. "He shouts down the chimney to know if I was ready for him."

"'Ready and waiting,' I says.

"'Right,' he says; 'I'm coming in through the window.'

"'Wait a bit,' I says; 'I'll go down and move the ladder for you.'

"'It's all right,' he says; 'I can reach it.'

"'No, you can't,' I says. 'It's the other side of the chimney.'

"'I can get round,' he says.

"Well, before I knew what had happened, I hears him go, smack! I rushes to the window and looks out; I see him on the pavement, sitting up like.

"'Hullo, Jim,' I says. 'Have you hurt yourself?'

"'I think I'm all right,' he says, 'as far as I can tell. But I wish you'd come down. This bloke I've fallen on looks a bit sick.'"

The others headed their flimsy "Sad Accident," a title truthful but not alluring. I altered mine to "Plumber in a Hurry—Fatal Result." Saying as little as possible about the unfortunate sailor, I called the attention of plumbers generally to the coroner's very just remarks upon the folly of undue haste; pointed out to them, as a body, the trouble that would arise if somehow they could not cure themselves of this tendency to rush through their work without a moment's loss of time.

It established for me a useful reputation. The sub-editor of one evening paper condescended so far as to come out in his shirt-sleeves and shake hands with me.

"That's the sort of thing we want," he told me ; "a light touch, a bit of humour."

I snatched fun from fires (I sincerely trust the insurance premiums were not overdue) ; culled quaintness from street rows ; extracted merriment from catastrophes the most painful, and prospered.

(*Paul Kelver.*)

Verboten.

ANOTHER passion you must restrain in Germany is
that prompting you to throw things out of window.
Cats are no excuse. During the first week of my
residence in Germany I was awakened incessantly
by cats. One night I got mad. I collected a small
arsenal—two or three pieces of coal, a few hard pears,
a couple of candle ends, an odd egg I found on the
kitchen table, an empty soda-water bottle, and a few
articles of that sort,—and, opening the window,
bombarded the spot from where the noise appeared
to come. I do not suppose I hit anything ; I never
knew a man who did hit a cat, even when he could
see it, except, maybe, by accident when aiming at
something else. I have known crack shots, winners
of Queen's prizes—those sort of men,—shoot with
shot-guns at cats fifty yards away, and never hit
a hair. I have often thought that, instead of bull's-
eyes, running deer, and that rubbish, the really superior
marksman would be he who could boast that he had
shot the cat.

But, anyhow, they moved off ; maybe the egg
annoyed them. I had noticed when I picked it up
that it did not look a good egg ; and I went back
to bed again, thinking the incident closed. Ten
minutes afterwards there came a violent ringing of
the electric bell. I tried to ignore it, but it was too

persistent, and, putting on my dressing gown, I went down to the gate. A policeman was standing there. He had all the things I had been throwing out of the window in a little heap in front of him, all except the egg. He had evidently been collecting them. He said :

"Are these things yours ? "

I said : "They were mine, but personally I have done with them. Anybody can have them—you can have them."

" What cats ? " he asked.

He ignored my offer. He said :

"You threw these things out of window."

"You are right," I admitted ; "I did."

"Why did you throw them out of window ? " he asked. A German policeman has his code of questions arranged for him ; he never varies them, and he never omits one.

"I threw them out of the window at some cats," I answered.

"What cats ? " he asked.

It was the sort of question a German policeman would ask. I replied with as much sarcasm as I could put into my accent that I was ashamed to say I could not tell him what cats. I explained that, personally, they were strangers to me ; but I offered, if the police would call all the cats in the district together, to come round and see if I could recognise them by their yaul.

The German policeman does not understand a joke, which is perhaps on the whole just as well, for I believe there is a heavy fine for joking with any German uniform ; they call it "treating an official with contumely." He merely replied that it was not the duty of the police to help me recognise the cats ; their duty was merely to fine me for throwing things out of window.

I asked what a man was supposed to do in Germany when woke up night after night by cats, and he explained that I could lodge an information against the owner of the cat, when the police would proceed to caution him, and, if necessary, order the cat to be destroyed. Who was going to destroy the cat, and what the cat would be doing during the process, he did not explain.

I asked him how he proposed I should discover the owner of the cat. He thought for a while, and then suggested that I might follow it home. I did not feel inclined to argue with him any more after that ; I should only have said things that would have made the matter worse. As it was, that night's sport cost me twelve marks ; and not a single one of the four German officials who interviewed me on the subject could see anything ridiculous in the proceedings from beginning to end.

(*Three Men on the Bummel.*)

Morning at " Beggarbush."

I KNEW that if he slept at " Beggarbush " he would be up in time ; I have slept there myself, and I know what happens. About the middle of the night, as you judge, though in reality it may be somewhat later, you are startled out of your first sleep by what sounds like a rush of cavalry along the passage, just outside your door. Your half-wakened intelligence fluctuates between burglars, the Day of Judgment, and a gas explosion. You sit up in bed and listen intently. You are not kept waiting long ; the next moment a door is violently slammed, and somebody, or something, is evidently coming downstairs on a tea-tray.

" I told you so," says a voice outside, and immediately some hard substance, a head one would say from the ring of it, rebounds against the panel of your door.

By this time you are charging madly round the room for your clothes. Nothing is where you put it overnight, the articles most essential have disappeared entirely ; and meanwhile the murder, or revolution, or whatever it is, continues unchecked. You pause for a moment, with your head under the wardrobe, where you think you can see your slippers, to listen to a steady, monotonous thumping upon a distant door. The victim, you presume, has taken refuge there ; they mean to have him out and finish him. Will you be in time ? The knocking ceases, and a voice, sweetly reassuring in its gentle plaintiveness, asks meekly :

" Pa, may I get up ? "

You do not hear the other voice, but the responses are :

" No, it was only the bath—no, she ain't really hurt,—only wet, you know. Yes, ma, I 'll tell 'em what you say. No, it was a pure accident. Yes ; good-night, papa."

Then the same voice, exerting itself so as to be heard in a distant part of the house, remarks :

" You 've got to come upstairs again. Pa says it isn't time yet to get up."

You return to bed, and lie listening to somebody being dragged upstairs, evidently against their will. By a thoughtful arrangement the spare rooms at " Beggarbush " are exactly underneath the nurseries. The same somebody, you conclude, still offering the most creditable opposition, is being put back into bed. You can follow the contest with much exactitude, because every time the body is flung down upon the spring mattress, the bedstead, just above your head, makes a sort of jump ; while every time the body succeeds in struggling out again, you are aware by the thud upon the floor. After a time the struggle wanes, or maybe the bed collapses ; and you drift back into sleep. But the next moment, or what seems to be the next moment, you again open your eyes under the consciousness of a presence. The door is being held ajar, and four solemn faces, piled one on top of the other, are peering at you, as though you were some natural curiosity kept in this particular room. Seeing you awake, the top face, walking calmly over the other three, comes in and sits on the bed in a friendly attitude.

"Oh!" it says, "we didn't know you were awake. I 've been awake some time."

"So I gather," you reply, shortly.

"Pa doesn't like us to get up too early," it continues. "He says everybody else in the house is liable to be disturbed if we get up. So, of course, we mustn't."

The tone is one of gentle resignation. It is instinct with the spirit of virtuous pride, arising from the consciousness of self-sacrifice.

"Don't you call this being up?" you suggest.

"Oh, no ; we 're not really up, you know, because we 're not properly dressed." The fact is self-evident. "Pa 's always very tired in the morning," the voice continues ; "of course, that 's because he works hard all day. Are you ever tired in the morning?"

At this point he turns and notices, for the first time, that the three other children have also entered, and are sitting in a semi-circle on the floor. From their attitude it is clear they have mistaken the whole thing for one of the slower forms of entertainment, some comic lecture or conjuring exhibition, and are waiting patiently for you to get out of bed and do something. It shocks him, the idea of their being in the guest's bedchamber. He peremptorily orders them out. They do not answer him, they do not argue ; in dead silence, and with one accord they fall upon him. All you can see from the bed is a confused tangle of waving arms and legs, suggestive of an intoxicated octopus trying to find bottom.

Not a word is spoken ; that seems to be the etiquette of the thing. If you are sleeping in your pyjamas, you spring from the bed, and only add to the confusion ; if you are wearing a less showy garment, you stop where you are and shout commands, which are utterly unheeded. The simplest plan is to leave it to the eldest boy. He does get them out after a while, and closes the door upon them. It re-opens immediately, and one, generally Muriel, is shot back into the room. She enters as from a catapult. She is handicapped by having long hair, which can be used as a convenient handle. Evidently aware of this natural disadvantage, she clutches it herself tightly in one hand, and punches with the other. He opens the door again, and cleverly uses her as a battering-ram against the wall of those without. You can hear the dull crash as her head enters among them, and scatters them. When the victory is complete, he comes back and resumes his seat on the bed. There is no bitterness about him ; he has forgotten the whole incident.

" I like the morning," he says, " don't you ? "

" Some mornings," you agree, " are all right ; others are not so peaceful."

He takes no notice of your exception ; a far-away look steals over his somewhat ethereal face.

" I should like to die in the morning," he says ; " everything is so beautiful then."

" Well," you answer, " perhaps you will, if your father ever invites an irritable man to come and sleep here, and doesn't warn him beforehand."

He descends from his contemplative mood, and becomes himself again.

" It 's jolly in the garden," he suggests ; " you

wouldn't like to get up and have a game of cricket, would you ? "

It was not the idea with which you went to bed, but now, as things have turned out, it seems as good a plan as lying there hopelessly awake ; and you agree.

You learn, later in the day, that the explanation of the proceeding is that you, unable to sleep, woke up early in the morning, and thought you would like a game of cricket. The children, taught to be ever courteous to guests, felt it their duty to humour you. Mrs. Harris remarks at breakfast that at least you might have seen to it that the children were properly dressed before you took them out ; while Harris points out to you, pathetically, how, by your one morning's example and encouragement, you have undone his labour of months.

(*Three Men on the Bummel.*)

The Wisdom of Uncle Podger.

THE wheel business settled, there arose the ever-lasting luggage question.

" The usual list, I suppose," said George, preparing to write.

That was wisdom I had taught them. I had learned it myself years ago from my Uncle Podger.

" Always, before beginning to pack," my Uncle would say, " make a list."

He was a methodical man.

" Take a piece of paper "—he always began at the beginning—" put down on it everything you can possibly require ; then go over it and see that it contains nothing you can possibly do without. Imagine yourself in bed ; what have you got on ? Very well, put it down—together with a change. You get up ; what do you do ? Wash yourself. What do you wash yourself with ? Soap ; put down soap. Go on till you have finished. Then take your clothes. Begin at your feet ; what do you wear on your feet ? Boots, shoes, socks ; put them down. Work up till you get to your head. What else do you want besides clothes ? A little brandy ; put it down. A corkscrew ; put it down. Put down everything, then you don't forget anything."

That is the plan he always pursued himself. The

list made, he would go over it carefully, as he always advised, to see that he had forgotten nothing. Then he would go over it again, and strike out everything it was possible to dispense with.

Then he would lose the list.

(Three Men on the Bummel.)

The Princess sends Paul a Ring.

IT was an evening in Brussels. Strolling idly after dinner, the bright lights of a theatre invited me to enter. It was somewhat late ; the second act had commenced. I slipped quietly into my seat, the only one vacant at the extreme end of the front row of the first *rang ;* then looking down upon the stage, met her eyes. A little later an attendant whispered to me that Madame G—— would like to see me ; so at the fall of the curtain I went round. Two men were in the dressing-room smoking, and on the table were some bottles of champagne. She was standing before her glass, a loose shawl about her shoulders.

"Excuse my shaking hands," she said. "This damned hole is like a furnace ; I have to make up fresh after each act."

She held them out for my inspection with a laugh ; they were smeared with grease.

"D'you know my husband ? " she continued. "Baron G—— ; Mr. Paul Kelver."

The Baron rose. He was a red-faced, pot-bellied little man. "Delighted to meet Mr. Kelver," he said, speaking in excellent English. "Any friend of my wife's is always a friend of mine."

He held out his fat, perspiring hand. I was not in the mood to attach much importance to ceremony.

I bowed and turned away, careless whether he was offended or not.

"I am glad I saw you," she continued. "Do you remember a girl called Barbara? You and she were rather chums, years ago."

"Yes," I answered, "I remember her."

"Well, she died, poor girl, three years ago." She was rubbing paint into her cheeks as she spoke. "She asked me if ever I saw you to give you this. I have been carrying it about with me ever since."

"*Quite a pretty little romance,*" laughed the Baron.

She took a ring from her finger. It was the one ring Barbara had worn as a girl, a chrysolite set plainly in a band of gold. I had noticed it upon her hand the first time I had seen her, sitting in my father's office framed by the dusty books and papers. She dropped it into my outstretched palm.

"Quite a pretty little romance," laughed the Baron.

"That's all," added the woman at the glass. "She said you would understand."

From under her painted lashes she flashed a glance

at me. I hope never to see again that look upon a woman's face.

"Thank you," I said. "Yes, I understand. It was very kind of you. I shall always wear it."

Placing the ring upon my finger, I left the room.

(Paul Kelver.)

The Billiard Lesson.

THERE is a friend of mine, an old sea-captain. He is the sort of man that when the three balls are lying in a straight line, tucked up under the cushion, looks pleased ; because then he knows he can make a cannon and leave the red just where he wants it. An Irish youngster named Malooney, a college chum of Dick's, was staying with us ; and the afternoon being wet, the Captain said he would explain it to Malooney, how a young man might practise billiards without any danger of cutting the cloth. He taught him how to hold the cue, and he told him how to make a bridge. Malooney was grateful, and worked for about an hour. He did not show much promise. He is a powerfully built young man, and he didn't seem able to get it into his head that he wasn't playing cricket. Whenever he hit a little low the result was generally lost ball. To save time—and damage to furniture—Dick and I fielded for him. Dick stood at long-stop, and I was short-slip. It was dangerous work, however, and when Dick had caught him out twice running, we agreed that we had won, and took him in to tea. In the evening— none of the rest of us being keen to try our luck a second time—the Captain said, that just for the joke of the thing he would give Malooney eighty-five and play him a hundred up. To confess the truth, I find no

particular fun myself in playing billiards with the
Captain. The game consists, as far as I am concerned,
in walking round the table, throwing him back the balls,
and saying " Good ! " By the time my turn comes I
don't seem to care what happens : everything seems
against me. He is a kind old gentleman and he means
well, but the tone in which he says " Hard lines ! "
whenever I miss an easy stroke irritates me. I feel
I 'd like to throw the balls at his head and fling the
table out of window. I suppose it is that I am in a fretful
state of mind, but the mere way in which he chalks his
cue aggravates me. He carries his own chalk in his
waistcoat pocket—as if our chalk wasn't good enough
for him—and when he has finished chalking, he smooths
the tip round with his finger and thumb and taps the
cue against the table. " Oh ! go on with the game,"
I want to say to him ; " don't be so full of tricks."

The Captain led off with a miss in baulk. Malooney
gripped his cue, drew in a deep breath, and let fly.
The result was ten : a cannon and all three balls in
the same pocket. As a matter of fact, he made the
cannon twice ; but the second time, as we explained to
him, of course did not count.

" Good beginning ! " said the Captain.

Malooney seemed pleased with himself, and took
off his coat.

Malooney's ball missed the red on its first journey
up the table by about a foot, but found it later on
and sent it into a pocket.

" Ninety-nine plays nothing," said Dick, who was
marking. " Better make it a hundred and fifty, hadn't
we, Captain ? "

"Well, I'd like to get in a shot," said the Captain, "before the game is over. Perhaps we had better make it a hundred and fifty, if Mr. Malooney has no objection."

"Whatever you think right, sir," said Rory Malooney.

Malooney finished his break for twenty-two, leaving himself hanging over the middle pocket and the red tucked up in baulk.

"Nothing plays a hundred and eight," said Dick.

"When I want the score," said the Captain, "I'll ask for it."

"Beg pardon, sir," said Dick.

"I hate a noisy game," said the Captain.

The Captain, making up his mind without much waste of time, sent his ball under the cushion, six inches outside baulk.

"What will I do here?" asked Malooney.

"I don't know what you will do," said the Captain; "I'm waiting to see."

Owing to the position of the ball, Malooney was unable to employ his whole strength. All he did that turn was to pocket the Captain's ball and leave himself under the bottom cushion, four inches from the red. The Captain said a nautical word, and gave another miss. Malooney squared up to the balls for a third time. They flew before him, panic-stricken. They banged against one another, came back and hit one another again for no reason whatever. The red, in particular, Malooney had succeeded apparently in frightening out of its wits. It is a stupid ball, generally speaking, our red—its one idea to get under a cushion and watch the game. With Malooney it soon found it was safe nowhere on the table. Its only hope was pockets. I may have been mistaken, my eye may have been deceived by the rapidity of the play, but it seemed to me that the red never waited to be hit. When it saw Malooney's ball coming for it at the rate of forty miles an hour, it just made for the nearest pocket. It rushed round the table looking for pockets. If, in its excitement, it passed an empty pocket, it turned back and crawled in. There were times when in its terror it jumped the table and took shelter under the sofa or behind the side-board. One began to feel sorry for the red.

The Captain had scored a legitimate thirty-eight, and Malooney had given him twenty-four, when it really seemed as if the Captain's chance had come. I could have scored myself as the balls were then.

" Sixty-two plays one hundred and twenty-eight. N o w then, Captain, game in your hands," said Dick.

We gathered round. The children left their play. It was a pretty picture : the bright young faces, eager with

It seemed to me that the red never waited to be hit.

expectation, the old worn veteran squinting down his cue, as if afraid that watching Malooney's play might have given it the squirms.

"Now follow this," I whispered to Malooney. "Don't notice merely what he does, but try and understand why he does it. Any fool—after a little practice, that is—can hit a ball. But why do you hit it ? What happens after you 've hit it ? What——"

"Hush," said Dick.

The Captain drew his cue back and gently pushed it forward.

"Pretty stroke," I whispered to Malooney ; "now, that 's the sort——"

I offer, by way of explanation, that the Captain by this time was probably too full of bottled-up language to be master of his nerves. The ball travelled slowly past the red. Dick said afterwards that you couldn't have put so much as a sheet of paper between them.

It comforts a man, sometimes, when you tell him this ; and at other times it only makes him madder.

It travelled on and passed the white—you could have put quite a lot of paper between it and the white—and dropped with a contented thud into the top left-hand pocket.

"Why does he do that ? " Malooney whispered. Malooney has a singularly hearty whisper.

Dick and I got the women and children out of the room as quickly as we could, but of course Veronica managed to tumble over something on the way— Veronica would find something to tumble over in the desert of Sahara ; and a few days later I overheard expressions, scorching their way through the nursery door, that made my hair rise up. I entered, and found Veronica standing on the table. Jumbo was sitting upon the music-stool. The poor dog himself was looking scared, though he must have heard a bit of language in his time, one way and another.

"Veronica," I said, "are you not ashamed of yourself ? You wicked child, how dare you——"

"It's all right," said Veronica. "I don't really mean any harm. He's a sailor, and I have to talk to him like that, else he don't know he's being talked to."

I pay hard-working, conscientious ladies to teach this child things right and proper for her to know. They tell her clever things that Julius Cæsar said ; observations made by Marcus Aurelius that, pondered over, might help her to become a beautiful character. She complains that it produces a strange buzzy feeling in her head ; and her mother argues that perhaps her brain is of the creative order, not intended to remember much—thinks that perhaps she is going to be something

A good round-dozen oaths the Captain must have let fly before Dick and I succeeded in rolling her out of the room. She had only heard them once, yet, so far as I could judge, she had got them letter perfect.

The Captain, now no longer under the necessity of employing all his energies to suppress his natural instincts, gradually recovered form, and eventually the game stood at one hundred and forty-nine all, Malooney to play. The Captain had left the balls in a position that would have disheartened any other opponent than Malooney. To any other opponent than Malooney the Captain would have offered irritating sympathy. "Afraid the balls are not rolling well for you to-night," the Captain would have said ; or, "Sorry, sir, I don't seem to have left you very much." To-night the Captain wasn't feeling playful.

"Well, if he scores off that !" said Dick.

"Short of locking up the balls and turning out the lights, I don't myself see how one is going to stop him," sighed the Captain.

The Captain's ball was in hand. Malooney went for the red and hit—perhaps it would be more correct to say, frightened—it into a pocket. Malooney's ball, with the table to itself, then gave a solo performance, and ended up by breaking a window. It was what the lawyers call a nice point. What was the effect upon the score ?

Malooney argued that, seeing he had pocketed the red before his own ball left the table, his three should be counted first, and that therefore he had won. Dick maintained that a ball that had ended up in a flower-bed couldn't be deemed to have scored anything. The Captain declined to assist. He said that, although he had been playing billiards for upwards of forty years, the incident was new to him. My own feeling was that of thankfulness that we had got through the game without anybody being really injured. We agreed that the person to decide the point would be the editor of *The Field*.

It remains still undecided. The Captain came into my study next morning. He said : "If you haven't written that letter to *The Field*, don't mention

L

my name. They know me on *The Field*. I would rather it did not get about that I have been playing with a man who cannot keep his ball within the four walls of a billiard-room."

(They and I.)

The Window Ajar.

MR. AIRLIE, picking daintily at his food, continued his stories : of philanthropists who paid starvation wages : of femininists who were a holy terror to their women folk : of socialists who travelled first-class and spent their winters in Egypt or Monaco : of stern critics of public morals who preferred the society of youthful affinities to the continued company of elderly wives : of poets who wrote divinely about babies' feet and whose children hated them.

"Do you think it 's all true ? " Joan whispered to her host.

He shrugged his shoulders. "No reason why it shouldn't be," he said. "I 've generally found him right.

"I 've never been able myself," he continued, "to understand the Lord's enthusiasm for David. I suppose it was the Psalms that did it."

Joan was about to offer comment, but was struck dumb with astonishment on hearing McKean's voice : it seemed he could talk. He was telling of an old Scotch peasant farmer. A mean, cantankerous old cuss whose curious pride it was that he had never given anything away. Not a crust, nor a sixpence, nor a rag ; and never would. Many had been the attempts to make him break his boast : some for the joke of the thing and some for the need ; but none had ever succeeded. It was his one claim to distinction and he guarded it.

One evening it struck him that the milk-pail, standing just inside the window, had been tampered with. Next day he marked with a scratch the inside of the pan, and returning later, found the level of the milk had sunk

One evening it struck him that the milk-pail, standing just inside the window, had been tampered with.

by half an inch. So he hid himself and waited ; and at twilight the next day the window was stealthily pushed open, and two small terror-haunted eyes peered round the room. They satisfied themselves that no one was about and a tiny hand clutching a cracked jug was thrust swiftly in and dipped into the pan ; and the window softly closed.

He knew the thief, the grandchild of an old bedridden dame who lived some miles away on the edge of the moor. The old man stood long, watching the small cloaked figure till it was lost in the darkness. It was not till he lay upon his dying bed that he confessed it. But each evening, from that day, he would steal into the room and see to it himself that the window was left ajar.

(*All Roads lead to Calvary.*)

Harris to the Rescue.

THE beautiful wood of the Eilenriede bounds Hanover on the south and west, and here occurred a sad drama in which Harris took a prominent part.

We were riding our machines through this wood on the Monday afternoon in the company of many other cyclists, for it is a favourite resort with the Hanoverians on a sunny afternoon, and its shady pathways are then filled with happy, thoughtless folk. Among them rode a young and beautiful girl on a machine that was new. She was evidently a novice on the bicycle. One felt instinctively that there would come a moment when she would require help, and Harris, with his accustomed chivalry, suggested that we should keep near her. Harris, as he occasionally explains to George and to myself, has daughters of his own, or, to speak more correctly, a daughter, who as the years progress will no doubt cease practising catherine wheels in the front garden, and will grow up into a beautiful and respectable young lady. This naturally gives Harris an interest in all beautiful girls up to the age of thirty-five or thereabouts ; they remind him, so he says, of home.

We had ridden for about two miles, when we noticed, a little ahead of us in a space where five ways met, a man with a hose, watering the roads.

A man with a hose, watering the roads.

The pipe, supported at each joint by a pair of tiny wheels, writhed after him as he moved, suggesting a gigantic worm, from whose open neck, as the man, gripping it firmly with both hands, pointing it now this way, and now that, now elevating it, now depressing it, poured a strong stream of water at the rate of about a gallon a second.

" What a much better method than ours," observed Harris enthusiastically. Harris is inclined to be chronically severe on all British institutions. " How much simpler, quicker, and more economical ! You see, one man by this method can in five minutes water a stretch of road that would take us with our clumsy lumbering cart half an hour to cover."

George, who was riding behind me on the tandem, said, " Yes, and it is also a method by which with a little carelessness a man could cover a good many people in a good deal less time than they could get out of the way."

George, the opposite to Harris, is British to the core. I remember George quite patriotically indignant with Harris once for suggesting the introduction of the guillotine into England.

" It is so much neater," said Harris.

" I don't care if it is," said George ; " I 'm an Englishman ; hanging is good enough for me."

" Our water-cart may have its disadvantages," continued George, " but it can only make you uncomfortable about the legs, and you can avoid it. This is the sort of machine with which a man can follow you round the corner and upstairs."

" It fascinates me to watch them," said Harris. " They are so skilful. I have seen a man from the corner of a crowded square in Strassburg cover every inch of ground, and not so much as wet an apron string. It is marvellous how they judge their distance. They will send the water up to your toes, and then bring it over your head so that it falls around your heels. They can—— "

" Ease up a minute," said George.

I said : " Why ? "

He said : " I am going to get off and watch the rest of this show from behind a tree. There may be great performers in this line, as Harris says ; this particular artist appears to me to lack something. He has just soused a dog, and now he's busy watering a sign-post. I am going to wait till he has finished."

" Nonsense," said Harris ; " he won't wet you."

" That is precisely what I am going to make sure of," answered George, saying which he jumped off, and, taking up a position behind a remarkably fine elm, pulled out and commenced filling his pipe.

I did not care to take the tandem on by myself, so I stepped off and joined him, leaving the machine against a tree. Harris shouted something or other about our being a disgrace to the land that gave us birth, and rode on.

The next moment I heard a woman's cry of distress. Glancing round the stem of the tree, I perceived that it proceeded from the young and elegant lady before mentioned, whom, in our interest concerning the road-waterer, we had forgotten. She was riding her machine steadily and straightly through a drenching shower of water from the hose. She appeared to be too paralysed either to get off or turn her wheel aside. Every instant she was becoming wetter, while the man with the hose, who was either drunk or blind, continued to pour water upon her with utter indifference. A dozen voices yelled imprecations upon him, but he took no heed whatever.

Harris, his fatherly nature stirred to its depths, did at this point what, under the circumstances, was quite the right and proper thing to do. Had he acted throughout with the same coolness and judgment he then displayed, he would have emerged from that incident the hero of the hour, instead of, as happened, riding away followed by insult and threat. Without a moment's hesitation he spurted at the man, sprang to the ground, and, seizing the hose by the nozzle, attempted to wrest it away.

What he ought to have done, what any man retaining his common sense would have done the moment he got his hands upon the thing, was to turn off the tap. Then he might have played football with the man, or battledore and shuttlecock as he pleased ; and the twenty or thirty people who had rushed forward to assist would have only applauded. His idea, however, as he explained to us afterwards, was to take away the hose from the man, and, for punishment, turn it upon the fool himself. The waterman's idea appeared to be the same, namely, to retain the hose as a weapon with which to soak Harris. Of course, the result was that, between them, they soused every dead and living thing for fifty yards, except themselves. One furious man, too drenched to care what more happened to him, leapt into the arena and also took a hand. The

L*

three among them proceeded to sweep the compass with that hose. They pointed it to heaven, and the water descended upon the people in the form of an equinoctial storm. They pointed it downwards, and sent the water in rushing streams that took people off their feet, or caught them about the waist line, and doubled them up.

Not one of them would loosen his grip upon the hose, not one of them thought to turn the water off. You might have concluded they were struggling with some primeval force of nature. In forty-five seconds, so George said, who was timing it, they had swept that circus bare of every living thing except one dog, who, dripping like a water nymph, rolled over by the force of water, now on this side, now on that, still gallantly staggered again and again to its feet to bark defiance at what it evidently regarded as the powers of hell let loose.

Men and women left their machines upon the ground, and flew into the woods. From behind every tree of importance peeped out wet, angry heads.

At last, there arrived upon the scene one man of sense. Braving all things, he crept to the hydrant, where still stood the iron key, and screwed it down. And then from forty trees began to creep more or less soaked human beings, each one with something to say.

At first I fell to wondering whether a stretcher or a clothes basket would be the more useful for the conveyance of Harris's remains back to the hotel. I consider that George's promptness on that occasion saved Harris's life. Being dry, and therefore able to run quicker, he was there before the crowd. Harris was for explaining things, but George cut him short.

"You get on that," said George, handing him his bicycle, "and go. They don't know we belong to you, and you may trust us implicitly not to reveal the secret. We'll hang about behind, and get in their way. Ride zig-zag in case they shoot."

(*Three Men on the Bummel.*)

The Angel and the Author.

I HAD a vexing dream one night, not long ago : it was about a fortnight after Christmas. I dreamt I flew out of the window in my nightshirt. I went up and up. I was glad that I was going up. " They have been noticing me," I thought to myself. " If anything, I have been a bit too good. A little less virtue and I might have lived longer. But one cannot have everything." The world grew smaller and smaller. The last I saw of London was the long line of electric lamps bordering the Embankment ; later nothing remained but a faint luminosity buried beneath darkness. It was at this point of my journey that I heard behind me the slow, throbbing sound of wings.

I turned my head. It was the Recording Angel. He had a weary look ; I judged him to be tired.

" Yes," he acknowledged, " it is a trying period for me, your Christmas time."

" I am sure it must be," I returned ; " the wonder to me is how you get through it all. You see at Christmas time," I went on, " all we men and women become generous, quite suddenly. It is really a delightful sensation."

" You are to be envied," he agreed.

" It is the first Christmas number that starts me off," I told him ; " those beautiful pictures—the sweet child looking so pretty in her furs, giving Bovril with her own dear little hands to the shivering street arab; the good old red-faced squire shovelling out plum pudding to the crowd of grateful villagers. It makes me yearn to borrow a collecting box and go round doing good myself.

"And it is not only me—I should say I," I continued; "I don't want you to run away with the idea that I am the only good man in the world. That's what I like about Christmas, it makes everybody good. The lovely sentiments we go about repeating! the noble deeds we do! from a little while before Christmas up to, say, the end of January! why noting them down must be a comfort to you."

"Yes," he admitted, "noble deeds are always a great joy to me."

"They are to all of us," I said; "I love to think of all the good deeds I myself have done. I have often thought of keeping a diary—jotting them down each day. It would be so nice for one's children."

He agreed there was an idea in this.

"That book of yours," I said, "I suppose, now, it contains all the good actions that we men and women have been doing during the last six weeks?" It was a bulky looking volume.

Yes, he answered, they were all recorded in the book.

It was more for the sake of talking than anything else that I kept up with him. I did not really doubt his care and conscientiousness, but it is always pleasant to chat about one's self. "My five shillings subscription to the *Daily Telegraph's* Sixpenny Fund for the Unemployed—got that down all right?" I asked him.

Yes, he replied, it was entered.

" As a matter of fact, now I come to think of it,"
I added, " it was ten shillings altogether. They spelt
my name wrong the first time."

Both subscriptions had been entered, he told me.

" Then I have been to four charity dinners," I
reminded him ; " I forget what the particular charity
was about. I know I suffered the next morning.
Champagne never does agree with me. But, then,
if you don't order it people think you can't afford it,
Not that I don't like it. It 's my liver, if you understand. If I take more—— "

He interrupted me with the assurance that my
attendance had been noted.

" Last week I sent a dozen photographs of myself,
signed, to a charity bazaar."

He said he remembered my doing so.

" Then let me see," I continued, " I have been to
two ordinary balls. I don't care much about dancing,
but a few of us generally play a little bridge ; and to
one fancy dress affair. I went as Sir Walter Raleigh.
Some men cannot afford to show their leg. What I
say is, if a man can, why not ? It isn't often that one
gets the opportunity of really looking one's best."

He told me all three balls had been duly entered ;
and commented upon.

" And, of course, you remember my performance
of Talbot Champneys in *Our Boys* the week before last,
in aid of the Fund for Poor Curates," I went on. " I
don't know whether you saw the notice in the *Morning
Post*, but—— "

He again interrupted me to remark that what
the *Morning Post* man said would be entered, one

way or the other, to the critic of the *Morning Post*,
and had nothing to do with me. "Of course not,"
I agreed ; "and between ourselves, I don't think the
charity got very much. Expenses, when you come to
add refreshments and one thing and another, mount up.
But I fancy they rather liked my Talbot Champneys."

He replied that he had been present at the
performance, and had made his own report.

I also reminded him of the four balcony seats I
had taken for the monster show at His Majesty's
in aid of the Fund for the Destitute British in
Johannesburg. Not all the celebrated actors and
actresses announced on the posters had appeared, but
all had sent letters full of kindly wishes ; and the
others—all the celebrities one had never heard of—had
turned up to a man. Still, on the whole, the show
was well worth the money. There was nothing to
grumble at.

There were other noble deeds of mine. I could
not remember them at the time in their entirety.
I seemed to have done a good many. But I did
remember the rummage sale to which I sent all my old
clothes, including a coat that had got mixed up with
them by accident, and that I believe I could have worn
again. And also the raffle I had joined for a motor-car.

The Angel said I really need not be alarmed,
that everything had been noted, together with other
matters I, may be, had forgotten.

I felt a certain curiosity. We had been getting
on very well together—at least, so it had seemed to me.
I asked him if he would mind my seeing the book.
He said there could be no objection. He opened it
at the page devoted to myself, and I flew a little higher,

and looked down over his shoulder. I can hardly believe it, even now—that I could have dreamt anything so foolish :

He had got it all down wrong !

Instead of to the credit side of my account he had put the whole bag of tricks to my debit. He had mixed them up with my sins—with my acts of hypocrisy, vanity, self-indulgence. Under the head of Charity he had but one item to my credit for the past six months : my giving up my seat inside a tramcar late one wet night, to a dismal-looking old woman, who had not even the politeness to say " thank you," she seemed just half asleep. According to this idiot, all the time and money I had spent responding to these charitable appeals had been wasted.

I was not angry with him, at first. I was willing to regard what he had done as merely a clerical error.

" You have got the items down all right," I said (I spoke quite friendly), " but you have made a slight mistake—we all do now and again : you have put them down on the wrong side of the book. I only hope this sort of thing doesn't occur often."

What irritated me as much as anything was the grave, passionless face the Angel turned upon me.

" There is no mistake," he answered.

" No mistake ! " I cried. " Why, you blundering ——— "

He closed the book with a weary sigh.

I felt so mad with him, I went to snatch it out of his hand. He did not do anything that I was aware of, but at once I began falling. The faint luminosity beneath me grew, and then the lights of London seemed shooting up to meet me. I was coming down on the clock tower at Westminster. I gave myself a convulsive twist, hoping to escape it, and fell into the river.

And then I awoke.

But it stays with me : the weary sadness of the Angel's face.

(*The Angel and the Author.*)

Malvina of Brittany.

It commenced, so I calculate, about the year
2000 B.C., or, to be more precise—for figures are not
the strong point of the old chroniclers—when King
Heremon ruled over Ireland and Harbundia was Queen
of the White Ladies of Brittany, the fairy Malvina
being her favourite attendant. It is with Malvina
that this story is chiefly concerned. Various quite
pleasant happenings are recorded to her credit. The
White Ladies belonged to the "good people," and,
on the whole, lived up to their reputation. But in
Malvina, side by side with much that is commendable,
there appears to have existed a most reprehensible
spirit of mischief, displaying itself in pranks that,
excusable, or at all events understandable, in, say, a
pixy or a pigwidgeon, strike one as altogether unworthy
of a well-principled White Lady, posing as the friend
and benefactress of mankind. For merely refusing to
dance with her—at midnight, by the shores of a mountain lake ; neither the time nor the place calculated
to appeal to an elderly gentleman, suffering possibly
from rheumatism—she on one occasion transformed
an eminently respectable proprietor of tin mines
into a nightingale, necessitating a change of habits
that to a business man must have been singularly
irritating. On another occasion a quite important
queen, having had the misfortune to quarrel with

Malvina over some absurd point of etiquette in connection with a lizard, seems, on waking the next morning, to have found herself changed into what one judges, from the somewhat vague description afforded by the ancient chroniclers, to have been a sort of vegetable marrow.

Such changes, according to the Professor, who is prepared to maintain that evidence of an historical nature exists sufficient to prove that the White Ladies formed at one time an actual living community, must be taken in an allegorical sense. Just as modern lunatics believe themselves to be china vases or poll-parrots, and think and behave as such, so it must have been easy, the Professor argues, for beings of superior intelligence to have exerted hypnotic influence upon the superstitious savages by whom they were surrounded, and who, intellectually considered, could have been little more than children.

"Take Nebuchadnezzar." I am still quoting the Professor. "Nowadays we should put him into a strait-waistcoat. Had he lived in Northern Europe instead of Southern Asia, legend would have told us how some Kobold or Stromkarl had turned him into a composite amalgamation of a serpent, a cat and a kangaroo." Be that as it may, this passion for change —in other people—seems to have grown upon Malvina until she must have become little short of a public nuisance, and eventually it landed her in trouble.

The incident is unique in the annals of the White Ladies, and the chroniclers dwell upon it with evident satisfaction. It came about through the betrothal of King Heremon's only son, Prince Gerbot, to the Princess Berchta of Normandy. Malvina seems to have said nothing, but to have bided her time. The White Ladies of Brittany, it must be remembered, were not fairies pure and simple. Under certain conditions they were capable of becoming women, and this fact, one takes it, must have exerted a disturbing influence upon their relationships with eligible male mortals. Prince Gerbot may not have been altogether blameless. Young men in those sadly unenlightened days may not, in their dealings with ladies, white or otherwise, have always been the soul of discretion and propriety. One would like to think the best of her.

But even the best is indefensible. On the day appointed for the wedding she seems to have surpassed herself. Into what particular shape or form she altered the wretched Prince Gerbot ; or into what shape or form she persuaded him that he had been altered, it really, so far as the moral responsibility of Malvina is concerned, seems to be immaterial ; the chronicle does not state ; evidently something too indelicate for a self-respecting chronicler to even hint at. As, judging from other passages in the book, squeamishness does not seem to have been the author's literary failing, the sensitive reader can feel only grateful for the omission. It would have been altogether too harrowing.

It had, of course, from Malvina's point of view, the desired effect. The Princess Berchta appears to have given one look and then to have fallen fainting into the arms of her attendants. The marriage was postponed indefinitely, and Malvina, one sadly suspects, chortled. Her triumph was short-lived.

Unfortunately for her, King Heremon had always been a patron of the arts and science of his period.

The Princess Berchta appears to have fallen fainting into the arms of her attendants.

Among his friends were to be reckoned magicians, genii, the Nine Korrigans or Fays of Brittany—all sorts of parties capable of exerting influence, and, as events proved, only too willing. Ambassadors waited upon Queen Harbundia; and Harbundia, even had she wished, as on many previous occasions, to stand by her favourite, had no alternative. The fairy Malvina was called upon to return to Prince Gerbot his proper body and all therein contained.

She flatly refused. A self-willed, obstinate fairy, suffering from swelled head. And then there was that personal note. Merely that he should marry the Princess Berchta! She would see King Heremon, and Anniamus, in his silly old wizard's robe, and the

Fays of Brittany, and all the rest of them——! A really nice White Lady may not have cared to finish the sentence, even to herself. One imagines the flash of the fairy eye, the stamp of the fairy foot. What could they do to her, any of them, with all their clacking of tongues and their wagging of heads? She, an immortal fairy! She would change Prince Gerbot back at a time of her own choosing. Let them attend to their own tricks and leave her to mind hers. One pictures long walks and talks between the distracted Harbundia and her refractory favourite—appeals to reason, to sentiment: "For my sake." "Don't you see?" "After all, dear, and even if he did."

It seems to have ended by Harbundia losing all patience. One thing there was she could do that Malvina seems either not to have known of or not to have anticipated. A solemn meeting of the White Ladies was convened for the night of the midsummer moon. The place of meeting is described by the ancient chroniclers with more than their usual exactitude. It was on the land that the magician Kalyb had, ages ago, raised up above all Brittany to form the grave of King Taramis. The "Sea of the Seven Islands" lay to the north. One guesses it to be the ridge formed by the Arree Mountains. "The Lady of the Fountain" appears to have been present, suggesting the deep green pool from which the river D'Argent takes its source. Roughly speaking, one would place it half-way between the modern towns of Morlaix and Callac. Pedestrians, even of the present day, speak of the still loneliness of that high plateau, treeless, houseless, with no sign of human hand there but that high, towering monolith round which the shrill winds moan incessantly. There, possibly on some broken fragment of these great grey stones, Queen Harbundia sat in judgment. And the judgment was—and from it there was no appeal—that the fairy Malvina should be cast out from among the community of the White Ladies of Brittany. Over the face of the earth she should wander, alone and unforgiven. Solemnly from the book of the roll-call of the White Ladies the name of Malvina was struck out for ever.

The blow must have fallen upon Malvina as heavily as it was unexpected. Without a word, without one backward look, she seems to have departed. One pictures the white, frozen face, the wide-open, unseeing eyes, the trembling, uncertain steps, the groping hands, the deathlike silence clinging like grave-clothes round about her.

From that night the fairy Malvina disappears from the book of the chroniclers of the White Ladies of Brittany, from legend and from folklore whatsoever. She does not appear again in history till the year A.D. 1914.

(*Malvina of Brittany*.)

A Lost Leader.

WE had a frugal breakfast at half-past four, and started away at five. Our road lay over a mountain, and from enquiries made in the village it appeared to be one of those roads you cannot possibly miss. I suppose everybody knows this sort of road. I foresaw evil from the very first, and before we had accomplished a couple of miles we came up with it. The road divided into three. A worm-eaten sign-post indicated that the path to the left led to a place that we had never heard of—that was on no map. Its other arm, pointing out the direction of the middle road, had disappeared. The road to the right, so we all agreed, clearly led back again to the village.

" Well, what shall we do ? " said Harris.

Now I happen to possess the bump of locality. It is not a virtue ; I make no boast of it. It is merely an animal instinct that I cannot help. That things occasionally get in my way—mountains, precipices, rivers, and such like obstructions—is no fault of mine. My instinct is correct enough ; it is the earth that is wrong. I led them by the middle road. That the middle road had not character enough to continue for any quarter of a mile in the same direction ; that after three miles up and down hill it ended abruptly in a wasps' nest, was not a thing that should have been laid to my door. If the middle road had gone in the direction it ought to have done, it would have taken us to where we wanted to go, of that I am convinced.

Even as it was, I would have continued to use this gift of mine to discover a fresh way had a proper spirit been displayed towards me. But I am not an angel—I admit this frankly—and I decline to exert myself for the ungrateful and the ribald. Besides, I doubt if George and Harris would have followed me further in any event. Therefore it was that I washed my hands of the whole affair, and that Harris entered upon the vacancy.

"Well," said Harris, "I suppose you are satisfied with what you have done?"

"I am quite satisfied," I replied from the heap of stones where I was sitting. "So far, I have brought you with safety. I would continue to lead you further, but no artist can work without encouragement. You appear dissatisfied with me because you do not know where you are. For all you know, you may be just where you want to be. But I say nothing as to that; I expect no thanks. Go your own way; I have done with you both."

I spoke, perhaps, with bitterness, but I could not help it. Not a word of kindness had I had all the weary way.

"Do not misunderstand us," said Harris; "both George and myself feel that without your assistance we should never be where we are now. For that we give you every credit. But instinct is liable to error. What I propose to do is to substitute for it Science, which is exact. Now, where's the sun?"

"Don't you think," said George, "that if we made

our way back to the village, and hired a boy for a mark to guide us, it would save time in the end ? "

" It would be wasting hours," said Harris, with decision. " You leave this to me. I have been reading about this thing, and it has interested me." He took out his watch, and began turning himself round and round.

" It 's as simple as A B C," he continued. " You point the short hand at the sun, then you bisect the segment between the short hand and the twelve, and thus you get the north."

He worried up and down for a while, then he fixed it.

" Now I 've got it," he said ; " that 's the north, where that wasps' nest is. Now give me the map."

We handed it to him, and seating himself facing the wasps, he examined it.

" Todtmoos from here," he said, " is south by south-west."

" How do you mean, from here ? " asked George.

" Why, from here, where we are," returned Harris.

" But where are we ? " said George.

This worried Harris for a time, but at length he cheered up.

" It doesn't matter where we are," he said. " Wherever we are, Todtmoos is south by south-west. Come on, we are only wasting time."

" I don't quite see how you make it out," said George, as he rose and shouldered his knapsack ; " but I suppose it doesn't matter. We are out for our health, and it 's all pretty ! "

" We shall be all right," said Harris, with cheery confidence. " We shall be in at Todtmoos before ten, don't you worry. And at Todtmoos we will have something to eat."

He said that he, himself, fancied a beefsteak, followed by an omelette. George said that, personally, he intended to keep his mind off the subject until he saw Todtmoos.

We walked for half an hour, then emerging upon an opening, we saw below us, about two miles away, the village through which we had passed that morning. It had a quaint church with an outside staircase, a somewhat unusual arrangement.

The sight of it made me sad. We had been walking hard for three hours and a half, and had accomplished, apparently, about four miles. But Harris was delighted.

" Now, at last," said Harris, " we know where we are."

" I thought you said it didn't matter," George reminded him.

" No more it does, practically," replied Harris, " but it is just as well to be certain. Now I feel more confidence in myself."

" I 'm not so sure about that being an advantage," muttered George. But I do not think Harris heard him.

" We are now," continued Harris, " east of the sun, and Todtmoos is south-west of where we are. So that if—— "

He broke off. " By-the-by," he said, " do you remember whether I said the bisecting line of that segment pointed to the north or to the south ? "

" You said it pointed to the north," replied George.

" Are you positive ? " persisted Harris.

" Positive," answered George ; " but don't let

that influence your calculations. In all probability you were wrong."

Harris thought for a while ; then his brow cleared.

"That 's all right," he said ; "of course, it 's the north. It must be the north. How could it be the south ? Now we must make for the west. Come on."

"I am quite willing to make for the west," said George ; "any point of the compass is the same to me. I only wish to remark that, at the present moment, we are going dead east."

"No we are not," returned Harris ; "we are going west."

"We are going east, I tell you," said George.

"I wish you wouldn't keep saying that," said Harris ; "you confuse me."

"I don't mind if I do," returned George ; "I would rather do that than go wrong. I tell you we are going dead east."

"What nonsense !" retorted Harris ; "there 's the sun."

"I can see the sun," answered George, "quite distinctly. It may be where it ought to be, according to you and Science, or it may not. All I know is, that when we were down in the village, that particular hill with that particular lump of rock upon it was due north of us. At the present moment we are facing due east."

"You are quite right," said Harris ; "I forgot for the moment that we had turned round."

"I should get into the habit of making a note of it, if I were you," grumbled George ; "it 's a manœuvre that will probably occur again more than once."

We faced about, and walked in the other direction. At the end of forty minutes' climbing we again emerged upon an opening, and again the village lay just under our feet. On this occasion it was south of us.

"This is very extraordinary," said Harris.

"I see nothing remarkable about it," said George. "If you walk steadily round a village it is only natural that now and then you get a glimpse of it. Myself, I am glad to see it. It proves to me that we are not utterly lost."

"It ought to be the other side of us," said Harris.

"It will be in another hour or so," said George, "if we keep on."

I said little myself; I was vexed with both of them; but I was glad to notice George evidently growing cross with Harris. It was absurd of Harris to fancy that he could find the way by the sun.

"I wish I knew," said Harris thoughtfully, "for certain whether that bisecting line points to the north or to the south."

"I should make up my mind about it," said George; "it's an important point."

"It's impossible it can be the north," said Harris, "and I'll tell you why."

"You needn't trouble," said George; "I am quite prepared to believe it isn't."

"You said just now it was," said Harris, reproachfully.

"I said nothing of the sort," retorted George. "I said you said it was—a very different thing. If you think it isn't, let's go the other way It'll be a change, at all events."

So Harris worked things out according to the contrary calculation, and again we plunged into the wood ; and again after half an hour's stiff climbing we came in view of that same village. True, we were a little higher, and this time it lay between us and the sun.

" I think," said George, as he stood looking down at it, " this is the best view we 've had of it, as yet. There is only one other point from which we can see it. After that, I propose we go down into it and get some rest."

" I don't believe it 's the same village," said Harris ; " it can't be."

" There 's no mistaking that church," said George. " But don't be discouraged. Which way do we go now ? "

" I don't know," said Harris, " and I don't care. I I have done my best ; you 've done nothing but grumble and confuse me."

" I may have been critical," admitted George ; " but look at the thing from my point of view. One of you says he 's got an instinct, and leads me to a wasps' nest in the middle of a wood."

" I can't help wasps building in a wood," I replied.

" I don't say you can," answered George. " I am not arguing ; I am merely stating incontrovertible facts. The other one, who leads me up and down hill for hours on scientific principles, doesn't know the north from the south, and is never quite sure whether he 's turned round or whether he hasn't. Personally, I profess to no instincts beyond the ordinary, nor am I a scientist. But two fields off I can see a man. I am going to offer him the worth of the hay he is cutting, which I estimate at one mark fifty pfennig, to leave his work, and lead me to within sight of Todtmoos. If you two fellows like to follow, you can. If not, you can start another system and work it out by yourselves."

George's plan lacked both originality and aplomb, but at the moment it appealed to us. Fortunately, we had worked round to a very short distance away from the spot where we had originally gone wrong ; with the result that, aided by the gentleman of the scythe, we recovered the road, and reached Todtmoos four hours later than we had calculated to reach it with an appetite that took forty-five minutes' steady work in silence to abate.

(*Three Men on the Bummel.*)

The Makers of War.

ONE topic that never lost its interest was : Who made wars ? Who hounded the people into them, and kept them there, tearing at one another's throats ? They never settled it.

"God knows I didn't want it, speaking personally," said a German prisoner one day, with a laugh. "I had been working at a printing business sixteen hours a day for seven years. It was just beginning to pay me, and now my wife writes me that she has had to shut the place up and sell the machinery to keep them all from starving."

"But couldn't you have done anything to stop it ? " demanded a Frenchman, lying next to him. "All your millions of Socialists, what were they up to ? What went wrong with the Internationale, the Universal Brotherhood of Labour, and all that Tra-la-la ? "

The German laughed again. "Oh, they know their business," he answered. "You have your glass of beer and go to bed, and when you wake up in the morning you find war has been declared ; and you keep your mouth shut—unless you want to be shot for a traitor. Not that it would have made much difference," he added. "I admit that. The ground had been too well prepared. England was envious of our trade. King Edward had been plotting our destruction. Our papers were full of translations from yours, talking about ' *La Revanche!* ' We were told that you had been lending money to Russia to enable her to build railways, and that when they were complete France and Russia would fall upon us suddenly. ' The Fatherland in danger ! ' It may be lies or it may not ; what is one to do ? What would you have done— even if you could have done anything ? "

" He 's right," said a dreamy-eyed looking man, laying down the book he had been reading. " We should have done just the same. ' My country, right or wrong.' After all, it is an ideal."

A dark, black-bearded man raised himself painfully upon his elbow. He was a tailor in the Rue Parnesse, and prided himself on a decided resemblance to Victor Hugo.

" It 's a noble ideal," he said. " *La Patrie!* The great Mother. Right or wrong, who shall dare to harm her ? Yes, if it was she who rose up in her majesty and called to us." He laughed. " What does it mean in reality : Germania, Italia, La France, Britannia ? Half a score of pompous old muddlers with their fat wives egging them on : sons of the fools before them ; talkers who have wormed themselves into power by making frothy speeches and fine promises. My Country ! " he laughed again. " Look at them. Can't you see their swelling paunches and their flabby faces ? Half a score of ambitious politicians, gouty old financiers, bald-headed old toffs, with their waxed moustaches and false teeth. That 's what we mean when we talk about ' My Country ' : a pack of selfish, soulless, muddle-headed old men. And whether they 're right or whether they 're wrong, our duty is to fight at their bidding—to bleed for them, to die for them, that

M

they may grow more sleek and prosperous." He sank back on his pillow with another laugh.

Sometimes they agreed it was the newspapers that made war—that fanned every trivial difference into a vital question of national honour—that, whenever there was any fear of peace, re-stoked the fires of hatred with their never-failing stories of atrocities. At other times they decided it was the capitalists, the traders, scenting profit for themselves. Some held it was the politicians, dreaming of going down to history as Richelieus or as Bismarcks. A popular theory was that cause for war was always discovered by the ruling classes whenever there seemed danger that the workers were getting out of hand. In war, you put the common people back in their place, revived in them the habits of submission and obedience. Napoleon the Little, it was argued, had started the war of 1870 with that idea. Russia had welcomed the present war as an answer to the Revolution that was threatening Czardom. Others contended it was the great munition industries, aided by the military party; the officers impatient for opportunities of advancement, the strategists eager to put their theories to the test. A few of the more philosophical shrugged their shoulders. It was the thing itself that sooner or later was bound to go off of its own accord. Half every country's energy, half every country's time and money was spent in piling up explosives. In every country envy and hatred of every other country was preached as a religion. They called it patriotism. Sooner or later the spark fell.

A wizened little man had been listening to it all one day. He had a curiously rat-like face, with round, red, twinkling eyes, and a long, pointed nose that twitched as he talked.

"I 'll tell you who makes all the wars," he said. "It 's you and me, my dears : we make the wars. We love them. That 's why we open our mouths and swallow all the twaddle that the papers give us ; and cheer the fine, black-coated gentlemen when they tell us it 's our sacred duty to kill Germans, or Italians, or Russians, or anybody else. We are just crazy to kill something : it doesn't matter what. If it 's to be Germans, we shout ' *A Berlin !* ' ; and if it 's to be Russians we cheer for Liberty. I was in Paris at the time of the Fashoda trouble. How we hissed the English in the cafés. And how they glared back at us ! They were just as eager to kill us. Who makes a dog fight ? Why, the dog. Anybody can do it. Who could make us fight each other, if we didn't want to ? Not all the King's horses and all the King's men. No, my dears, it 's we make the wars. You and me, my dears."

(*All Roads lead to Calvary*.)

How to Write a Play.

I HAD written a few farces, comediettas, and they had been successful. But the chief piece of the evening is a serious responsibility. A young man may be excused for hesitating. It can make, but also it can mar him. A comic opera above all other forms of art— if I may be forgiven for using the sacred word in connection with such a subject—demands experience.

I explained my fears. I did not explain that in my desk lay a four-act drama throbbing with humanity, with life, with which it had been my hope —growing each day fainter—to take the theatrical public by storm, to establish myself as a serious playwright.

" It 's very simple," urged Hodgson. " Provide A—— plenty of comic business ; you ought to be able to do that all right. Give G—— something pretty in waltz time, and D—— a part in which she can change her frock every quarter of an hour or so, and the thing is done.

" I 'll tell you what," continued Hodgson. " I 'll take the whole crowd down to Richmond on Sunday. We 'll have a coach, and leave the theatre at half-past ten. It will be an opportunity for you to study them. You 'll be able to have a talk with them and get to know just what they can do. A—— has ideas in his head ; he 'll explain them to you. Then, next week, we 'll draw up a contract and set to work."

It was too good an opportunity to let slip, though I knew that if successful I should find myself pinned down firmer than ever to my rôle of jester. But it is remunerative, the writing of comic opera.

A small crowd had gathered in the Strand to see us start.

"Nothing wrong, is there ? " inquired the leading lady, in a tone of some anxiety, alighting a quarter of an hour late from her cab. " It isn't a fire, is it ? "

" Merely assembled to see you," explained Mr. Hodgson, without raising his eyes from his letters.

"Oh, good gracious ! " cried the leading lady, " do let us get away quickly."

" Box seat, my dear," returned Mr. Hodgson.

The leading lady, accepting the proffered assistance of myself and three other gentlemen, mounted the ladder with charming hesitation. Some delay in getting off was caused by our low comedian, who twice, making believe to miss his footing, slid down again into the arms of the stolid doorkeeper. The crowd, composed for the most part of small boys, approving the endeavour to amuse them, laughed and applauded. Our low comedian, thus encouraged, made a third attempt upon his hands and knees, and, gaining the roof, sat down upon the tenor, who smiled somewhat mechanically.

The first dozen or so 'buses we passed our low comedian greeted by rising to his feet and bowing profoundly, afterwards falling back upon either the tenor or myself. Except by the tenor and myself his performance appeared to be much appreciated.

Charing Cross passed, and nobody seeming to be interested in our progress, to the relief of the tenor and myself, he settled down.

"People sometimes ask me," said the low comedian, brushing the dust off his knees, "why I do this sort of thing off the stage. It amuses me.

"I was coming up to London the other day from Birmingham," he continued. "At Willesden, when the ticket collector opened the door, I sprang out of the carriage and ran off down the platform. Of course, he ran after me, shouting to all the others to stop me. I dodged them for about a minute. You wouldn't believe the excitement there was. Quite fifty people left their seats to see what it was all about. I explained to them when they caught me that I had been travelling second with a first-class ticket, which was the fact.

People think I do it to attract attention. I do it for my own pleasure."

"It must be a troublesome way of amusing oneself," I suggested.

"Exactly what my wife says," he replied; "she

He attracted a certain amount of attention by balancing the horn upon his nose.

can never understand the desire that comes over us all, I suppose, at times, to play the fool. As a rule, when she is with me I don't do it."

" She is not here to-day ? " I asked, glancing round.

" She suffers from headaches," he answered, " she hardly ever goes anywhere."

" I 'm sorry." I spoke not out of mere politeness ; I really did feel sorry.

During the drive to Richmond this irrepressible desire to amuse himself got the better of him more than once or twice. Through Kensington he attracted a certain amount of attention by balancing the horn upon his nose. At Kew he stopped the coach to request of a young ladies' boarding school change for sixpence. At the foot of Richmond Hill he caused a crowd to assemble while trying to persuade a deaf old gentleman in a Bath-chair to allow his man to race us up the hill for a shilling.

At these antics and such-like our party laughed uproariously, with the exception of Hodgson, who had his correspondence to attend to, and an elegant young lady of some social standing who had lately emerged from the divorce court with a reputation worth to her in cash a hundred pounds a week.

Arriving at the hotel, a quarter of an hour or so before lunch time, we strolled into the garden. Our low comedian, observing an elderly gentleman of dignified appearance sipping a glass of Vermouth at a small table, stood for a moment rooted to the earth with astonishment, then, making a bee-line for the stranger, seized and shook him warmly by the hand. We exchanged admiring glances with one another.

" Charlie is in good form to-day," we told one another, and followed at his heels.

The elderly gentleman had risen ; he looked puzzled.

" And how 's Aunt Martha ? " asked him our low comedian. " Dear old Aunt Martha ! Well, I am glad ! You do look bonny ! How is she ? "

" I 'm afraid—— " commenced the elderly gentleman.

Our low comedian started back. Other visitors had gathered round.

" Don't tell me anything has happened to her ! Not dead ? Don't tell me that ! "

He seized the bewildered gentleman by the shoulders, and presented to him a face distorted by terror.

" I really have not the faintest notion what you are talking about," returned the gentleman, who seemed annoyed. " I don't know you."

" Not know me ? Do you mean to tell me you 've forgotten—— ? Isn't your name Steggles ? "

" No, it isn't," returned the stranger somewhat shortly.

" My mistake," replied our low comedian. He tossed off at one gulp what remained of the stranger's Vermouth and walked away rapidly.

The elderly gentleman, not seeing the humour of the joke, one of our party to soothe him explained to him that it was A——, *the* A——,—Charlie A——.

" Oh, is it ? " growled the elderly gentleman. " Then will you tell him from me that when I want his damned tomfoolery I 'll come to the theatre and pay for it."

" What a disagreeable man ! " we said, as, following our low comedian, we made our way into the hotel.

During lunch he continued in excellent spirits ; kissed the bald back of the waiter's head, pretending to mistake it for a face, called for hot mustard and water, made believe to steal the silver, and when the finger bowls arrived, took off his coat and requested the ladies to look the other way.

After lunch he became suddenly serious, and slipping his arm through mine, led me by unfrequented paths.

" Now, about this new opera," he said ; " we don't want any of the old stale business. Give us something new."

I suggested that to do so might be difficult.

" Not at all," he answered. " Now my idea is this. I am a young fellow, and I 'm in love with a girl."

I promised to make a note of it.

" Her father, apoplectic old idiot—make him comic ; ' Damme, sir ! By gad ! ' all that sort of thing."

By persuading him that I understood what he meant, I rose in his estimation.

" He won't have anything to say to me—thinks I 'm an ass. I 'm a simple sort of fellow—on the outside. But I 'm not such a fool as I look."

" You don't think we are getting too much out of the groove ? " I inquired.

His opinion was that the more so the better.

" Very well. Then, in the second act I disguise myself. I 'll come on as an organ grinder, sing a song in broken English, then as a policeman, or a young swell about town. Give me plenty of opportunity, that 's the great thing—opportunity to be really funny, I mean. We don't want any of the old stale tricks."

I promised him my support.

" Put a little pathos in it," he added ; " give me

M*

a scene where I can show them I 've something else
in me besides merely humour. We don't want to make
them howl, but just to feel a little. Let 's send them
out of the theatre saying, ' Well, Charlie 's often made
me laugh, but I 'm damned if I knew he could make me
cry before ! ' See what I mean ? "

I told him I thought I did.

The leading lady, meeting us on our return,
requested, with pretty tone of authority, everybody
else to go away and leave us. There were cries of
" Naughty ! " The leading lady, laughing girlishly,
took me by the hand and ran away with me.

" I want to talk to you," said the leading lady,
as soon as we had reached a secluded seat overlooking
the river, " about my part in the new opera. Now,
can't you give me something original ? Do."

Her pleading was so pretty, there was nothing
for it but to pledge compliance.

" I am so tired of being the simple village maiden,"
said the leading lady ; " what I want is a part with
some opportunity in it—a coquettish part. I can
flirt," assured me the leading lady archly. " Try
me."

I satisfied her of my perfect faith.

" You might," said the leading lady, " see your way
to making the plot depend upon me. It always seems
to me that the woman's part is never made enough of
in comic opera. I am sure a comic opera built round
a woman would be a really great success. Don't
you agree with me, Mr. Kelver ? " pouted the leading
lady, laying her pretty hand on mine. " We are
much more interesting than the men—now, aren't
we ? "

Personally, as I told her, I agreed with her.

The tenor, sipping tea with me on the balcony, beckoned me aside.

"About this new opera," said the tenor; "doesn't it seem to you the time has come to make more of the story—that the public might prefer a little more human interest and a little less clowning?"

I admitted that a good plot was essential.

"It seems to me," said the tenor, "that if you could write an opera round an interesting love story, you would score a success. Of course, let there be plenty of humour, but reduce it to its proper place. As a support, it is excellent; when it is made the entire structure, it is apt to be tiresome—at least, that is my view."

I replied with sincerity that there seemed to be much truth in what he said.

"Of course, so far as I am personally concerned," went on the tenor, "it is immaterial. I draw the same salary whether I'm on the stage five minutes or an hour. But when you have a man of my position in the cast, and give him next to nothing to do—well, the public are disappointed."

"Most naturally," I commented.

"The lover," whispered the tenor, noticing the careless approach towards us of the low comedian, "that's the character they are thinking about all the time—men and women both. It's human nature. Make your lover interesting—that's the secret."

Waiting for the horses to be put to, I became aware of the fact that I was standing some distance from the others in company with a tall, thin, somewhat oldish-looking man. He spoke in low, hurried tones, fearful evidently of being overheard and interrupted.

" You 'll forgive me, Mr. Kelver," he said—" Trevor, Marmaduke Trevor. I play the Duke of Bayswater in the second act."

I was unable to recall him for the moment; there were quite a number of small parts in the second act. But glancing into his sensitive face, I shrank from wounding him.

" A capital performance," I lied. " It has always amused me."

He flushed with pleasure. " I made a great success some years ago," he said, " in America with a soda-water syphon, and it occurred to me that if you could, Mr. Kelver, in a natural sort of way, drop in a small part leading up to a little business with a soda-water syphon, it might help the piece."

I wrote him his soda-water scene, I am glad to remember, and insisted upon it, in spite of a good deal of opposition. Some of the critics found fault with the incident, as lacking in originality. But Marmaduke Trevor was quite right, it did help a little.

Our return journey was an exaggerated repetition of our morning drive. Our low comedian produced hideous noises from the horn, and entered into contests of running wit with 'bus-drivers—a decided mistake from his point of view, the score generally remaining with the 'bus-driver. At Hammersmith, seizing the opportunity of a block in the traffic, he assumed the rôle of cheap-jack, and standing up on the back seat, offered all our hats for sale at temptingly low prices.

" Got any ideas out of them ? " asked Hodgson, when the time came for us to say good-night.

" I 'm thinking, if you don't mind," I answered, " of going down into the country and writing the piece quietly, away from everybody."

(Paul Kelver.)

Robina on Marriage.

"I SHALL never marry," said Robina. "At least, I hope I shan't."

"Why ' hope ' ? " I asked.

"Because I hope I shall never be idiot enough," she answered. "I see it all so clearly. I wish I didn't. Love ! it 's only an ugly thing with a pretty name. It will not be me that he will fall in love with. He will not know me until it is too late. How can he ? It will be merely with the outside of me—my pink-and-white skin, my rounded arms. I feel it sometimes when I see men looking at me, and it makes me mad. And at other times the admiration in their eyes pleases me. And that makes me madder still."

The moon had slipped behind the wood. She had risen, and, leaning against the porch, was standing with her hands clasped. I fancy she had forgotten me. She seemed to be talking to the night.

"It 's only a trick of Nature to make fools of us," she said. " He will tell me I am all the world to him ; that his love will outlive the stars—will believe it himself at the time, poor fellow ! He will call me a hundred pretty names, will kiss my feet and hands. And if I 'm fool enough to listen to him, it may last " —she laughed ; it was rather an ugly laugh—" six months ; with luck perhaps a year, if I 'm careful

not to go out in the east wind and come home with a
red nose, and never let him catch me in curl papers.
It will not be me that he will want : only my youth,
and the novelty of me, and the mystery. And when
that is gone——"

She turned to me. It was a strange face I saw
then in the pale light, quite a fierce little face. She
laid her hands upon my shoulders, and I felt them cold.
"What comes when it is dead ?" she said. "What
follows ? You must know. Tell me. I want the
truth."

Her vehemence had arisen so suddenly. The little
girl I had set out to talk with was no longer there.
To my bewilderment, it was a woman that was
questioning me.

I drew her down beside me. But the childish face
was still stern.

"I want the truth," she said ; so that I answered
very gravely :

"When the passion is passed ; when the glory
and the wonder of Desire—Nature's eternal ritual of
marriage, solemnising, sanctifying it to her commands
—is ended ; when, sooner or later, some grey dawn
finds you wandering bewildered in once familiar places,
seeking vainly the lost palace of youth's dreams ;
when Love's frenzy is faded, like the fragrance of the
blossom, like the splendour of the dawn ; there will
remain to you, just what there was before—no more,
no less. If passion was all you had to give to one
another, God help you. You have had your hour of
madness. It is finished. If greed of praise and worship
was your price—well, you have had your payment.
The bargain is complete. If mere hope to be made

happy was your lure, one pities you. We do not make each other happy. Happiness is the gift of the gods, not of man. The secret lies within you, not without. What remains to you will depend not upon what you *thought*, but upon what you *are*. If behind the lover there was the man—behind the impossible goddess of his love-sick brain some honest, human woman, then life lies not behind you, but before you.

" Life is giving, not getting. That is the mistake we most of us set out with. It is the work that is the joy, not the wages ; the game, not the score. The lover's delight is to yield, not to claim. The crown of motherhood is pain. To serve the State at cost of ease and leisure ; to spend his thought and labour upon a hundred schemes, is the man's ambition. Life is doing, not having. It is to gain the peak the climber strives, not to possess it. Fools marry thinking what they are going to get out of it : good store of joys and pleasure, opportunities of self-indulgence, eternal soft caresses—the wages of the wanton. The rewards of marriage are toil, duty, responsibility—manhood, womanhood. Love's baby talk you will have outgrown. You will no longer be his ' Goddess,' ' Angel,' ' Popsy Wopsy,' ' Queen of his heart.' There are finer names than these : wife, mother, priestess in the temple of humanity. Marriage is renunciation, the sacrifice of self upon the altar of the race. ' A trick of Nature ' you call it. Perhaps. But a trick of Nature compelling you to surrender yourself to the purposes of God."

I fancy we must have sat in silence for quite a long while ; for the moon, creeping upward past the wood, had flooded the fields again with light before Robina spoke.

"Then all love is needless," she said, "we could do better without it, choose with more discretion. If it is only something that worries us for a little while and then passes, what is the sense of it ? "

"You could ask the same question of Life itself," I said ; " 'something that worries us for a little while, then passes.' Perhaps the 'worry,' as you call it, has its uses. Volcanic upheavals are necessary to the making of a world. Without them the ground would remain rock-bound, unfitted for its purposes. That explosion of Youth's pent-up forces that we term Love serves to the making of man and woman. It does not die, it takes new shape. The blossom fades as the fruit forms. The passion passes to give place to peace. The trembling lover has become the helper, the comforter, the husband."

"But the failures," Robina persisted ; "I do not mean the silly or the wicked people ; but the people who begin by really loving one another, only to end in disliking—almost hating one another. How do *they* get there ? "

"Sit down," I said, "and I will tell you a story."

(*They and I.*)

Saint Montmorency.

To look at Montmorency you would imagine that he was an angel sent upon the earth, for some reason withheld from mankind, in the shape of a small fox-terrier. There is a sort of Oh-what-a-wicked - world - this-is-and - how-I-wish-I-could -do-something - to-make -it - better- and - nobler expression about Montmorency that has been known to bring the tears into the eyes of pious old ladies and gentlemen.

When he first came to live at my expense, I never thought I should be able to get him to stop long. I used to sit down and look at him, as he sat on the rug and looked up at me, and think : " Oh, that will never live. He will be snatched up to the dog bright skies in a chariot, that is what will happen to him."

But, when I had paid for about a dozen chickens that he had killed ; and had dragged him, growling and kicking, by the scruff of his neck, out of a hundred and fourteen street fights ; and had had a dead cat brought round for my inspection by an irate female, who called me a murderer ; and had been summoned by the man next door but one for having a ferocious dog at large, that had kept him pinned up in his own tool-shed, afraid to venture his nose outside the door for over two hours on a cold night ;

and had learned that the gardener, unknown to myself, had won thirty shillings by backing him to kill rats against time, then I began to think that maybe they 'd let him remain on earth for a bit longr,e after all.

(Three Men in a Boat.)

The Unknown.

How long Joan remained there she was never quite
sure. There was little difference between day and
night. After it had been quiet for an hour or so,
Madame Lelanne would go out, to return a little later
with a wounded man upon her back ; and when one
died, she would throw him across her shoulder and
disappear again up the steps. Sometimes it was
a Frenchman and sometimes a German she brought
in. One gathered that the fight for the village still
continued. There was but little they could do for
them beyond dressing their wounds and easing their
pain. Joan and the little chemist took it in turns
to relieve one another. If Madame Lelanne ever slept,
it was when she would sit in the shadow behind the
stove, her hands upon her knees. Dubos had been
in the house when it had fallen. Madame Lelanne
had discovered him pinned against a wall underneath
a great oak beam that had withstood the falling débris.
His beard had been burnt off, but otherwise he had
been unharmed.

She seemed to be living in a dream. She could not
shake from her the feeling that it was not bodies but
souls that she was tending. The men themselves
gave colour to this fancy of hers. Stripped of their
poor, stained, tattered uniforms, they were neither

French nor Germans. Friend or foe ! it was already but a memory. Often, awakening out of a sleep, they would look across at one another and smile as to a comrade. A great peace seemed to have entered there. Faint murmurs as from some distant troubled world would steal at times into the silence. It brought a pang of pity, but it did not drive away the quiet that dwelt there.

Once, someone who must have known the place and had descended the steps softly, sat there among them and talked with them. Joan could not remember seeing him enter. Perhaps unknowing, she had fallen to sleep for a few minutes. Madame Lelanne was seated by the stove, her great coarse hands upon her knees, her patient, dull, slow-moving eyes fixed upon the speaker's face. Dubos was half standing half resting against the

The speaker sat a little way apart.

table, his arms folded upon his breast. The wounded men had raised themselves upon the straw and were listening. Some leant upon their elbows, some sat with their hands clasped round their knees, and one, with head bent down, remained with his face hidden in his hands.

The speaker sat a little way apart. The light from the oil lamp, suspended from the ceiling, fell upon his face. He wore a peasant's blouse. It seemed to her a face she knew. Possibly she had passed him in the village street and had looked at him without remembering. It was his eyes that for long years afterwards still haunted her. She did not notice at the time what language he was speaking. But there were none who did not understand him.

" You think of God as of a great King," he said, " a Ruler who orders all things : who could change all things in the twinkling of an eye. You see the cruelty and wrong around you. And you say to yourselves : ' He has ordered it. If He would, He could have willed it differently.' So that in your hearts you are angry with Him. How could it be otherwise ? What father, loving his childrem would see them suffer wrong, when by stretching out a hand he could protect them : turn their tears to gladness ? What father would see his children doing evil to one another and not check them : would see them following ways leading to their destruction, and not pluck them back ? If God has ordered all things, why has He created evil, making His creatures weak and sinful ? Does a father lay snares for his children : leading them into temptation : delivering them unto evil ?

" There is no God, apart from Man.

"God is a spirit. His dwelling-place is in man's heart. We are His fellow-labourers. It is through man that He shall one day rule the world.

"God is knocking at your heart, but you will not open to Him. You have filled your hearts with love of self. There is no room for Him to enter in.

"God whispers to you : ' Be pitiful. Be merciful. Be just.' But you answer Him : ' If I am pitiful, I lose my time and money. If I am merciful, I forego advantage to myself. If I am just, I lessen my own profit, and another passes me in the race.'

"And yet in your inmost thoughts you know that you are wrong : that love of self brings you no peace. Who is happier than the lover, thinking only how to serve ? Who is the more joyous : he who sits alone at the table, or he who shares his meal with a friend ? It is more blessed to give than to receive. How can you doubt it ? For what do you toil and strive but that you may give to your children, to your loved ones, reaping the harvest of their good ?

"Who among you is the more honoured ? The miser or the giver : he who heaps up riches for himself or he who labours for others ?

"Who is the true soldier ? He who has put away self. His own ease and comfort, even his own needs, his own safety : they are but as a feather in the balance when weighed against his love for his comrades, for his country. The true soldier is not afraid to love. He gives his life for his friend. Do you jeer at him ? Do you say he is a fool for his pains ? No, it is his honour, his glory.

"God is love. Why are you afraid to let Him in ? Hate knocks also at your door and to him you open wide. Why are you afraid of love? All things are created by love. Hate can but destroy. Why choose you death instead of life? God pleads to you. He is waiting for your help."

And one answered him.

"We are but poor men; what can we do? Of what use are such as we?"

The young man looked at him and smiled.

"You can ask that," he said: "you, a soldier? Does the soldier say: 'I am of no use. I am but a poor man of no account. Who has need of such as I?' God has need of all. There is none that shall not help to win the victory. It is with his life the soldier serves. Who were they whose teaching moved the world more than it has ever yet been moved by the teaching of the wisest? They were men of little knowledge, of but little learning, poor and lowly. It was with their lives they taught.

"Cast out self, and God shall enter in, and you shall be One with God. For there is none so lowly that he may not become the Temple of God: there is none so great that he shall be greater than this."

The speaker ceased. There came a faint sound at which she turned her head; and when she looked again he was gone.

(All Roads lead to Calvary.)

The Return.

THIS world was a school, so he viewed it, for the making of men ; and the one thing essential to a man was strength. One gathered the impression of a deeply religious man. In these days he would, no doubt, have been claimed as a theosophist ; but his beliefs he had made for, and adapted to, himself—to his vehement, conquering temperament. God needed men to serve Him—to help Him. So, through many changes, through many ages, God gave men life ; that by contest and by struggle they might ever increase in strength ; to those who proved themselves most fit the sterner task, the humbler beginnings, the greater obstacles. And the crown of well-doing was ever victory. He appeared to have convinced himself that he was one of the chosen, that he was destined for great ends. He had been a slave in the time of the Pharaohs ; a priest in Babylon ; had clung to the swaying ladders in the sack of Rome ; had won his way into the councils when Europe was a battlefield of contending tribes ; had climbed to power in the days of the Borgias.

To most of us, I suppose, there come at odd moments haunting thoughts of strangely familiar, far-off things ; and one wonders whether they are memories or dreams. We dismiss them as we grow older and the present with its crowding interests shuts them out ; but in youth they were more persistent. With him they appeared to have remained, growing in reality. His recent existence, closed under the white sheet in the hut behind me as I read, was only one chapter of the story ; he was looking forward to the next.

He wondered, so the letter ran, whether he would have any voice in choosing it. In either event he was curious of the result. What he anticipated confidently were new opportunities, wider experience. In what shape would these come to him ?

The letter ended in a strange request. It was that, on returning to England, I should continue to think of him : not of the dead man I had known, the Jewish banker, the voice familiar to me, the trick of speech, of manner—all such being but the changing clothes— but of the man himself, the soul of him, that would seek and perhaps succeed in revealing itself to me.

A postscript concluded the letter, to which at the time I attached no importance. He had made a purchase of the hut in which he had died. After his removal it was to remain empty.

I folded the letter and placed it among other papers, and passing into the hut took a farewell glance at the massive, rugged face. The mask might have served a sculptor for the embodiment of strength. He gave one the feeling that having conquered death he was sleeping.

I did what he had requested of me. Indeed, I could not help it. I thought of him constantly. That may have been the explanation of it.

I was bicycling through Norfolk, and one afternoon, to escape a coming thunderstorm, I knocked at the door of a lonely cottage, on the outskirts of a common.

The woman, a kindly bustling person, asked me in ; and hoping I would excuse her, as she was busy ironing, returned to her work in another room. I thought myself alone, and was standing at the window watching the pouring rain. After a while, without knowing why, I turned. And then I saw a child seated on a high chair behind a table in a dark corner of the room. A book of pictures was open before it, but it was looking at me. I could hear the sound of the woman at her ironing in the other room. Outside there was the steady thrashing of the rain. The child was looking at me with large, round eyes filled with a terrible pathos. I noticed that the little body was misshapen. It never moved ; it made no sound ; but I had the feeling that out of those strangely wistful eyes something was trying to speak to me. Something was forming itself before me—not visible to my sight ; but it was there, in the room. It was the man I had last looked upon as, dying, he sat beside me in the hut below the Jungfrau. But something had happened to him. Moved by instinct I went over to him and lifted him out of his chair, and with a sob the little wizened arms closed round my neck and he clung to me crying—a pitiful, low, wailing cry.

Hearing his cry, the woman came back. A comely, healthy-looking woman. She took him from my arms and comforted him.

"He gets a bit sorry for himself at times," she explained. "At least, so I fancy. You see, he can't run about like other children, or do anything without getting pains."

"Was it an accident ? " I asked.

"No," she answered, "and his father as fine a man

as you would find in a day's march. Just a visitation of God, as they tell me. Sure I don't know why. There never was a better little lad, and clever, too, when he's not in pain. Draws wonderfully."

The storm had passed. He grew quieter in her arms, and when I promised to come again and bring him a new picture-book, a little grateful smile flickered across the drawn face, but he would not talk.

(Malvina of Brittany.)

On the Inadvisability of Following Advice.

"THERE are people like that," he broke out, as we turned, "people who will go about giving advice. I 'll be getting six months over one of them, I 'm always afraid. I remember a pony I had once." (I judged the man to be a small farmer; he talked in a wurzelly tone. I don't know if you understand what I mean, but an atmosphere of wurzels was the thing that somehow he suggested.) "It was a thorough-bred Welsh pony, as sound a little beast as ever stepped. I 'd had him out to grass all the winter, and one day in the early spring I thought I 'd take him for a run. I had to go to Amersham on business. I put him into the cart, and drove him across; it is just ten miles from my place. He was a bit uppish, and had lathered himself pretty freely by the time we reached the town.

"A man was at the door of the hotel. He says, ' That 's a good pony of yours.'

"' Pretty middling,' I says.

"' It doesn't do to overdrive 'em when they're young,' he says.

"I says, ' He 's done ten miles, and I 've done most of the pulling. I reckon I 'm a jolly sight more exhausted than he is.'

"I went inside and did my business, and when

I came out the man was still there. ' Going back up the hill ? ' he says to me.

"Somehow I didn't cotton to him from the beginning. ' Well, I 've got to get the other side of it,' I says ; ' and unless you know any patent way of getting over a hill without going up it, I reckon I am.'

" He says, ' You take my advice : give him a pint of old ale before you start.'

" ' Old ale,' I says ; ' why, he 's a teetotaler.'

" ' Never you mind that,' he answers ; ' you give him a pint of old ale. I know these ponies ; he 's a good 'un, but he ain't set. A pint of old ale, and he 'll take you up that hill like a cable tramway, and not hurt himself.'

" I don't know what it is about this class of man. One asks oneself afterwards why one didn't knock his hat over his eyes and run his head into the nearest horse-trough. But at the time one listens to them. I got a pint of old ale in a hand bowl, and brought it out. About half-a-dozen chaps were standing round, and of course there was a good deal of chaff.

" ' You 're starting him on the downward course, Jim,' says one of them. ' He 'll take to gambling, rob a bank, and murder his mother. That 's always the result of a glass of ale, 'cording to the tracts.'

" ' He won't drink it like that,' says another ; ' it 's as flat as ditch water. Put a head on it for him.'

" ' Ain't you got a cigar for him ? " says a third.

" ' A cup of coffee and a round of buttered toast would do him a sight more good, a cold day like this,' says a fourth.

" I 'd half a mind then to throw the stuff away, or drink it myself ; it seemed a piece of bally nonsense, giving good ale to a four-year-old pony ; but the moment the beggar smelt the bowl he reached out his head, and lapped it up as though he 'd been a Christian ; and I jumped into the cart and started off, amid cheers. We got up the hill pretty steady. Then the liquor began to work into his head. I 've taken home a drunken man more than once ; and there 's pleasanter jobs than that. I 've seen a drunken woman, and they 're worse. But a drunken Welsh pony I never want to have anything more to do with so long as I live. Having four legs, he managed to hold himself up ; but as to guiding himself, he couldn't ; and as for letting me do it, he wouldn't. First we were one side of the road, and then we were the other. When we were not either side, we were crossways in the middle. I heard a bicycle bell behind me, but I dared not turn my head. All I could do was to shout to the fellow to keep where he was.

" ' I want to pass you,' he sang out, so soon as he was near enough.

" ' Well, you can't do it,' I called back.

" ' Why can't I ? ' he answered. ' How much of the road do *you* want ? "

" ' All of it, and a bit over,' I answered him, ' for this job, and nothing in the way.'

" He followed me for half a mile, abusing me ; and every time he thought he saw a chance he tried to pass me. But the pony was always a bit too smart for him. You might have thought the brute was doing it on purpose.

" ' You 're not fit to be driving,' he shouted. He was quite right ; I wasn't. I was feeling just about dead beat.

" ' What do you think you are,' he continued,—
' a musical ride ? ' (He was a common sort of fellow.)
' Who sent *you* home with the washing ? '

" Well, he was making me wild by this time.
' What 's the good of talking to me ? ' I shouted back.
' Come and blackguard the pony if you want to blackguard anybody. I 've got all I can do without the
help of that alarm clock of yours. Go away ; you 're
only making him worse.'

" ' What 's the matter with the pony ? ' he called
out.

" ' Can't you see ? ' I answered. ' He 's drunk.'

" Well, of course it sounded foolish ; the truth
often does.

" ' One of you 's drunk,' he retorted ; ' for two pins
I 'd come and haul you out of the cart.'

" I wish to goodness he had ! I 'd have given something to be out of that cart. But he didn't have the
chance. At that moment the pony gave a sudden
swerve ; and I take it he must have been a bit too close.
I heard a yell and a curse, and at the same instant
I was splashed from head to foot with ditch-water.
Then the brute bolted. A man was coming along,
asleep on the top of a cartload of windsor chairs.
It 's disgraceful the way those wagoners go to sleep ;
I wonder there are not more accidents. I don't think
he ever knew what had happened to him. I couldn't
look round to see what became of him ; I only saw him
start. Halfway down the hill a policeman holla'd to
me to stop ; I heard him shouting out something
about furious driving. Half a mile this side of Chesham
we came upon a girls' school walking two and two—
a ' crocodile,' they call it, I think. I bet you those

girls are still talking about it. It must have taken the old woman a good hour to collect them together again.

"It was market day in Chesham; and I guess there has not been a busier market-day in Chesham before or since. We went through the town at about thirty miles an hour. I 've never seen Chesham so lively, it 's a sleepy hole as a rule. A mile outside the town I sighted the High Wycombe coach. I didn't feel I minded much; I had got to that pass when it didn't seem to matter to me what happened; I only felt curious. A dozen yards off the coach the pony stopped dead; that jerked me off the seat to the bottom of the cart. I couldn't get up because the seat was on top of me. I could see nothing but the sky, and occasionally the head of the pony, when he stood upon his hind legs. But I could hear what the driver of the coach said, and I judged he was having trouble also.

"'Take that damn circus out of the road,' he shouted. If he 'd had any sense, he 'd have seen how helpless I was. I could hear his cattle plunging about; they are like that, horses,—if they see one fool, then they all want to be fools.

"'Take it home, and tie it up to its organ,' shouted the guard.

"Then an old woman went into hysterics, and began laughing like a hyena. That started the pony off again, and, as far as I could calculate by watching the clouds, we did another four miles at the gallop. Then he thought he 'd try to jump a gate, and finding, I suppose, that the cart hampered him, he started kicking it to pieces. I 'd never have thought a cart

N

could have been separated into so many pieces, if I hadn't seen it done. When he had got rid of everything but half a wheel and the splashboard he bolted again. I remained behind with the other ruins, and glad I was to get a little rest. He came back later in the afternoon, and I was pleased to sell him the next week for a five-pound note : it cost me about another ten to repair myself.

" To this day, I am chaffed about that pony, and the local Temperance Society made a lecture out of me. That 's what comes of following advice."

(*Second Thoughts of an Idle Fellow.*)

See England First.

To tell the truth, it was the journey more than the play that tempted me. To be a great traveller has always been one of my cherished ambitions. I yearn to be able to write in this sort of strain :—

" I have smoked my fragrant Havana in the sunny streets of old Madrid, and I have puffed the rude and not sweet-smelling calumet of peace in the draughty wigwam of the Wild West ; I have sipped my evening coffee in the silent tent, while the tethered camel browsed without upon the desert grass, and I have quaffed the fiery brandy of the North while the reindeer munched his fodder beside me in the hut, and the pale light of the midnight sun threw the shadows of the pines across the snow ; I have felt the stab of lustrous eyes that, ghostlike, looked at me

from out veil-covered faces in Byzantium's narrow
ways, and I have laughed back (though it was wrong
of me to do so) at the saucy, wanton glances of the
black-eyed girls of Jedo; I have wandered where
' good '—but not too good—Haroun Alraschid crept
disguised at nightfall, with his faithful Mesrour by
his side; I have stood upon the bridge where Dante
watched the sainted Beatrice pass by; I have floated
on the waters that once bore the barge of Cleopatra;
I have stood where Cæsar fell; I have heard the soft
rustle of rich, rare robes in the drawing-rooms of
Mayfair, and I have heard the teeth-necklaces rattle
around the ebony throats of the belles of Tongataboo;
I have panted beneath the sun's fierce rays in India,
and frozen under the icy blasts of Greenland; I have
mingled with the teeming hordes of old Cathay, and,
deep in the great pine forests of the Western World,
I have lain, wrapped in my blanket, a thousand miles
beyond the shores of human life."

B., to whom I explained my leaning towards this
style of diction, said that exactly the same effect
could be produced by writing about places quite handy.
He said :—

" I could go on like that without having been
outside England at all. I should say :

" ' I have smoked my fourpenny shag in the sanded
bars of Fleet Street, and I have puffed my twopenny
Manilla in the gilded halls of the Criterion ; I have
quaffed my foaming beer of Burton where Islington's
famed Angel gathers the little thirsty ones beneath her
shadowing wings, and I have sipped my tenpenny
ordinaire in many a garlic-scented *salon* of Soho.
On the back of the strangely-moving ass I have urged

—or, to speak more correctly, the proprietor of the ass, or his agent, from behind has urged—my wild career across the sandy heaths of Hampstead, and my canoe has startled the screaming wild-fowl from their lonely haunts amid the sub-tropical regions of Battersea. Adown the long, steep slope of One Tree Hill have I rolled from top to foot, while laughing maidens of the East stood round and clapped their hands and yelled ; and, in the old-world garden of that pleasant Court, where played the fair-haired children of the ill-starred Stuarts, have I wandered long through mazy paths, my arm entwined about the waist of one of Eve's sweet daughters, while her mother raged around indignantly on the other side of the hedge, and never seemed to get any nearer to us. I have chased the lodging-house Norfolk Howard to his watery death by the pale lamp's light ; I have, shivering, followed the leaping flea o'er many a mile of pillow and sheet, by the great Atlantic's margin. Round and round, till the heart—and not only the heart—grows sick, and the mad brain whirls and reels, have I ridden the small, but extremely hard, horse, that may, for a penny, be mounted amid the plains of Peckham Rye ; and high above the heads of the giddy throngs of Barnet (though it is doubtful if anyone among them was half so giddy as was I) have I swung in highly-coloured car, worked by a man with a rope. I have trod in stately measure the floor of Kensington's Town Hall (the tickets were a guinea each, and included refreshments—when you could get to them through the crowd), and on the green sward of the forest that borders eastern Anglia by the oft-sung town of Epping I have performed quaint ceremonies in a ring ; I have mingled with the teeming hordes of Drury Lane on Boxing Night, and, during the run of a high-class piece, I have sat in lonely grandeur in the front row of the gallery, and wished that I had spent my shilling instead in the Oriental halls of the Alhambra.'

" There you are," said B., " that is just as good as yours ; and you can write like that without going more than a few hours' journey from London."

(*Diary of a Pilgrimage*.)

Dream Children.

"WHY didn't you have better children?" sobbed Robina; "we are none of us any good to you."

"You are not the children I wanted, I confess," I answered.

"That 's a nice kind thing to say!" retorted Robina indignantly.

"I wanted such charming children," I explained— "my idea of charming children; the children I had imagined for myself. Even as babies you disappointed me."

Robina looked astonished.

"You, Robina, were the most disappointing," I complained. "Dick was a boy. One does not calculate upon boy angels; and by the time Veronica arrived I had got more used to things. But I was so excited when you came. The Little Mother and I would steal at night into the nursery. 'Isn't it wonderful,' the Little Mother would whisper, to think it all lies hidden there: the little tiresome child, the sweetheart they will one day take away from us, the wife, the mother?' 'I am glad it is a girl,' I would whisper; 'I shall be able to watch her grow into womanhood. Most of the girls one comes across in books strike one as not perhaps quite true to life. It will give me such an advantage to have a girl of my own. I shall keep a note-book, with a lock and key, devoted to her.' "

" Did you ? " asked Robina.

" I put it away," I answered ; " there were but a few pages written on. It came to me quite early in your life that you were not going to be the model heroine. I was looking for the picture baby, the clean, thoughtful baby, with its magical, mystical smile. I wrote poetry about you, Robina, but you would slobber and howl. Your little nose was always having to be wiped, and somehow the poetry did not seem to fit you. You were at your best when you were asleep, but you would not even sleep when it was expected of you. I think, Robina, that the fellows who draw the pictures for the comic journals of the man in his night-shirt with the squalling baby in his arms must all be single men. The married man sees only sadness in the design. It is not the mere discomfort. If the little creature were ill or in pain we should not think of that. It is the reflection that we, who meant so well, have brought into the world just an ordinary fretful human creature with a nasty temper of its own : that is the tragedy, Robina. And then you grew into a little girl. I wanted the soulful little girl with the fathomless eyes, who would steal to me at twilight and question me concerning life's conundrums."

" But I used to ask you questions," grumbled Robina, " and you would tell me not to be silly."

" Don't you understand, Robina ? " I answered. " I am not blaming you, I am blaming myself. We are like children who plant seeds in a garden, and then are angry with the flowers because they are not what we expected. You were a dear little girl ; I see that now, looking back. But not the little girl I had in my mind. So I missed you, thinking of the little girl you were not. We do that all our lives, Robina. We are always looking for the flowers that do not grow, passing by, trampling underfoot, the blossoms round about us. It was the same with Dick. I wanted a naughty boy. Well, Dick was naughty, no one can say that he was not. But it was not my naughtiness. I was prepared for his robbing orchards. I rather hoped he would rob orchards. All the high-spirited boys in books rob orchards, and become great men. But there were not any orchards handy. We happened to be living in Chelsea at the time he ought to have been robbing orchards : that, of course, was my fault. I did not think of that. He stole a bicycle that a lady had left outside the tea-room in Battersea Park, he and another boy, the son of a common barber, who shaved people for three-halfpence. I am a

Republican in theory, but it grieved me that a son of mine could be drawn to such companionship. They contrived to keep it for a week—till the police found it one night, artfully hidden behind bushes. Logically, I do not see why stealing apples should be noble and stealing bicycles should be mean, but it struck me that way at the time. It was not the particular steal I had been hoping for.

"I wanted him wild; the hero of the book was ever in his college days a wild young man. Well, he was wild. It cost me three hundred pounds to keep that breach of promise case out of Court; I had never imagined a breach of promise case. Then he got drunk, and bonneted a bishop in mistake for a 'bull-dog.' I didn't mind the bishop. That by itself would have been wholesome fun. But to think that a son of mine should have been drunk!"

"He has never been drunk since," pleaded Robina. "He had only three glasses of champagne and a liqueur: it was the liqueur—he was not used to it. He got into the wrong set. You cannot in college belong to the wild set without getting drunk occasionally."

"Perhaps not," I admitted. "In the book the wild young man drinks without ever getting drunk. Maybe there is a difference between life and the book. In the book you enjoy your fun, but contrive somehow to escape the licking: in life the licking is the only thing sure. It was the wild young man of fiction I was looking for, who, a fortnight before the exam., ties a wet towel round his head, drinks strong tea, and passes easily with honours. He tried the wet towel, he tells me. It never would keep in its place. Added to which it gave him neuralgia; while the strong tea gave him indigestion. I used to picture myself the proud, indulgent father lecturing him for his wildness—turning away at some point in the middle of my tirade to hide a smile. There was never any smile to hide. I feel that he has behaved disgracefully, wasting his time and my money."

" He is going to turn over a new leaf," said Robina : " I am sure he will make an excellent farmer."

" I did not want a farmer," I explained ; " I wanted a Prime Minister. Children, Robina, are very disappointing. Veronica is all wrong. I like a mischievous child. I like reading stories of mischievous children : they amuse me. But not the child who puts a pound of gunpowder into a red-hot fire, and escapes with her life by a miracle."

" And yet, I daresay," suggested Robina, " that if one put it into a book—I mean that if you put it into a book, it would read amusingly."

" Likely enough," I agreed. " Other people's troubles can always be amusing. As it is, I shall be in a state of anxiety for the next six months, wondering, every moment that she is out of my sight, what new devilment she is up to. The Little Mother will be worried out of her life, unless we can keep it from her."

" Children will be children," murmured Robina, meaning to be comforting.

" That is what I am complaining of, Robina. We are always hoping that ours won't be. She is full of faults, Veronica, and they are not always nice faults. She is lazy—lazy is not the word for it."

" She is lazy," Robina was compelled to admit.

" There are other faults she might have had and welcome," I pointed out ; " faults I could have taken an interest in and liked her all the better for. You children are so obstinate. You will choose your own faults. Veronica is not truthful always. I wanted a family of little George Washingtons, who could not tell a lie. Veronica can. To get herself out of trouble —and provided there is any hope of anybody believing her—she does."

"We all of us used to when we were young," Robina maintained ; "Dick used to, I used to. It is a common fault with children."

"I know it is," I answered. "I did not want a child with common faults. I wanted something all my own. I wanted you, Robina, to be my ideal daughter. I had a girl in my mind that I am sure would have been charming. You are not a bit like her. I don't say she was perfect, she had her failings, but they were such delightful failings—much better than yours, Robina. She had a temper—a woman without a temper is insipid ; but it was that kind of temper that made you love her all the more. Yours doesn't, Robina. I wish you had not been in such a hurry, and had left me to arrange your temper for you. We should all of us have preferred mine. It had all the attractions of a temper without the drawbacks of the ordinary temper."

"Couldn't use it up, I suppose, for yourself, Pa ? " suggested Robina.

"It was a lady's temper," I explained. "Besides," as I asked her, "what is wrong with the one I have ? "

"Nothing," answered Robina. Yet her tone conveyed doubt.

(They and I.)

Uncle Podger goes to Town.

WE caught the train by the skin of our teeth, as the saying is, and reflecting upon the events of the morning, as we sat gasping in the carriage, there passed vividly before my mind the panorama of my Uncle Podger, as on two hundred and fifty days in the year he would start from Ealing Common by the nine-thirteen train to Moorgate Street.

From my Uncle Podger's house to the railway station was eight minutes' walk. What my uncle always said was :

"Allow yourself a quarter of an hour, and take it easily."

What he always did was to start five minutes before the time and run. I do not know why, but this was the custom of the suburb. Many stout City gentlemen lived at Ealing in those days—I believe some live there still—and caught early trains to Town. They all started late ; they all carried a black bag and a newspaper in one hand, and an umbrella in the other ; and for the last quarter of a mile to the station, wet or fine, they all ran.

Folks with nothing else to do, nursemaids chiefly and errand boys, with now and then a perambulating costermonger added, would gather on the common of a fine morning to watch them pass, and cheer the most deserving. It was not a showy spectacle. They did not run well, they did not even run fast; but they were earnest, and they did their best. The exhibition appealed less to one's sense of art than to one's natural admiration for conscientious effort.

Occasionally a little harmless betting would take place among the crowd.

"Two to one agin the old gent in the white weskit!"

"Ten to one on old Blowpipes, bar he don't roll over hisself 'fore 'e gets there!"

"Heven money on the Purple Hemperor!"—a nickname bestowed by a youth of entomological tastes upon a certain retired military neighbour of my uncle's,—a gentleman of imposing appearance when stationary, but apt to colour highly under exercise.

My uncle and the others would write to the *Ealing Press* complaining bitterly concerning the supineness of the local police; and the editor would add spirited leaders upon the Decay of Courtesy among the Lower Orders, especially throughout the Western Suburbs.   But no good ever resulted.

It was not that my uncle did not rise early enough ; it was that troubles came to him at the last moment.

The first thing he would do after breakfast would be to lose his newspaper.   We always knew when Uncle Podger had lost anything, by the expression of astonished indignation with which, on such occasions, he would regard the world in general.   It never occurred to my Uncle Podger to say to himself :

" I am a careless old man.   I lose everything : I never know where I put anything.   I am quite incapable of finding it again for myself.   In this respect I must be a perfect nuisance to everybody about me. I must set to work and reform myself."

On the contrary, by some peculiar course of reasoning, he had convinced himself that whenever he lost a thing it was everybody else's fault in the house but his own.

" I had it in my hand here not a minute ago ! " he would exclaim.

From his tone you would have thought he was living surrounded by conjurers, who spirited away things from him merely to irritate him.

" Could you have left it in the garden ? " my aunt would suggest.

" What should I want to leave it in the garden for ?   I don't want a paper in the garden ; I want the paper in the train with me."

" You haven't put it in your pocket ? "

" God bless the woman !   Do you think I should be standing here at five minutes to nine looking for it if I had it in my pocket all the while ? *Do* you think I 'm a fool ? "

Here somebody would exclaim, " What 's this ? " and hand him from somewhere a paper neatly folded.

" I do wish people would leave my things alone," he would growl, snatching at it savagely.

He would open his bag and put it in, and then glancing at it, he would pause, speechless with sense of injury.

" What 's the matter ? " aunt would ask.

" The day before yesterday's ! " he would answer, too hurt even to shout, throwing the paper down upon the table.

If only sometimes it had been yesterday's it would have been a change. But it was always the day before yesterday's ; except on Tuesday ; then it would be Saturday's.

We would find it for him eventually ; as often as not he was sitting on it. And then he would smile, not genially, but with the weariness that comes to a man who feels that fate has cast his lot among a band of hopeless idiots.

" All the time, right in front of your noses—— ! " He would not finish the sentence ; he prided himself on his self-control.

(*Three Men on the Bummel.*)

Why Didn't He Marry the Girl?

WHAT is wrong with marriage, anyhow ? I find myself pondering this question so often, when reading high-class literature. I put it to myself again the other evening, during a performance of *Faust*. Why could not Faust have married the girl ? I would not have married her myself for any consideration whatsoever ; but that is not the argument. Faust, apparently, could not see anything amiss with her. Both of them were mad about each other. Yet the idea of a quiet, unostentatious marriage with a week's honeymoon, say, in Vienna, followed by a neat little cottage *orné*, not too far from Nürnberg, so that their friends could have come out to them, never seems to have occurred to either of them.

There could have been a garden. Marguerite might have kept chickens and a cow. That sort of girl, brought up to hard work and by no means too well educated, is all the better for having something to do. Later, with the gradual arrival of the family, a good, all-round woman might have been hired in to assist. Faust, of course, would have had his study and got to work again ; that would have kept him out of further mischief. The idea that a brainy man, his age, was going to be happy with nothing to do all day but fool round a petticoat was ridiculous from the beginning.

Valentine—a good fellow, Valentine, with nice ideas—
would have spent his Saturdays to Monday with them.
Over a pipe and a glass of wine, he and Faust would
have discussed the local politics.

He would have danced the children on his knee,
have told them tales about the war—taught the eldest
boy to shoot. Faust, with a practical man like
Valentine to help him, would probably have invented
a new gun. Valentine would have got it taken up.
Things might have come of it. Sybil, in course of
time, would have married and settled down—perhaps
have taken a little house near to them. He and
Marguerite would have joked—when Mrs. Sybil was
not around—about his early infatuation. The old
mother would have toddled over from Nürnberg—
not too often, just for the day.

The picture grows upon one the more one thinks of
it. Why did it never occur to them ? There would
have been a bit of a bother with the Old Man. I can
imagine Mephistopheles being upset about it, thinking
himself swindled. Of course, if that was the reason—
if Faust said to himself :

" I should like to marry the girl, but I won't do it ;
it would not be fair to the Old Man ; he has been to
a lot of trouble working this thing up ; in common
gratitude I cannot turn round now and behave like a
decent sensible man ; it would not be playing the game "
—if this was the way Faust looked at the matter
there is nothing more to be said. Indeed, it shows him
in rather a fine light—noble, if quixotic.

If, on the other hand, he looked at the question
from the point of view of himself and the girl, I think
the thing might have been managed. All one had to do

in those days when one wanted to get rid of the Devil was to show him a sword hilt. Faust and Marguerite could have slipped into a church one morning, and have kept him out of the way with a sword hilt till the ceremony was through. They might have hired a small boy :

" You see the gentleman in red ? Well, he wants us and we don't want him. That is the only difference between us. Now, you take this sword, and when you see him coming show him the hilt. Don't hurt him ; just show him the sword and shake your head. He will understand."

The old gentleman's expression, when subsequently Faust presented him to Marguerite, would have been interesting :

" Allow me, my wife. My dear, a—a friend of mine. You may remember meeting him that night at your aunt's."

As I have said, there would have been ructions ; but I do not myself see what could have been done. There was nothing in the bond to the effect that Faust should not marry, so far as we are told. The Old Man had a sense of humour. My own opinion is that, after getting over the first annoyance, he himself would have seen the joke. I can even picture him looking in now and again on Mr. and Mrs. Faust. The children would be hurried off to bed. There would be, for a while, an atmosphere of constraint.

But the Old Man had a way with him. He would have told one or two stories at which Marguerite would have blushed, at which Faust would have grinned. I can see the old fellow occasionally joining the homely social board. The children, awed at first, would have sat silent, with staring eyes. But, as I have said, the Old Man had a way with him. Why should he not have reformed? The good woman's unconsciously exerted influence—the sweet childish prattle! One hears of such things. Might he not have come to be known as " Nunkie "?

(*Idle Ideas in* 1905.)

The Fawn Gloves.

ALWAYS he remembered her as he saw her first : the little spiritual face, the little brown shoes pointing downwards, their toes just touching the ground ; the little fawn gloves folded upon her lap. He was not conscious of having noticed her with any particular attention : a plainly-dressed, childish-looking figure alone on a seat between him and the setting sun. Even had he felt curious his shyness would have prevented his deliberately running the risk of meeting her eyes. Yet immediately he had passed her he saw her again, quite clearly : the pale oval face, the brown shoes, and, between them, the little fawn gloves folded one over the other. All down the Broad Walk and across Primrose Hill, he saw her silhouetted against the sinking sun. At least that much of her : the wistful face and the trim brown shoes and the little folded hands ; until the sun went down behind the high chimneys of the brewery beyond Swiss Cottage, and then she faded.

She was there again the next evening, precisely in the same place. Usually he walked home by the Hampstead Road. Only occasionally, when the beauty of the evening tempted him, would he take the longer way by Regent Street and through the Park. But so often it made him feel sad, the quiet Park, forcing upon him the sense of his own loneliness.

He would walk down merely as far as the Great Vase, so he arranged with himself. If she were not there— it was not likely that she would be—he would turn back into Albany Street. The newsvendors' shops with their display of the cheaper illustrated papers, the second-hand furniture dealers with their faded engravings and old prints, would give him something to look at, to take away his thoughts from himself. But seeing her in the distance, almost the moment he had entered the gate, it came to him how disappointed he would have been had the seat in front of the red tulip bed been vacant. A little away from her he paused, turning to look at the flowers. He thought that, waiting his opportunity, he might be able to steal a glance at her undetected. Once for a moment he did so, but venturing a second time their eyes met, or he fancied they did, and blushing furiously he hurried past. But again she came with him, or, rather, preceded him. On each empty seat between him and the sinking sun he saw her quite plainly : the pale oval face and the brown shoes, and, between them, the fawn gloves folded one upon the other.

Only this evening, about the small, sensitive mouth there seemed to be hovering just the faintest suggestion of a timid smile. And this time she lingered with him past Queen's Crescent and the Malden Road, till he turned into Carlton Street. It was dark in the passage, and he had to grope his way up the stairs, but with his hand on the door of the bed-sitting room on the third floor he felt less afraid of the solitude that would rise to meet him.

All day long in the dingy back office in Abingdon Street, Westminster, where from ten to six each day he sat copying briefs and petitions, he thought over what he would say to her ; tactful beginnings by means of which he would slide into conversation with her. Up Portland Place he would rehearse them to himself. But at Cambridge Gate, when the little fawn gloves came in view, the words would run away, to join him again maybe at the gate into the Chester Road, leaving him meanwhile to pass her with stiff, hurried steps and eyes fixed straight in front of him. And so it might have continued, but that one evening she was no longer at her usual seat. A crowd of noisy children swarmed over it, and suddenly it seemed to him as if the trees and flowers had all turned drab. A terror gnawed at his heart, and he hurried on, more for the need of movement than with any definite object. And just beyond a bed of geraniums that had hidden his view she was seated on a chair, and stopping with a jerk absolutely in front of her, he said, quite angrily :

"Oh ! there you are ! "

Which was not a bit the speech with which he had intended to introduce himself, but served his purpose just as well—perhaps better.

She did not resent his words or the tone.

"It was the children," she explained. "They wanted to play ; so I thought I would come on a little farther."

Upon which, as a matter of course, he took the chair beside her, and it did not occur to either of them that they had not known one another since the beginning, when between St. John's Wood and Albany Street God planted a garden.

(*Malvina of Brittany.*)

How to be Healthy and Unhappy.

" THERE was a gent in Middle Temple Lane," said Mrs. Wilkins, " as I used to do for. It 's my belief as 'e killed 'imself worrying twenty-four hours a day over what 'e called 'is 'ygiene.

" Leastways 'e 's dead and buried now, which must be a comfort to 'imself, feeling as at last 'e 's out of danger. All 'is time 'e spent taking care of 'imself—didn't seem to 'ave a leisure moment in which to live. For 'alf an hour every morning 'e 'd lie on 'is back on the floor, which is a draughty place, I always 'old, at the best of times, with nothing on but 'is pyjamas, waving 'is arms and legs about, and twisting 'imself into shapes unnatural to a Christian. Then 'e found out that everything 'e 'd been doing on 'is back was just all wrong, so 'e turned over and did tricks on 'is stomach—begging your pardon for using the word—that you 'd 'ave thought more fit and proper to a worm than to a man. Then all that was discovered to be a mistake. There don't seem nothing certain in these matters. That's the awkward part of it, so it seems to me. 'E got 'imself a machine, by means of which 'e'd 'ang 'imself up to the wall, and behave for all the world like a beetle with a pin stuck through 'im, poor thing. It used to give me the shudders to catch sight of 'im through the 'alf-open door. For that was part of the game : you 'ad to 'ave a current of air through the room, the result of which was that for six months out of the year 'e'd be coughing and blowing 'is nose from morning to night. It was the new treatment, so 'e'd explain to me. You got yourself accustomed to draughts so that they didn't 'urt you, and if you died in the process that only proved that you never ought to 'ave been born.

" Then there came in this new Japanese business, and 'e'd 'ire a little smiling 'eathen to chuck 'im about 'is room for 'alf an hour every morning after breakfast. It got on my nerves after a while 'earing 'im being bumped on the floor every minute, or flung with 'is 'ead into the fire-place. But 'e always said it was doing 'im good. 'E'd argue that it freshened up 'is liver. It was 'is liver that 'e seemed to live for—didn't appear to 'ave any other interest in life. It was the same with 'is food. One year it would be nothing but meat, and next door to raw at that. One of them medical papers 'ad suddenly discovered that we were intended to be a sort of wild beast. The wonder to me is that 'e didn't go out 'unting chickens with a club, and bring 'em 'ome and eat 'em on the mat without any further fuss. For drink it would be boiling water that burnt my fingers merely 'andling the glass. Then some other crank came out with the information that every other crank was wrong—which, taken by itself, sounds natural enough—that meat was fatal to the 'uman system. Upon that 'e becomes all at once a raging, tearing vegetarian, and trouble enough I 'ad learning twenty different ways of cooking beans, which didn't make, so far as I could ever see, the slightest difference— beans they were, and beans they tasted like, whether you called them *ragoût à la maison,* or cutlets *à la Pompadour.* But it seemed to please 'im.

"Then vegetarianism turned out to be the mistake of our lives. It seemed we made an error giving up monkeys' food. That was our natural victuals ; nuts with occasional bananas. As I used to tell 'im, if that was so, then for all we 'ad got out of it we might just as well 'ave stopped up a tree—saved rent and shoe leather. But 'e was one of that sort that don't seem able to 'elp believing everything they read in print. If one of those papers 'ad told 'im to live on the shells and throw away the nuts, 'e 'd have made a conscientious endeavour to do so, contending that 'is failure to digest them was merely the result of vicious training—didn't seem to 'ave any likes or dislikes of 'is own. You might 'ave thought 'e was just a bit of public property made to be experimented upon.

"One of the daily papers interviewed an old gent, as said 'e was a 'undred, and I will say from 'is picture as any'ow 'e looked it. 'E said it was all the result of never 'aving swallowed anything 'ot, upon which my gentleman for a week lives on cold porridge, if you 'll believe me ; although myself I 'd rather 'ave died at fifty and got it over. Then another paper dug up from somewhere a sort of animated corpse that said 'e was a 'undred and two, and attributed the unfortunate fact to 'is always 'aving 'ad 'is food as 'ot as 'e could swallow it. A bit of sense did begin to dawn upon 'im then, but too late in the day, I take it. 'E 'd played about with 'imself too long. 'E died at thirty-two, looking to all appearance sixty, and you can't say as 'ow it was the result of not taking advice.

"We talk a lot about it," thought Mrs. Wilkins, "but it does not seem to me that we are very much better off than before we took to worrying ourselves for twenty-four 'ours a day about 'ow we are going to live. Lord ! to read the advertisements in the papers you would think as 'ow flesh and blood was never intended to 'ave any natural ills. ' Do you ever 'ave a pain in your back ? ' because, if so, there 's a picture of a kind gent who 's willing for one and sixpence halfpenny to take it quite away from you—make you look forward to scrubbing floors, and standing over the wash-tub six hours at a stretch like to a beanfeast. ' Do you ever feel as though you don't want to get out of bed in the morning ? ' that 's all to be cured by a bottle of their stuff—or two at the outside. Four children to keep, and a sick 'usband on your 'ands used to get me over it when I was younger. I used to fancy it was just because I was tired.

" There's some of them seem to think," continued Mrs. Wilkins, " that if you don't get all you want out of this world, and ain't so 'appy as you 've persuaded yourself you ought to be, that it's all because you ain't taking the right medicine. Appears to me there's only one doctor as can do for you, all the others talk as though they could, and 'e only comes to each of us once, and then 'e makes no charge."

(*The Angel and the Author.*)

All Roads lead to Calvary.

"ALL roads lead to Calvary." It was curious how the words had dwelt with her, till gradually they had become a part of her creed. She remembered how at first they had seemed to her a threat, chilling her with fear. They had grown to be a promise : a hope held out to all. The road to Calvary ! It was the road to life. By the giving up of self we gained God.

And suddenly a great peace came to her. One was not alone in the fight. God was with us : the great Comrade. The evil and the cruelty all round her : she was no longer afraid of it. God was coming. Beyond the menace of the passing day, black with the war's foul aftermath of evil dreams and hatreds, she saw the breaking of the distant dawn. The devil should not always triumph. God was gathering His labourers.

God was conquering. Unceasing through the ages, God's voice had crept round man, seeking entry. Through the long darkness of that dim beginning, when man knew no law but self, unceasing, God had striven : until at last one here and there, emerging from the brute, had heard—had listened to the voice of love and pity, and in that hour, unknowing, had built to God a temple in the wilderness.

Labourers together with God. The mighty host

of those who through the ages had heard the voice of God and had made answer. The men and women in all lands who had made room in their hearts for God. Still nameless, scattered, unknown to one another : still powerless as yet against the world's foul law of hate, they should continue to increase and multiply, until one day they should speak with God's voice and should be heard. And a new world should be created.

God. The tireless Spirit of eternal creation, the Spirit of Love. What else was it that out of formlessness had shaped the spheres, had planned the orbits of the suns. The law of gravity we named it. What was it but another name for Love, the yearning of like for like, the calling to one another of the stars. What else but Love had made the worlds, had gathered together the waters, had fashioned the dry land. The cohesion of elements, so we explained it. The clinging of like to like. The brotherhood of the atoms.

God. The Eternal Creator. Out of matter, lifeless void, He had moulded His worlds, had ordered His endless firmament. It was finished. The greater task remained : the Universe of mind, of soul. Out of man it should be created. God in man and man in God : made in like image : fellow labourers together with one another : together they should build it. Out of the senseless strife and discord, above the chaos and the tumult should be heard the new command : " Let there be Love."

(All Roads lead to Calvary.)